*A
Harlequin
Romance*

WELCOME
TO THE WONDERFUL WORLD
of Harlequin Romances!

Interesting, informative and entertaining,
each Harlequin Romance portrays an appealing
love story. Harlequin Romances take you
to faraway places — places with real people
facing real love situations — and
you become part of their story.

As publishers of Harlequin Romances, we're extremely
proud of our books (we've been publishing
them since 1954). We're proud also that Harlequin
Romances are North America's most-read
paperback romances.

Eight new titles are released every month and are
sold at nearly all book-selling stores across
Canada and the United States.

A free catalogue listing all available Harlequin Romances
can be yours by writing to the

HARLEQUIN READER SERVICE,
M.P.O. Box 707, Niagara Falls, N.Y. 14302.
Canadian address: Stratford, Ontario, Canada.

or use order coupon at back of book.

We sincerely hope you enjoy reading
this Harlequin Romance.

Yours truly,

THE PUBLISHERS
        Harlequin Romances

GOLDEN HARVEST

by

STELLA FRANCES NEL

HARLEQUIN BOOKS   TORONTO
WINNIPEG

Original hard cover edition published in 1973
by Mills & Boon Limited

© Stella Frances Nel 1973

SBN 373-01708-1

Harlequin edition published August, 1973

To
my beloved daughter

CHAPTER 1

THE child sat perfectly still on the sun-warmed rock, quite unaware of the creepy thing that was slowly making its way to the exposed part of her thin little thigh. Tangled hair shone red in the bright sun and her sleeveless shirt hung over brief shorts. The girl's slight body tensed as the first tug vibrated her rod and Jane realised, with her heart in her mouth, that the moment would come when the fish swallowed the bait and the child would strike, leaning back with the movement. Right within reach of that tiny, poisonous tail!

Jane Wheeler slid fast and silently down the bank, a sweep of her arm pushed the child off the rock just as the line became taut in the water. She made a wild grab at the ratchet-whirring rod that had been flung aside with a yelp of fright at her sudden onslaught.

'Sorry, chicken, I had to do that, don't be scared—take your rod, he's still on the hook. I'll explain in a minute why I tackled you!' Jane was out of breath with her double effort, but she managed a wide smile at the startled little redhead. With one hand she held the line taut, her other hand stretched out to grip and guide the child's confused fingers back on to the rod. A keen fisherman herself, Jane knew the thrill of landing a fish all on one's own, scorpion and fright not excepted!

She released her hold and stepped back to watch a remarkable recovery as the little mite switched her attention to the effort of bringing in her catch. The hooked victim was zig-zagging in a most alarming manner, being equally determined not be landed. Jane forgot her own dishevelled state as the excitement mounted and was ready with a willing hand as a good-sized Yellow flopped on the bank. The two girls knelt down, the young one held the fish while the older girl

7

extricated the hook from a gaping mouth.

'You sure had luck, chick. I've tried twice at this same spot and only netted a couple of gillie-winkies!' Jane's brown eyes met the large grey ones for the first time. 'I'm Jane Wheeler, from across the river.'

'I'm Sandy—Sandra Saxon.' The little redhead was excited and stroked the quivering fish with a hesitant finger. Curiosity overcame pride of achievement. 'Why did you push me off that rock? I didn't even see you——'

'Come, I'll show you. First put your fish in that bag, he's quite likely to jump back into the water.' Jane waited and then led Sandy to her former perch, found a stick and started to poke in the crevices. The tiny red devil came out fighting, tail curved in an arch across its back. 'Scorpy was about three millimetres from your thigh and, believe me, that tail is loaded with venom. I was stung once and for more than a week my elbow and arm was horribly swollen and burned like fire. If you're allergic it can be quite dangerous. Look at him—if he gets any angrier he'll sting himself!' Unable to kill the creature, Jane hooked her stick in the circle of the arched tail and swung it across the water, releasing the stick as well.

'Why didn't you kill it?' Sandy asked in surprise.

Jane scuffed the grass with the toe of her moccasin. 'Well, you know how it is, he's so tiny and rather valiant and—and——'

'I know egsackerly how you feel,' Sandy confided. 'Matter o' fact I feel like putting my poor fish back in the water, but,' temptation fought with pride, 'I'd like Grant to see it.'

'No, you can't do that, fish are legit game,' Jane compensated.

'Legit——?' Grey eyes circled the child's face and then brightened knowingly. 'Oh, like having married babies, it's legitimate to keep him?'

'Wherever——!' Jane covered her astonishment with a grin. 'Well, I guess it's the same—er—principle,' she added under her breath, 'if you have a licence.'

'Mara explained the difference, so it's all right. Mara is my mother. Thank you for saving my life, Jane.' The upturned

8

face was piquantly grave.

'You're from the Estates, the Saxon family?' Aunt Janet had spoken of the vast orange orchards and cattle ranch across the river. On her two excursions to this part of the river Jane had marvelled at the march of orderly trees and the insidiously sweet scent of orange blossoms that invaded the air and nostrils.

'Yes. Mara is mod'lling pretty clothes in Johannesburg, so I'm having my holiday with Grant—it's super!' Sandy smiled happily. 'Are you on holiday too?'

'No, not quite a holiday. My mother has been very ill and we came here because the climate will make her better quickly. We come from Port Elizabeth. Is Grant Saxon . . . .' Jane whirled as a flurry behind them drew her attention.

'Missy Sandy, the Boss said for me to go wit' you and you no dinkum wait fo' me!' A reproachful ebony face peered at them through the parted clump of pampas grass.

'Oh, Lemmy, you took ages and—come and see what I catched,' Sandy answered inelegantly, and clutched a dark hand to drag the young African to her net-bag.

'Ow, missy, that is too good!' Velvety eyes rolled whitely. 'We go now. Lena cook, you eat, hey?'

'Yes, Lemmy.' Sandy turned to Jane. 'Will you come again tomorrow if Grant lets me come? He's going to smack my launching pad, if he knows I slipped 'way from Lemmy— he's my bodyguard. I'd better give my fish to this boy to shut his mouth. Will you come, Jane?'

Jane pursed her mouth sternly and a small hand was lifted appealingly. 'I know what you're going to say, if you weren't here that scorpy would've bited me, and I'm naughty 'cos I slipped Lemmy. I promise I won't do it again . . . please, Jane?'

Jane bit back a smile. 'Okay, mate, but let's make it the morning after tomorrow. I've some work to catch up with tomorrow.'

'That's fab. If Grant 'llows me to come I'll be here at seven o'clock. 'Bye, Jane.' At the top of the bank Sandy turned to wave at her new friend.

Jane walked back along the river bank to the stepping

stones where she had crossed over and recalled, with a smile, the worldly way Sandra Saxon, aged approximately nine years, had repeated her mother's lesson on the law of legitimation. Mara Saxon, modelling pretty clothes in the golden city. Uncle Bart had remarked that Saxon Estates was one of the largest and wealthiest in that area, so it could not be financial embarrassment that took Sandy's mother away from her home. The child's affection for Grant Saxon was very evident, even though she had grimaced at the thought of a heavy parental hand on her 'launching pad'. Jane did not approve of parents who allowed their children to call them by name instead of the loving and cosy 'Mum' and 'Daddy'. She herself had a loving mum, but was denied the presence of a comforting daddy.

The girl's thoughts turned inwardly to her own misery and shock when her mother had nearly died of pneumonia. Elizabeth Wheeler had lost her husband five years previously. It was a bitter blow for her and Jane, losing a loving husband and wonderful father respectively. Elizabeth went to work for a thriving departmental store and, within a year, had become their top buyer in the rag trade. They maintained their standard of living and she was able to see her daughter through a course of typing and book-keeping. The terrible rain and flooding of Port Elizabeth, the destitution and ravage that followed, will long remain in the memories of its inhabitants. The savage swirl of waters had trapped Elizabeth's car as she was returning home and her consequent battle against the elements had resulted in the inflammation of lungs that had never been very healthy.

Her brother-in-law and his wife had sympathised and urged Elizabeth to make her home with them. The climate was ideal and there were towns within reach if Jane wanted to continue working. They personally would be only too thankful if Jane would consider helping on the farm, for Aunt Janet had hurt her back and needed young hands to do the chores she could no longer handle, also to be companion to their two sons when they were home from boarding school.

Bart Wheeler had met them at Nelspruit and they had

called at the hostel for his two sons, Anthony and Michael, whose holidays coincided. The remainder of the trip was done in his roomy Combi. That was two weeks ago and already Elizabeth looked better, with colour in her thin cheeks and brightness in her eyes as she became interested in her new surroundings. Jane had not quibbled about giving up an interesting job for the sake of her mother's health; they had made a tidy sum from the sale of their house and furniture and Mum was not ever going to work so hard again. Not while she, Jane Wheeler, was capable of caring for her.

She approached the farmhouse from the backlands, through lush green lucerne and past the hen-houses and runs —that was her chore tomorrow, to clean out that mess! In the kitchen doorway she stopped short as two startled miscreants dropped the lid of the biscuit barrel with a loud clang.

'Tony—Mick! It took me all day to bake that lot, it's supposed to last for weeks, and look at your bulging pockets! Give—you're not that hungry.' Jane made a sudden dive at them.

Tony, with a superior length of fifteen years, sidestepped neatly behind her and clamped long arms around her slender body, pinning her flailing arms. Twelve-year-old Mick lowered and curled round her ankles, taking great care not to crush his bulging pockets.

Tony hissed in her ear, 'Good strategy, what? You were saying, sweet coz?'

'Let me go, you hooligans! Put back those tarts and biscuits——' Jane panted in her effort to free herself.

'Darling Jane, we haven't had it so good for years. Mum hasn't baked for simply ages—well, since she hurt her back. Are you going to deprive us of delectation while the going's good?' Tony nuzzled her ears and nipped delicately on a rosy lobe.

Jane jerked her head away, long chestnut hair fell forward to obstruct her vision and her shirt worked its way up under the pinioning arms to bare a tanned midriff. Mick was trying his best to plait her legs. A large shadow blocked the outer door just as Jane gave a peculiar judo grunt and subsided limply, catching her tormentors off guard. She whipped Tony's leg up, he lost balance to fall on top of his brother and the girl rolled out of reach.

The shadow surveyed the jumbled mass. 'Boys, you're slipping—a mere schoolgirl can do that?' it inquired sarcastically.

Jane peeped through a curtain of tumbled hair and hurriedly pulled her shirt down. The shadow resolved into a tall, massive-shouldered stranger.

'Is there a sober warder in this asylum with whom I can consult?' He asked, and stepped over the tangled heap to help himself to a fistful of biscuits.

Jane hopped lightly to her feet and swept back a cascade of nut-brown hair. Tony extricated himself shamefacedly while Mick explored the damage in biscuit-filled pockets.

'Hi, Grant. That was a sneak defence we weren't prepared for from this female—er—schoolgirl,' Tony hastened to justify their downfall, a sly grin sliding over Jane.

Wood-smoke eyes surveyed her critically. 'Do they teach judo tricks at the schools now?'

'Yes—I mean no.' Couldn't this dark stranger with the startling contrast of grey eyes see that she was no schoolgirl?

Tony remembered his manners. 'Meet cousin Jane Wheeler, the mighty atom from Port Elizabeth—she baked those cookies. Mr. Grant Saxon of Saxon Estates.'

'Oh? I was given to understand that your cousin was a working girl. Is there another sister? Your baking's not bad, Jane, but your method of discipline is somewhat drastic.' He sounded so tauntingly arrogant that Jane felt immediate hackles rising and stiffened her back haughtily.

'Reprehensible behaviour requires drastic methods, Mr. Saxon. Thanks for the wild compliment on my baking. How do you do.' Her rumpled appearance belied her manner, but she managed a natty sangfroid as she leaned over the table and selected a cigarette from the box that rested there.

A dark eyebrow shot up as Grant Saxon watched her action. He hesitated for a measurable, mocking moment then leaned forward with his lighter.

'Advanced methods at the schools, surely, or are the super-

12

intendents ignorant of the fact that their scholars smoke?'

Her schooldays being well in the past, Jane could answer in all honesty. She took time for a slightly defiant puff on the offending weed. 'No, teacher lacks knowledge of my ignominious habits. I've also noticed that parents are more advanced, teaching the very young the laws of legitimacy and—otherwise. Tony, you may keep what you have taken, but remember in future, be moderate with your colossal appetite or no more bakings from me!'

Grant leaned against the dresser. 'That centre crack sounds suspiciously like young Sandra's gossip. Her mother certainly has some odd notions which could fall under the category of modern teachings. Sandy told me about the lady,' he stressed the last word, 'who saved her from an awful fate. Where was Lemmy—he's supposed to watch her every move?'

Sandy had evidently not disclosed the full story. 'He was around someplace. I happened to be above her on the bank a —and got there first.' Jane didn't care for his sarcastic stress on the 'lady' part. Her cheeks felt hot as she visualised Saxon's first glimpse of her on the floor with the boys, hair wildly disarrayed and her shirt practically around her neck! Anyway, he had no right to come barging in at the back door, like a tramp. He was the great Saxon of Saxon Estates and should behave accordingly. Furthermore, if he thought Sandy's mother's notions were odd, why didn't he nip them in the bud?

Mick moved to the door. 'If you're looking for Dad he's down at the pig runs. I'll go call him...' Tony followed hastily.

Grant Saxon and Jane Wheeler took stock of each other. Her hazel-brown eyes lowered before the compelling, levelling grey stare. Not before she had noticed the dark frame of thick eyelashes and an almost black ring around the outer rim of blue-grey iris. Irish eyes, smudged in with a sooty finger. Sandy's hair was red, she obviously had her mother's colouring. He had a strong, square jaw, well-defined mouth and black hair that looked alive and springy. He was indolently at ease in his contemplation and Jane felt prickles

13

up her spine, as if this tableau would stretch through eternity if she did not make the first move to break it up.

'Would you care to step through to the living-room, Mr. Saxon? Uncle Bart should be here any moment. Mum and Aunt Janet have gone to Kiepersol, I think, on some mysterious jaunt. I'll make coffee.'

Grant turned in the passage doorway, filling its frame with lengthy leanness. 'There's evidently been a great deception. You're not so schoolgirlish after all, not with all those ins and—outs. A bit on the skinny side . . . how is your mother?'

Jane straightened indignantly and tried to flatten her 'ins and outs'. She answered coldly, 'My mother is much better, thank you. The change of air is most beneficial.'

'Good.' Grant frowned darkly. 'I had intended to speak to Bart concerning a responsible post for Elizabeth Wheeler's daughter; he had assured me she was a reserved and competent young woman, but now,' he looked disparagingly at her scuffed moccasins, rumpled shirt and long, untidy hair, 'I'm having second thoughts.' He disappeared down the passage, leaving an infuriated young woman absolutely speechless!

She rattled the cups with a quivering hand as she heard her uncle greeting the insufferable man with easy familiarity. Post for a responsible person indeed! Grant Saxon had caught her at a disadvantage. He was absolutely beastly, and she would take great pleasure in telling him exactly what to do with his job at the first opportunity, just let him dare approach her . . .!

Jane firmly intended to help her aunt straighten out the sadly neglected homestead; since her fall poor Aunt Janet hadn't been so active and her normal duties had fallen into a state of disrepair. After all that was back to normal then Jane felt she could consider an outside post. With the money she and her mother had saved and collected she could afford to invest in a small car, for future transport to wherever employment took her.

For some obscure reason Jane slipped into her room, intending to change into a cool frock. The reason clarified when she held up a daffodil cotton with tan saddle-stitching;

14

she wanted to show Grant Saxon that she could look all of her twenty-one years! With an abrupt movement she thrust the dress back on its hanger. He would guess her intention and jump to the conclusion that she was angling after his job—to the devil with appearances! Jane tucked her plaid shirt firmly into the old jeans, retied her hair and walked back to the kitchen. For good measure, she ran a finger across the blackened kettle and thoughtfully stroked her forehead. (She simply must tackle that kettle and stove, they were in a shocking state.)

She stomped down the passage with the tray and managed clumsily to spill a satisfactory amount from the brimming cups as she set it down on the low table between the two men. She smiled sweetly in their general direction and turned to leave, but her uncle stopped her at the doorway.

'Oh, Jane, just a minute, dear. I believe you've met Mr. Saxon, in the kitchen?'

'Yes,' Jane acknowledged stonily. Teller of tales, her eyes shot silent accusation at the lanky, khaki-clad visitor. He returned her gaze blandly and the deliberate smudges suddenly felt like hot brand marks as grey eyes circled her face and a smile glimmered on well-cut lips.

'Grant came to find out if you were interested in office and general work, on the Estates. It would be conveniently near——'

'Me?' Jane opened wide eyes in astonishment. 'Why, Uncle dear, a girl of my tender years couldn't possibly cope with such a responsible position. Thanks all the same, Mr. Saxon.' She smiled vaguely, turned on her heel to leave and caught the loop of her jeans on the jutting lock of the door. She jerked savagely and proceeded down the passage to the tune of a deep male chuckle . . . !

Later, as Jane rinsed the cups and helped Alphina, the buxom coloured maid, to prepare the vegetables for supper, she looked through the window and glimpsed the two men beyond the lucerne lands, at the edge of Bart's orange grove. Grant Saxon was gesticulating with his arms and her uncle showed evident agreement with whatever was being expressed. Alphina followed her gaze.

15

'Dat Boss is ver' pertickuler 'bout dem fruit, de black boys sees him dey jump like grasshoppers!'

Jane took a second look at the figures. 'Mr. Saxon seems to be giving the orders, not the Boss?'

'He be *mongaka*, de big Boss, missy Jane,' came the astonishing reply.

'You mean Mr. Saxon is ... those trees belong to him? But this land belongs to my uncle!' Jane was utterly bewildered.

'Yes'm, I dunno fo' sure——' Alphina shrugged plump shoulders and turned to the stove. Jane gazed at her back in perplexity. This was something that had to be explained more clearly, as soon as possible ...

She had no opportunity that afternoon, for Bart Wheeler went off in the Combi and only came back in time for supper. Elizabeth and Janet also came late and, at the table, excitedly revealed the secret of their jaunt to Sabie—a knitting machine, to be paid for and used jointly. A visit to various shops and friends had resulted in a batch of satisfactory orders for knitted garments. They intended to widen the list of customers, from Nelspruit and Barberton to a wide circling of Lydenburg, Graskop and Pilgrims Rest. Elizabeth's eyes shone as she and Janet outlined their big plans and Bart remarked wryly that one little machine was not going to be sufficient if all their ideas bore fruit. He was pleased to see his wife bright and lively again; she had been rather depressed since her fall down the steps and the coming of Elizabeth and Jane had cheered her considerably.

Elizabeth felt that the profits she and Janet hoped to make on this knitting venture would help towards her and Jane's keep; her independent spirit demanded a return for the goodness of her brother-in-law and his wife in providing a home for them. Janet would also benefit; she knew spans of busy wives who would be only too pleased to pay for what they considered a tiresome chore, and her back could stand this particular labour.

'Grant can give his measurements, and Sandy's. I'll insist he be one of our first customers,' Janet declared, with a determined glint in her eyes.

16

'What about his—Mara—isn't it? Why can't she knit for them and stay at home where she's needed, instead of modelling——'

'Oh, that one, you wouldn't find her burying all that glamour in the wilds. The world's axis would slip the day Mara Saxon takes a knitting needle in her hand!'

Jane was genuinely puzzled. 'It can't be much of a life for Sandy and Grant, with her away most of the time?'

Bart looked thoughtful. 'Well, Jane, it's always been her job, since before her marriage, and she loves it. Sandy is much better off at boarding school than being towed along where her mother's work takes her. Grant doesn't mind, he's very fond of Sandy and she loves spending her holidays on the Estate. So everybody's happy. Grant had word from Mara, she's coming for a long rest when her present assignment is completed. She's very beautiful—red hair and the most remarkable green eyes.'

'And Grant Saxon is satisfied with the arrangement? If she's so beautiful he surely would want her with them?' Jane felt she was harping on that theme, but she felt an irresistible urge to find the reason for a man like Saxon allowing his wife to flit around at will. He looked strong-minded, virile and sure of himself, not the sort of man to let any female boss him around...

Janet gave a small, mirthless laugh. 'Quite frankly, she has an unsettling effect on Sandy and, I'm almost certain, on Grant as well—although he clams up mighty quick when it comes to a discussion on Mara's not-so-fine points. Mick, stop stuffing your mouth like that, a body would swear you're starving!'

Tony started to laugh, caught Jane's stern eye that warned against revealing their morning tussle and subsided meekly.

Lying in her bed that night, Jane's thoughts nagged again on the Saxon set-up. The man was definitely good-looking and, in the brief time she had been in his presence, Jane had instantly become aware of a vibrant aliveness about him; such a man would surely want his beautiful wife at their home constantly, not only at spaced intervals? Especially with a young child to care for and love?

17

Uncle Bart and Aunt Janet seemed to have accepted the state of affairs with an indolent contempt that Jane found hard to understand. They were usually very proper about the sanctity of a home and all it entailed. Jane snuggled deeper. What concerned her most was the set-up right here at Mimosa. Alphina must be wrong in her facts ... she would speak to her uncle in the morning.

CHAPTER 2

JANE reeled in and came to sit beside Sandy, taking care to sit outside striking distance: Fishermen were known for frustrated anger when their bait was taken only to have some silly chump get in the way of the strike! She cast a glance at the large hamper which Lemmy had so carefully deposited in the shade of a willow. Judging by size, enough tucker to feed an army ... she had only brought a flask of tea and home-made biscuits. Tony and Mick had begged to join them, after they had wheedled her destination, and Jane warned them to bring their own vittles. They had the 'disgustingly menial' job of cleaning out the pig runs, so would be down much later. Jane had cleaned the hen-houses the day before and felt she had earned the right to enjoy her early start with Sandy.

Yesterday Bart had left early in the Combi and had come back fairly late, tired and grumpy, so she could not speak on the subject that was causing her worry. Jane could not bring herself to approach her aunt on the matter and decided to speak to Uncle Bart after supper tonight, when he was re-laxed and enjoying a quiet smoke on the verandah.

Sandy intercepted Jane's glance at the hamper. 'Lena packed lots 'cause Grant's got a big appetite—so've I, but I don't get fat. Do you like chicken sammidges too, Jane?' The little redhead had taken an immediate fancy to her new friend. She was different from her mother, who wouldn't be

18

seen dead in the worn shirt and blue shorts that Jane was wearing.

'Grant—what has his appetite got to do with the size of your hamper?' Jane asked sharply, her suspicions aroused before Sandy confirmed them.

'He's coming to have tea with us. I did tell him about my fish and slipping that boy. Last night I told him 'cause my conscious was guilty.' Sandy looked piously for approbation.

'So why is he coming to tea?' Jane smiled her approval of Sandy's confession while she thought wryly, he's coming to check the child's safety with that scatterbrained, juvenile Wheeler girl . . .

'Because I'm as keen on fishing as the next, and a break is indicated, in the presence of two charming ladies.' Grant's deep voice floated down the bank and Jane turned a startled face to the lithe figure towering above her.

Colour flooded, then receded most annoyingly in her cheeks; the mere presence of this man reduced her reactions to teenage ditherings. Something about him, a magnetism she could not define, rang bells of warning; look out, Jane, watch out, there's danger in the air. She recoiled inwardly from this ominous feeling. What danger could he have for her? She didn't even like him; he was—exasperating!

Grant lowered negligently on to a rock a yard away from her and flicked his hat back rakishly, amusement lurking in discerning grey eyes as he waited for her tongue to unknot.

'Good morning, Mr. Saxon,' Jane murmured stiffly, and was relieved when Sandy placed her rod in the cleft stick and launched herself like a saucy rocket at him, diverting his attention momentarily. The youngster plopped on to his lap and twined thin arms around a tanned neck. 'Can we eat now, I'm starving to death! Did you bring your rod? We haven't been lucky yet—Jane says Tony and Mick are coming too—mm, you smell delicious!' She sniffed ecstatically and burrowed deeper into the open neck of his shirt.

Jane felt sudden laughter bubbling as she noticed a deepening colour rise up the exposed neck to suffuse and brighten well-shaped ears. Her own poise was regained at the thought that even a wealthy, temporal Saxon could not always control nature's embarrassing blushes! He did smell rather strange—a mixture of green orange leaves, hay, shaving soap and tobacco—an intriguing combination.

'Cut it out, you little squib, that's my Chanel Number Five you're busy licking off. I didn't shower in it for your benefit!' Grant tickled the child into a state of delighted hysterics.

Jane swallowed the bubbling laughter and asked demurely, 'A new sort of bait for the fish, Mr. Saxon?'

'A new sort of bait, Miss Wheeler, period.' Over the tousled head wood-smoke eyes dwelt on her with deepening speculation.

Jane made a deliberate show of tilting her head to study the trees, scrub and river as if in search of something or someone and then turned back with an expressive shrug of her shoulders. A feathery prickle started up her spine at the amused stare that had replaced the speculative shine in his eyes. She was annoyed at the queer breathlessness that tightened her chest and the words that were meant to be uttered nonchalantly came out rather stiltedly. 'What a waste of good bait, and so expensive. Sandy may as well enjoy it.'

'Unappreciative girl! Doesn't it send your senses reeling just the tiniest bit?' Grant dared mockingly.

Jane stood upright and dusted the seat of her shorts. The man was out to bait her; time must hang heavy on his hands with the absence of his wife. But she, Jane Wheeler, was not going to be a temporary target, not by a long shot, for the amusement of any flirtatious-minded man!

'It certainly does not, Mr. Saxon,' she retorted, and walked away from his unsettling presence to open the flask of tea. Arranging the cups in a precise row, she slanted a quick backward glance. Grant was tying Sandy's ribbon with great concentration and calling to Lemmy to fetch his rod and tackle.

Sandy came to help Jane open the hamper and they set out plates of chicken and cucumber sandwiches, hard-boiled eggs and ripe tomatoes. By the time this was done, Grant had his line in the water and was settled very comfortably against the jutting root of a willow tree.

He looked so relaxed with his rather scruffy hat edged over his eyes that Jane forbore to call him. Instead, she walked over with the plate and steaming cup. Grant tipped his hat and watched lazily as she set it down within his reach. 'Thanks, Jane. Have you attempted a catch yet?'

'I gave up just before you arrived, Mr. Saxon.'

He squinted up at her, 'You may call me Grant——' and sounded so condescending that betraying colour whipped her cheeks.

'Big deal!' Her retort was only an indignant whisper as she turned away, followed by an involuntary squeal as a lithe body turned like a steel spring and her ankle was caught in a vice, making her come down inelegantly on her seat.

'Girls always fall at my feet even without bait lure, didn't you know?' Grant jeered, and brought a tanned, disturbing face closer. 'Sit still now, there's a good girl, and tell me why you're so very prickly. Are you like that with every stranger you meet, Jane Wheeler?'

Her heart began an absurd beat; his dark nearness was causing a strange effect ... Jane sat perfectly still while she tried to analyse her emotions. She did not like him very much; he was too arrogant and sure of himself; his derogatory manner infuriated her—and he was a married man with a small daughter.

'Well, Jane, is this hate at first sight?'

'I don't hate every stranger on sight, Mr. Saxon——'

'Grant.'

'—but then strangers don't usually treat me in an offending manner.' To her own ears Jane sounded absurdly prim, but that was exactly how she felt. A primness that covered wavering emotions which were quite unexplainable.

'My dear girl, have I offended you? I thought you liked horseplay, having seen you with the boys ...' Grant tried a penitent look. 'Did I hurt your delectable little ankle or is it your neat posterior that pains—or just your vanity? Actually I had to make a grab, you're like a will-o'-the-wisp, in order to have a serious little chat.'

'If that's your idea of an apology then I fear you haven't had much experience in that fine art, Mr.——'

21

'Grant.' The interpolation came firmly.

'—however, I will accept it as such.' Jane extricated her ankle from his grasp, brought her knees up and encircled them with her arms. 'What do you want to talk about, what serious discussion could you possibly have with me?'

A banshee yell rent the air. 'Your line, Grant, your line—just look at it!' Sandy screamed. Grant shot towards the singing ratchet and rod while Jane flattened herself in a good imitation of a starfish.

'Well, what do you know!' Grant exclaimed as they viewed the shining, wriggling fish with dark markings across its back. 'A Black bass, no less!'

Tony and Mick appeared on cue, to admire enviously. They were all for settling their bait then and there, but Grant allowed for tea and vittles before the ants invaded everything. The children were obviously fond and at ease with him and his comradely way with them was uncommonly surprising and pleasant to watch. He did not mention the supposedly serious discussion again until just before they packed up. Lemmy went off loaded with gear and the empty hamper. Grant took Sandy's hand and repeated his invitation to run Jane and the boys home in the Rover that he had parked under the trees.

'No, thanks ... Grant,' she still stumbled slightly on his name, 'I—we enjoy the walk and Mick promised to show me clumps of montbretias and agapanthus that are growing wild further downstream.' Within the last two hours Jane had overcome her strange antagonism, which had melted somewhat under his rather devastating personality. Grant Saxon could be quite charming when it suited him.

'Yes, I know the place. I'll be around later. I must see your uncle about certain things and I'd like you to be present, it concerns you as well.' It was politely worded but sounded like a definite demand, and Jane watched him and Sandy disappear over the bank with mixed feelings. She simply could not account for the butterfly condition under her ribs.

One thing for sure, she was determined to have that talk with her uncle before that broad-shouldered, rangy man arrived. Jane felt there might just be a connection between that subject of discussion and her state of mind.

The Combi was parked at the side of the house, so her uncle must be home. Elizabeth and Janet were setting out the knitting machine in the study which had been drastically converted to suit their needs. Bart's books and disorder were stacked neatly in a corner cupboard, his writing desk stood outside the door on the enclosed portion of the verandah. Janet assured him he would do far better there, it was so much cooler, and the poor man perforce agreed to this invasion of his territory, in the interests of Business!

Jane took her uncle's arm and persuaded him to walk with her to the bench under the trees in the back yard. Bart sat down and watched her quizzically, aware that his niece had something on her mind. 'Spit it out, Jane. If I can help—here I am.'

'Uncle Bart,' Jane studied her interclasped fingers, suddenly hesitant for fear he might think her presumptuous in sticking her nose into what did not concern her. Anxiety and a sincere wish for clarification made her lift her head and continue, 'Uncle, please don't think it's cheek or mere nosiness and interference on my part—would you care to tell me if Mr. Saxon has some hold on you? Is he perhaps a part-owner of your orchards and lands?'

Bart Wheeler studied the intense young face and gold-flecked brown eyes that withstood his scrutiny with a levelling sincerity. He withdrew his pipe from a jacket pocket and started to tamp down the tobacco with a stained thumb. 'What did you hear, and how, Jane?' he asked quietly.

'Alphina was rather confused on the set-up here. She happened to mention something about—Grant—being the big boss when we were watching you and him through the kitchen window, two days ago. I didn't want to question her or Aunt Janet, but I'm rather puzzled. She seemed to insinuate that he owned all the l-land.'

'Oh.' The pipe drew to his satisfaction and Bart spoke through a cloud of fragrant smoke. 'Grant Saxon is the big boss, Jane. He owns the land, house, in fact the entire property.'

Although her suspicions were finally confirmed a ripple of

23

astonishment contracted her throat and she stared at him wordlessly. Bartholomew Wheeler had lived here for more years than she could remember and there had never been a hint of evidence that he was in need, financially, or planning to sell his beloved farm. Why now——?

'Why, Uncle?' she managed at last.

'Well, dear, it's rather a long story, but I'll put it as briefly as possible. I wanted to spread out, tried my hand at tobacco and chose one of the worst, driest years. A complete flop it was, and I, who should have known better, also committed the unpardonable sin of neglecting my orchards. The results were black rot in the orange crop and a tobacco disaster. The expense of the tobacco sheds and new equipment put me badly in the red. Grant came to my aid and, being a decent chap, gave me a share in the business and took over in his own capable way. He's convinced that those sheds will still be of use and will pay their way when the young tobacco crop he planted matures ... I'm also on his wage sheet, all his chaps are provided with good living quarters and he insisted that I remain here, in my own home. Don't look so tragic, Jane. It's a satisfactory partnership and arrangement. The lands adjoin, to Grant's benefit, and Janet's and my roots have not been disturbed by having to consider the possibility of m-moving, if someone else had taken over.'

Jane watched him attend his pipe in the silence that followed.

'Meaning,' she stammered slightly, 'that you live here, only while you're willing and—able—to work for Grant? What happens if you become ill and unable—do you lose all this, your heritage——'

Bart put a rough brown hand on her knee. 'Don't be so upset and concerned, Jane dear. I have no intentions of giving up or losing my health. Grant and I get on very well and I'm not badly off financially now. He's a good, generous man, although a hard driver, and quite rightly so. I was very fortunate to have him as my neighbour and feel deeply in his debt—not financially, but for helping me keep my head above water at a critical time. A friend in time of need. I didn't mind selling out my heritage—as you call it—to such

24

a man and still have a share in it all. Actually I'm better off now, the load of responsibility has shifted; not that I want to shirk the work, but I'm getting older and he's a young man with more advanced ideas ... a man with a great store of vital enthusiasm. Tony and Mick will learn more from him and your aunt, and I have Grant Saxon's word that this will remain our home for life—with a pension clause in our contract.' He smiled confidently into the eyes that had mirrored mixed emotions at his explanations, with an intensity that varied their colour from gold to almost black.

'Yes, I understand, Uncle. Thank you for your confidence.' Jane's lashes dropped to her hands again. 'Mother and I, coming here, are really interlopers on Saxon property——'

'Just a minute, girl, let's get this straight: Grant knew that Janet and I wanted you to make your home with us; we're allowed to invite our families into our private homes. He not only persuaded but demanded that we send for you and Elizabeth, not only to visit but to make a permanent home with us. Which we were very happy to do, so don't let me hear any more of that sort of talk or I shall be very angry!' Back in his mouth, the old pipe belched smoke like an upgrading little engine.

Jane smiled a beguiling apology but persisted on the tangent of her mind. 'Do all the people on these estates work exclusively for the owners?'

'Of course, that's understood. He can't provide for outsiders and his men are happier when they have comfortable homes right on the job.'

A startling thought struck her. 'Was that why he—Grant —mentioned something about a job for me? Is it a real job, Uncle, or simply a made one to put me in a working category, not to be listed as an outsider?'

Smoke belched again, but her discerning relative understood and considered.

'I don't think it's a put-up job because, to my knowledge, the offices are short-staffed. Two girls are down with 'flu and one is leaving for Nelspruit to get hitched. If Grant mentions it again you can take it from there, if you feel so in-

25

clined. But remember, it's not necessary for you to seek out-side work. There's plenty for you to do right here, and you've already shown your worth with the chores you've undertaken. On the other hand, you have high qualifications in your own line of work and due respect should be given in the right direction. So, if such an opportunity is offered,' twinkling eyes creased at the corners, 'Grant pays damned well for services rendered!'

Jane smoothed an affectionate hand down his sleeve. 'Thanks, Uncle Bart, for being so patient with me. I do understand, and I think you're very brave to be so philo-sophical about your losses. Your loyalty to Grant Saxon is commendable—but anyone with half a brain can see the ad-vantages of being in a position to snap up fertile adjoining lands!'

For the second time that day a certain adjective was used when her relative said rather reproachfully, 'Jane, don't be so prickly about our neighbour. Get to know him before you judge too hastily. You didn't mention anything, but Tony told me that Grant spent the morning with you at the river; that's most unusual and surprising—he's for ever too busy to relax for a moment, never mind a full morning! A hard business man, difficult to assess at first or second meeting. His prestige is high, he's regarded with respect throughout the eastern Province and is really a good chap. Come on, Janey, why the prickles—did you have a tiff with Grant?'

Jane jumped up suddenly and showed pearly teeth in a wide smile. 'Listen to that list of virtues! And you're so right about me being hedgehoggy; firstly, he found me on the floor with the boys at our first meeting, in a dishevelled state; brought me most unbecomingly down on to my seat this morning, treats me with amused contempt and makes me feel ludicrous most of the time. Who wouldn't prickle? But for your sweet sake I'll endeavour to remain upright on my two feet as from now on and show due respect for such a para-gon——'

'Starting right now. The paragon approaches,' Bart ad-vised as a low-slung, high-powered car purred up the drive-way.

The door opened, long legs unfurled to be followed by the rest of a lithe body. Grant Saxon snicked the door shut, saw them and started to walk towards uncle and niece.

'Wow!' said Jane, her eyes glued to the sleek lines of the car. She ignored the driver.

'Car or driver?' Bart teased.

Brown eyes swivelled to the driver and Jane very nearly repeated her exclamation. He did look rather dashing. Brown tight-hipped trousers accentuated the slim hips and length of strong rangy legs. A tan polo-necked pullover, a mixed texture of wool and some silky stuff, contrasted sharply with the blue-grey smokiness of dark-lashed eyes. Grant moved with indolent grace. And Jane Wheeler felt a silly flutter in her breast as she watched him approach . . .

Well, any female, unless she were made of solid granite, would admire and feel a certain flutter at the sight of such broad shoulders, supple free-muscled stride and male vitality! Jane sternly put an end to the lyrical waxing of thought and forbore to answer her uncle's teasing remark.

Instead, she concentrated on composure and the quelling of rioting butterflies under her ribs, stuck a determined smile on her lips, and let her eyes wander back to the car.

Grant lifted a saluting hand, then turned slightly to follow the direction of the girl's eyes.

'Like it?'

She lifted her chin to meet his questioning glance. 'If 'tis permitted to use expressive slang when referring to that well-bred, sleek, autocratic, fabulous automobile? Definitely a snazzy job!'

His laughter, deep and vibrating, immediately disturbed and caused new havoc amongst the winged insects that Jane had managed to quell only moments ago.

'Bart, the lady approves!' Sunshine lent red glints to dark hair as Grant inclined his head. 'In appreciation of her outright and sincere flattery may I suggest Jane be given fifteen minutes to change into attire suitable to the occasion and I'll proceed to prove that performance equals beauty?'

Jane turned wide, bedazzled eyes to Bart. 'The inland dialect is so charming, but so hard to follow. Do I under-

27

stand rightly—we're referring and acclaiming the beauty and merits of the car and that I've been invited to share those delights——' She stopped abruptly. Now she had left herself wide open for whatever was coming. Her admiration for the car had been open, but she had not voiced her thoughts on the man ... that tongue of hers would always try to outsmart the rest of her!

Yes, 'whatever' was coming ... Jane was treated to a cool, amused, analytical stare, a diabolical eyebrow lifted knowledgeably.

'I realise my inimitable charm is quite as devastating, my performance can equal same, but,' Grant sighed regretfully, 'we were discussing the car. Maybe at some future date ... Yes, Jane, you're coming with me to the Mission Hospital. I suggest you slip into a dress, if you own one, my dear. You look very—er—cute in shorts or jeans, but it would be more circumspect to confront the medical staff and patients properly attired, don't you think?'

Jane's soft mouth opened and shut rather like that of the poor fish that had lain panting on the bank.

'Well! Of all the——' even white teeth clamped hard on a runaway tongue.

Bart touched her arm hastily. 'Janey, don't argue, run along and change before you're hijacked bodily, just as you are. It can happen, take it from one who knows.'

'On your way, a small request, for Janet and your mother to join us with coffee, while we wait for you? Fifteen minutes?' Grant bowed politely.

Jane's slim hands came defiantly to her hips, and Grant Saxon took a reflective step forward. She backed hastily, turned to look at the car and decided to capitulate. 'One's prepared to put up with anything for a ride in that beauty'— amending quickly as a dark eyebrow shot up again—'sorry, by anything I mean being ordered around. It's rather late, can we make it to the Mission and back in time for supper?'

'Dr. David expects us to stay for dinner, so there's no need to hurry back,' Grant stated calmly.

'But he doesn't know me or expect——'

'He's expecting both of us. I phoned him.'

Jane was transfixed and silent with the audacity of the man!

Grant Saxon lifted a negligent arm and studied his watch. 'Twelve minutes to go.'

She walked indoors breathing exasperation and gave her aunt his message through clenched teeth. Under a quick shower and while she dressed, Jane took stock of her jumbled emotions. She could quite easily have stood her ground and refused to go; this was a civilised world—and Grant wouldn't have really forced the issue, to lift her bodily as her uncle had warned? A niggling thorn in her mind pricked her into admission that she did want to go with—she compromised—in that sleek car, just to experience its performance and to meet the interesting people at the Mission.

Two white doctors, according to her aunt, and an attractive Sister-in-Charge, coloured nurses and clerical staff. One wing for European patients and the rest for Bantu in and out patients. Dr. David Muller, the elderly popular head, dedicated to his work, and his young assistant Dr. Peter Davis. The Sister, Pat Somebody—Jane could not recall her surname—was young, blonde and attractive.

Yes, she would go with Grant this time only, not let it become a habit. Uncle Bart didn't seem to think it strange for his niece to ride around with an attractive family man; he evidently trusted the estate owner considerably. However, she would refrain from accepting any further invitations, if they were forthcoming; she might become the target for unsavoury scandal if she were seen gadding about with Saxon too much, especially if his glamorous Mara got to hear of it! On second thoughts, maybe Grant was making this trip, taking this opportunity to have that talk that was mentioned earlier on?

Jane took a last quick survey of the girl in the mirror. Shoulder-length hair brushed to a silky sheen, a glimmer of eye-shadow and pearly lipstick. The short-sleeved cinnamon sheath showed the youthful contours of her slim figure and boosted her morale considerably after the derisive way her scruffiness and questioned lack of dress had been commented upon. Slim feet went into her newest buckled shoes, and with the comfort of feeling clean and well-groomed, Jane lifted her head proudly and descended the steps to where her family were in a worshipping huddle around Grant's car.

He was smiling at Elizabeth and turned to glance at the girl, taking in the slim brevity of her mini-dress, the wet shine of buckled shoes, back to the shining fall of hair and delicacy of features. His expression altered infinitesimally, something Jane saw but could not define but which sent a feathery play along her spine.

Tony opened the car door for Jane with great ceremony and Mick dashed to do the same for Grant. Elizabeth smiled at her daughter and dropped a wicked wink of approval in the direction of the owner of the super-car. Only Jane saw it, but it was so blatant, so unlike her conventional mother that the girl wondered for a shocked moment if Elizabeth knew that her daughter's escort was married. Of course she knew; they had discussed Mara and there was young Sandra to prove it!

The family waved cheerfully as the powerful car glided swiftly and silently down the avenue of pines.

The man behind the wheel did not offer small talk and Jane pushed back the puzzlement of her mother's strange behaviour to relax and enjoy the feel of comfort and power the 'snazzy job' instilled. She was entranced by the lovely scent and orderliness of orange trees stretching into the distance. The variable greens of pines and gums sloped lushly up the hills and closer, on the sides of the road, wild flowers peeped out in many brilliant colours amongst tree ferns and wild creepers.

Inevitably, her eyes were drawn back to the long brown hands manipulating the wheel with sure, firm ease. She lifted her head slightly and studied his neck and profile, relaxed yet revealing strength and certain arrogance which commanded one's attention.

Grant turned his head suddenly, met her intent gaze and his teeth gleamed whitely. 'Up to expectations?' The smile deepened into an unexpected dimple. 'And I'm referring to the car.'

Jane straightened from her relaxed position. He really was

30

a tease, but he had caught her studying him and teasing seemed to be part of his nature.

She answered naturally and enthusiastically. 'Absolutely super, marvellous suspension—it's like floating inches off the ground, and the engine's so silent. Synchromeshed?'

Grant's eyes crinkled at her enthusiasm. 'Automatic transmission, air-conditioned, button-control radio. You name it, this baby's got it!'

'You will show me the engine some time?' Jane closed her eyes dreamily. 'If I possessed a baby like this, I would travel all the time and see Africa. I bet these seats are convertible, the backs lower to form beds—you did say name it?'

His chuckle came deep and infectious. 'Caught me out first shot! No convertible seats, I'm afraid. I wasn't thinking of sleeping when I bought this car. Do you like travelling, Jane?'

'No more nor less than most ordinary folks. This car is highly conducive to such thoughts—one wouldn't tire easily on long journeys. I have visited the Cape and Natal, but inland, further north and east is still just an enchanting dream to me.'

'You should travel the Summit Route some day. It begins right here on your doorstep.'

'I've heard about Mount Anderson and the Pinnacle at Graskop. The Bridal Veil falls and Devil's Knuckles—Jock of the Bushveld route——'

'Blyde River Canyon and its Nature Reserve, God's Window and——' Grant continued as Jane paused for breath, 'the Devil's Pulpit. Near Bourke's Luck are the Potholes, a series of rockpools at the confluence of the Blyde and Treur rivers. They've built suspension bridges, and if you're prepared or brave enough to venture on them you have a clear view. A visit to Mount Sheba is a must—I believe two brothers from Kenya have built a fabulous hotel and the view is breathtaking. Then there's Kowyn's Pass which drops roughly one thousand five hundred feet down the escarpment within a matter of two miles and was named after a Bakwena Chief.'

'I've now made up my mind,' Grant went on, 'to take you

on that trip. It's been quite some time since I last travelled that way, and with this car and your enthusiasm I'll see and appreciate with new eyes. However, our humble Mission lies ahead and it's time to come down to earth and meet a dedicated mortal—David Muller.'

Jane had been so mesmerised by his deep voice and travelogue that she only realised now that they were beginning to wind through a number of white-washed buildings. Spaced at intervals, the long buildings were evidently wards for the sick and ailing. A number of Bantu were either sitting or walking about in a type of long white shirt with blue, knitted skull-caps on their black fuzzy hair. Grant followed a sign and pointer indicating the doctor's quarters and offices.

Her eyes saw groups of tiny piccaninnies, but her thoughts ran on Grant's sudden decision to take her on that Summit trip. It would be wonderful, but definitely not just the two of them? He could only mean when Mara came home. Jane Wheeler found her thoughts dribbling to a stop with unaccountable heaviness...

CHAPTER 3

GRANT ushered Jane through the reception office where coloured orderlies were busily engaged. The Bantu Staff Sister greeted them with a pearly smile of recognition for the Estate owner. She was clad in a crisp blue and white uniform with ranking blue belt and her white cap sat jauntily atop curly black hair.

'Sister Marion,' Grant put a hand on Jane's shoulder, 'this is Miss Wheeler who, with her mother, is now living with her relatives, Mr. and Mrs. Bart Wheeler.'

Sister Marion hesitated for only a second, then clasped Jane's outstretched hand. 'I'm honoured, ma'am. You wish to see Doctor Muller, please to come this way?' She spoke to a passing nurse in dialect and then politely motioned the two visitors to precede her down the cool stone-floored passage.

A door at the far end erupted violently and a blonde, uniformed girl turned sharply in the opening and straightened her cap while she spoke indignantly to an unseen occupant.

'I promise you, Peter Davis, if you lay a finger on me again I'll report you, so help me!'

'Well, what have we here, young Pat? Someone molesting you?'

The girl whirled with a startled squeak, a hand to her mouth as Grant spoke directly behind her.

'Grant Saxon, you devil!' She lifted a shaking hand to tuck another wisp of gold under her cap. 'Sorry, you startled me——'

'You seem to be between two devils, then, my beauty.' Grant drawled, and towered over her slight figure to peer into the room she had vacated so abruptly. 'Can only be one other and sure 'tis he, Pete the Knife! Do I smell nasty competition, sweet one?'

'That man couldn't compete with a—a zongololo!'

'That man' came into view. 'Certainly not! That creepy has a thousand arms and I only have two.' Peter Davis surveyed his hands disgustedly, looked up and caught sight of Jane in the background. A delighted eyebrow shot skywards.

'Move over, please, can't have my patients waiting. Grant, old boy, do you mind, your manly bulk is impeding progress —take Sister Pat away and smooth her feathers. I accidentally tipped her cap—no offence, y'know.'

Grant moved negligently, but his voice came with a sharp bite.

'Superintendent Wheeler has come to look into reported negligence and misbehaviour on the part of the staff. She has now registered first-hand knowledge——' Amused interest lurked in grey eyes as he watched the abrupt reaction of Doctor Davis and Sister Marais.

The Mission staff stiffened to attention. Peter ran a finger along his collar, buttoned the top button on his white coat and the blonde, petite Sister flushed to the tips of her ears and twined her hands nervously behind her back.

Peter's former rapt but now startled gaze shifted for a

33

moment from the lady 'superintendent' to Grant Saxon. He caught the mocking light in wood-smoke eyes and relaxed indignantly.

'I thought she was too young and unspoilt-looking to be a dreary inspector. You're an unmitigated goof, Grant, frightening the curl out of Pat's hair and right into my toenails! Wheeler? Elizabeth? No, this must be Jane, old Bart's niece. How do you do, Jane Wheeler. I can see by the innocent surprise on your face that you weren't on to this dirty trick Grant tried on us. Peter Davis, at your service.' Her hand was clasped tenderly.

'Not so much of your kind of service either. She's under my care. Jane, this is Pat Marais, Sister-in-Charge between times of warding off unwanted approaches of various males in the neighbourhood.'

Pat Marais acknowledged the introduction and immediately slanted blue eyes back to Grant. 'Excluding yours, Grant? Your approaches are the most difficult because,' her dancing gaze swept back to Jane, 'his are never there to ward off!' Slender shoulders sloped regretfully.

'Why didn't you tell me about this torch you're carrying, honey?' Grant teased, and Jane was more than ever convinced that, for a family man, he behaved most outrageously. And his bland statement that she, Jane, was under his care, designating himself calmly as her keeper—well!

'You've felt the scorching heat of my torch, but you remain hard, uncaring and unbeguiled, damn you, Saxon! How did you get into his clutches, Jane?' Pat wanted to know.

With all the flirtatious banter and the openly admiring eyes of Peter Davis fixed on her, Jane felt that things were getting slightly beyond her. She answered Pat airily enough, in a conspiratorial whisper. 'His car, Sister, lured me as inexorably as a bird is hypnotised by a snake. Absolutely magnetic, you know?'

Sister Marion had vanished from the flippant company and now an adjacent door opened and an elderly man in a white safari suit appeared, his hand outstretched to meet the firm clasp of Grant Saxon.

'Sorry to keep you waiting, Grant. I could distinctly hear my staff putting up an inferior show of entertaining, but couldn't free myself sooner to rescue you and——' he turned to Jane and a quick, piercing eye circled her face and rested for a long moment on her honey-flecked brown eyes.

'How do you do, Dr. Muller.' She found herself stammering under the close scrutiny of those piercing blue eyes.

Grant's deep voice interposed, 'Enough of this mutual admiration stuff. My feet wants up and my hand craves to clutch a glass of something wet and cool.'

Jane's hands were dropped. 'Jealousy gets you nowhere, old chap. Come, I've finished for the day, I hope, so let's move to my quarters.' He turned to his silent staff. 'You two may join us at dinner if—I repeat, if you manage to complete your duties and stop wasting hospital time on horseplay!' Jane's hand was tucked firmly in the crook of a wiry arm and they proceeded down the passage. Grant lowered a wickedly superior look on the two open-mouthed victims before falling into step beside Jane.

David Muller's quarters led off the main building under a connecting, open-sided canopied walk. The lounge contained scattered armchairs covered with faded but clean floral cretonnes, a few small tables and a long bookshelf that stretched across one entire wall. A battery-operated radio occupied one corner, next to it a low table stacked neatly with a small selection of records.

The doctor led Jane to his best armchair and Grant sank his length into the depths of another, across from her. A sharp clap brought a white-clad house-boy and David communicated his guests' choice of drinks. The two men chose whisky with ice and Jane settled for an iced passion-fruit. A silence that held a companionable quality enveloped the three occupants while they waited for the return of the house-boy with the tray. He set the tray on a table and withdrew in a polite backward shuffle.

'How is young Sandra?' David inquired of Grant.

The sun-browned Estate owner leaned his dark head back comfortably and grinned lobsidedly, 'Just fine. She has a new friend who's also keen on fishing, and that's tops with her.

Her friend is the sole subject of discussion at all times ... how she saved Sandra Saxon from an agonising death, how this understanding friend allowed her to land her first catch, which incidentally grows with each telling. How she, Sandy, pleads with her Maker every night to change her own 'orrible red hair to a nice, polished berry colour. This amazing friend truly doesn't mind getting dirty all over and, wonders never cease, she doesn't squirm or shudder away from threading nice juicy earthworms on to the hook. Quite unlike her mother, who's stuffy about a bit of dirt and squeals at the sight of a dear little worm. Sandra has a great pash for her new friend!'

Two pairs of eyes were on Jane. Her face had turned a bright pink, but she lifted her chin and outstared them defiantly.

'I like her too, very much. We would like to explore, your permission permitting, the gully and stream below the pines. We want to start a nature book, with pressed specimens and notes on what we see and find.'

David spoke before Grant could pass comment. 'That will be fine, I'm sure Grant won't mind. It's a good thing for the young to learn about nature at first hand. I'm very glad Sandy has found such a friend. Not many older girls would bother with the things that children find exciting and wonderful. Tell me about the rescue from agonising death?'

Jane's heart warmed towards the discerning doctor and while she explained she also silently wondered what Grant's thoughts would be on the comparison between mother and friend. Sandy would think it disparaging, but he would pass it off as a comparison seen through a child's adventurous eyes; he would rather have Mara just as she was, glamorous and fastidious, of that Jane was quite sure.

'That must have made our Sandra's day! And the glamorous Mara, have you heard from her, and how is the modelling profession progressing?' David voiced the direction of her thoughts.

Grant became intent on the golden liquid in his glass. His reply was laconic, but Jane noticed a pressure of hand that whitened the knuckles of the one holding the glass.

'She's doing well. Her tour ends this week-end. We can expect her soon; she's finally bought another car and insists on driving herself, instead of my usual motoring down to fetch her. Wants to show off her driving prowess, I guess.'

David's eyes narrowed slightly as he watched the tip of Grant's glass.

'That means she's finally overcome her aversion to driving, since the accident?'

'It means just that. Positive proof of a fault in the steering column, not her—the other—caused the tragedy.' Grant's lips were compressed.

'Yes, well.' David smiled again. 'Coming back to Sandy and her friend. Mara's going to be slightly ruffled at the competition. Sandy's worship has never wavered before. Come to think of it,' his blue eyes rested on the uncomprehending girl opposite him, 'those pretty feathers could be ruffled quite considerably!'

Grant Saxon lifted his head and stared at his friend for palpitating seconds before he stated with a cold finality, 'If you're harping back to a certain personal subject, I assure you the question doesn't arise, nor ever will.'

'Okay, Grant Saxon, don't knock your block. Just a reminder that no man can say with complete confidence that he's impervious to the insidious guile of the fair sex.'

Jane looked from the cold, closed face of Grant Saxon to the crinkled eyebrows of the older man in complete bewilderment. She had absolutely no idea why the teasing tones had suddenly become something that left a gleam of icy steel in wood-smoke eyes. She knew nothing of what they were alluding to when they spoke of Mara and accidents and ruffled feathers. Surely the doctor couldn't mean that she could cause a rift somehow? That was unthinkable and in bad taste, not the sort of thing she would expect of David Muller. No wonder the cold look had come into those eyes! It had also spoilt the air of ease that had pervaded the room ... until Mara Saxon was mentioned.

She turned with a sense of relief as voices heralded the appearance of Pat Marais and Peter Davis. David expelled a gusty breath and smiled at the pair while he called for more drinks.

Grant subsided deeper into his chair, lit a cigarette and allowed the smoke to drift across his face while he contemplated Jane in a disinterested way, almost as if he did not see, as if his eyes were turned inwards to match a secret brooding thought.

Jane turned a bright face to the newcomers, angry and bewildered at the stony, lifeless feeling under her heart. When they finally sat down to dinner Peter Davis made a point of engaging her attention, and it was not hard to return his friendly banter.

Pat Marais revealed gay social abilities as well, although she seemed somewhat obsessed with Grant and flirted outrageously whenever opportunity offered. His riposte had a derisive, mocking quality that only incited, instead of curbing her enthusiasm. Jane knew her own insides would curl up if a man returned her teasing with that certain inflection of voice that Saxon knew how to use to a fine art. He, a family man, evidently enjoyed a bit of offside bird-baiting in the absence of wifely restrictions!

The thought made her sniff contemptuously, harder than she intended. In the sudden silence that befalls most conversations, that sniff came loud and clear!

All heads swivelled in that direction. Grant, directly opposite her, leaned over and studied Jane with concern, the dark ring rimming the outer iris of his eyes blending into blue-grey pools.

'This is no time to start a cold, Jane.'

Jane squirmed at the sudden all-round scrutiny and answered with some asperity. 'Of course not. Can't one sniff in medical company without the worst being immediately diagnosed?'

Grant said coolly, 'I'm not included in the medical category, but Dr. Muller will bear me out, there's been a wide outbreak of Hong Kong 'flu in this vicinity. Did you have the precautionary injection last year? That was a mighty unusual sniff, young woman!'

'Well,' she retorted, guilty colour making her feel hot, 'that was simply an unexpected, ordinary snort—sniff—not a cold or impending 'flu—take my word.'

'I could take a test—prompt attention and all that?' Peter's eyes twinkled in anticipation.

His superior slanted an ominous eyebrow at his assistant. 'Very commendable, but quite unnecessary, Dr. Davis. I know every nuance of various sniffs, and that one sounded suspiciously like a—disdainful snort. Now, I wonder,' a piercing eye circled the table and came back to his slim, delightfully blushing guest, 'what caused it?'

Jane's lashes fanned her cheeks in confusion and she started to pleat her napkin with unsteady fingers. Pat laughed suddenly and waved her hand across the table to break the spell of staring eyes.

'You see how it is in a small community, Jane. Everything you do is analysed, even a sniff isn't allowed to pass unnoticed. Join me on my afternoon off, we'll creep into a bush hideout and sniff and snort disdainfully, disgustedly, vulgarly and to our hearts' content at everything and everyone we yearn to sniff at!'

Everybody had to laugh at her comical, commiserating expression, and Jane was very conscious of the moment when the direct grey gaze of Grant lowered as he leaned back in his chair. Only when he offered cigarettes did she lift her eyes to refuse mutely. David put a hand on her shoulder.

'Joking aside, Jane, we've really had a run of the illness and three of my office staff are flat on their backs. Have you any experience of clerical, elementary office work, and are you, by some miracle, free and willing to help out?'

Her beech-nut hair swung into a pleased affirmative, but Grant Saxon cut across her reply with astounding, maddening coolness.

'Sorry, old boy, we're also drastically short-staffed. Jane may, if she's willing and not too tired, give you a hand one or two afternoons a week if you're truly stuck. Otherwise, she'll be kept horribly busy in my own office!'

Under the mesmeric smile directed at her, Jane slowly expelled the smouldering breath that threatened her bosom to bursting point. Doctor Muller shrugged rueful shoulders.

'Trust big Saxon to be first on the field! Talent of any

description simply gravitates to the Estates, or should I say, is sucked in before any other poor devil gets the chance. Well, I'm grateful for any crumbs of help, every bit helps. I'll accept your offer, Grant, if Jane agrees.'

Smoke drifted up steadily from a brown hand and a dimple line deepened as Grant continued to look at the stunned girl.

'My new assistant will be up to her ears, but I'm sure she'll take pity on your suffering. I'll give you a ring on her free time and bring her over myself.'

Peter said, 'That's how the cards fall, Janey. Your life gets mapped out regardless; don't look so stunned. Has Mr. Dynamite forestalled me, or have I still the chance to invite you to the Club dance two weeks from now?'

The trend of talk and impudence of Grant's cool declaration had indeed stunned Jane and her eyes were still mutinous when she switched from the hypnotic gaze to look at Peter. Sanity returned as she mastered her thoughts and tongue.

'Thanks, I'd like that, Peter.' She managed to repress the sarcasm to a minimum, to turn her lips upwards. 'Mr. Saxon hasn't forestalled you at all. He's rather overpowering at times, but surely not omnipotent?' Turning to Pat, whose bright inquisitive eyes had jumped from one speaker to the next, 'Are you going to this dance, Pat? What are they like? Is the attendance good? I haven't even seen the Club.'

Grant interposed, 'Quite respectable, my dear. Pete may be quite a lad with the girls, but he'll look after you—no need for girlish qualms.'

Jane slanted furious eyes and thought wildly: You, Grant Saxon, should be the last man to jeer at Peter's way with girls, you're way ahead of him! And not even free to be that way; you're the one I would have girlish qualms about. Stating in that lordly manner that I'll be working for you, without even asking me first—we'll see about that, Saxon! Not everybody is a softie!

Through a mist of boiling thoughts she became conscious of Pat speaking.

'The only man I'd bow down to doesn't ask me, so I'll take

up the first offer that comes my way, being an eager beaver when it comes to dancing. My boss will probably put me on night duty to save my innocent soul and prevent me from making an ass of myself!'

'I'm quite sure you'll not lack escort, Pat. If this one man in your life is such a stodge, my advice is forget him, he's not worth further thought,' Grant comforted.

Pat looked at him through slitted eyes. 'Yeah!' she gritted, 'how closed and dense can a man get? I suppose Mara will be here by then, so you're accounted for?'

An imperceptible paused followed before Grant said with careless equanamity, 'Don't try to be too perceptive, Pat dear, it's unbecoming in the young. I may show up—depends——' he turned to David and inquired after the health of the Estate hands who were in the Mission for treatment.

Jane again felt a sense of puzzlement at some mystery in the atmosphere. The Mara situation definitely intrigued. All was not as it should be in the Saxon household, of that she was becoming very aware.

Later, Pat curled up on the couch in her bedroom while Jane visited the bathroom. She washed her hands and joined the blonde Sister, looking around curiously at the cosy room. 'Nice pad you've got here, Pat. Do you live in permanently, and have you a family in this vicinity?'

Pat uncurled and stood up, stretching her body languidly. 'Mum and Dad live in White River, I visit as often as permits and I've two younger brothers. Real stinkers, those two, but I love 'em all! I like it here, plenty of work but interesting. What do you think of Pete Davis?' she asked in a sudden tangent.

'Peter? I haven't had much time to delve deeply, but he strikes me as a good sort,' Jane answered cautiously.

'He's okay, a good doctor but an awful flirt.' Pat spoke offhandedly and shot another question, 'What do you make of Grant Saxon?'

Jane became more cautious; that question came with deeper intensity. 'There also I plead short acquaintance. He's slightly masterful—very sure of himself.'

'And yet you're already on his wage sheet ... and visiting

list? Do you like him?'

Jane grinned suddenly. 'Come now, Pat, one visit to the Mission, that's all! As for the wage sheet, I——' she almost blurted out the truth, that she herself had heard of that for the first time tonight. Something held her back. '—I do need the work and it's close at hand, practically on my doorstep, so to speak, very convenient all round. As for liking the man—well, it's hard to say——'

'I couldn't agree more! Grant Saxon is a strange man, you either fall madly or hate him like hell! He's a real paradox, one can hate and love him at the same time, and as elusive as the proverbial will-o'-the-wisp. I'm beginning to believe that Mara is the only one——' Pat stopped and dived to a lower drawer to extract a few tissues.

Jane waited and found her body tensed for the conclusion of Pat's beliefs. Her companion straightened up, tucked the tissues into her pocket and said casually, 'Shall we go?'

Feeling highly frustrated, Jane came to a decision. 'Pat, what happened in that accident, with Mara?'

Pat paused in the doorway. 'Oh, didn't you know? Mara was driving—rumour has it that she was slightly intoxicated, but I hear now that some driving gear was faulty. It's being investigated ... poor John was killed instantly.'

'John?' Jane felt shock streak through her system.

'Of course, you never knew him. One of the best, an awful tragedy, and Grant was absolutely and still is inconsolable. He loved his brother very dearly. John Saxon was two years younger than Grant, but they were like twin souls ... except where Mara was concerned. I hear she's coming back, and if I know her, she'll have her way, fair means or foul. Grant would be most annoyed if he heard my gossiping, but, just for the record, I can't stand that female. Let's go!'

Peter had been called away to attend a slight emergency and Pat hurried in his wake with a wave of her hand. David Muller walked to the car with Jane and Grant.

'Remember that offer of help, Grant,' was his parting reminder as they pulled away.

Jane waited until they were on the open road, steeling herself to question Grant's statement and foregone conclusion that she would accept his plan of employment. Somehow the heat had gone out of her resolution to confront him with angry reproaches. Since Pat's rather muddled explanation her heart had softened towards this tall, sun-browned man. Sorrow did not sit on his shoulder, but he must be grieving inwardly at the loss of a beloved brother. She still had no idea of where and when the tragedy had occurred nor how Mara became involved. Nevertheless she felt a strong wave of sympathy for Grant Saxon and decided not to probe further into his affairs or try to solve the puzzling Saxon set-up.

He disarmed her completely in the next few seconds.

'Jane, I'd like to thank you and say I admire your self-control for not letting me down in company. I saw the surprised anger on your face and, quite frankly, I surprised myself. I had no intention of startling you with that bald statement, fully intending to discuss it with you first. Remember the confidential talk I mentioned this morning? When David pleaded lack of staff and I could see your coming acceptance—well, it simply had to be said.'

Her reply was not immediate and Grant lifted his foot off the accelerator, slowing down to glance at his silent passenger. 'Don't be angry, Jane. I'm asking you now for your help at the office. Bart told me you would be seeking your type of employment, you live conveniently near and further transport will be provided. I really need your services desperately. Jane?'

The assured, self-contained Grant Saxon actually apologising and pleading! Her silly heart, already softened by sympathy and now made more malleable by his disarming explanation, capitulated completely even while her mind urged caution. If Pat had not told of his bereavement ...

'I'm not angry any more, but I certainly was astonishingly so, at your apparent high-handedness. However, I accept your explanation, and when would you like me to start?'

'Thanks, Jane Wheeler, I like the way you cut corners. As soon as possible?'

'Can you send for me tomorrow, and do I wear an overall?'

'Atta-girl! Transport will be waiting at seven-thirty and you're not going into the packing sheds ... my office is reasonably clean, so no overalls!' The car shot forward under pressure from a well-shod foot.

He left her at the front door with a smile and a word of thanks for her company. Jane leaned against the closed door until the diminishing sound of the car had died away, then walked slowly to her room with very mixed and undefinable emotions clouding her mind.

CHAPTER 4

THE birds chirping boisterously when she returned to her room from an early morning shower. Jane opened the windows to their full extent and leaned out precariously, filling her lungs with pure, dewy air.

She twisted back for her brush and lifted her hair, allowing the fresh breeze to tingle her scalp while she brushed the long, nut-brown strands. The new, sparkling morning gave her a feeling of buoyancy, a sense of fitness; she felt capable and ready for her new job and whatever else this day may hand out. She completed her toilet, then walked quietly down the passage and tapped softly on her mother's door before entering.

Elizabeth opened sleepy eyes, then came fully awake as she realised it was not her morning tea as expected but daughter Jane, trim and businesslike in a neat dress instead of jeans and shirt which were usually standard morning gear. 'Wh—what's happened, darling? You're dressed and—and——' she stammered in alarm. Jane smiled reassuringly. 'Not to worry, Mother. You are surveying a girl with a JOB! The Saxon Estates have acquired a brilliant new hand,' her smile turned mischievously gamin, 'I hope! I'm going to have a cup of that aromatic coffee I can smell brewing and then someone'll probably be here to pick me up. I've just nipped in to let you know and I'll give you more details this evening.'

She leaned over her astonished mother, gave her a kiss and a pat on the cheek and disappeared before one of many questions could formulate on the opened lips of her nearest and dearest!

Her uncle was seated at the kitchen table, a large cup of steaming black coffee under his appreciative nose. Bart raised shaggy eyebrows at his niece's neat appearance. She was usually up with the lark, but this was not her morning rig? Like a dewy bud, for sure, in her yellow linen dress with collar and cuffs that matched the highlights in her hair.

''Morning, Jane, going somewhere special?'

'Good morning, Uncle Bart.' Jane poured a cup of coffee and settled on the chair opposite him. 'I'm a working gal, no less.'

'Well, well, the boss sure doesn't waste time, I'll say!'

His tone unaccountably flustered her, taking it so for granted that it could only be Grant Saxon that had hired her. A resentful wish fluttered for a moment, that she could inform him that she was being employed by the Mission or somewhere else. Oh well, Grant had been her escort the previous evening, so it figured . . .

'Yes, he certainly doesn't. I think I was hijacked into this, last night. He declared, in front of witnesses, that I was a new addition to the Estate. If he hadn't been so fast and given me the idea that I would be letting the side down by denying his statement, I'd most probably be doing a spot of duty for Doctor Muller instead.' A sliver of indignation was evident in her explanation.

Bart assimilated her news, drawing deeply on his pipe. A strong chuckle mingled with pipesmoke. 'I see . . . Grant and his devious ways. He strikes fast and you find yourself loyal, willy-nilly, even while wondering what hit you!'

Jane sighed. 'How right you are, Barty dear. Now, about my chores here—can I change them from the morning to the evening?'

'Oh, don't worry about all that. I forgot to mention that I've hired a local handyman, Flip Olivier—bit of a rover,

45

can't stay in one place for long but good at whatever job's going. You should see him on a tractor, slices the ground like butter. He'll be available twice a week for the heavy work, cleaning the hen and pig runs and the garden. Not the sort of work for a girl anyway.'

'Oh, Uncle, I didn't find it such hard work,' Jane smiled, 'just very smelly.'

'I don't care greatly for the man,' said Bart, 'but he prefers to earn his keep that way, does the rounds of all the farmers, and we take turns to feed and pay him.'

A vehicle stopped at the side of the house and Jane rose hurriedly and grabbed her bag. Bart walked with her to the Land-Rover from which a coloured driver descended. He greeted them politely and swung round to hold the door for Jane. She settled herself and waved to Bart as they proceeded down the drive.

Tom, the driver, handled the Rover competently and Jane still felt that curious exhilaration as they sped through the sparkling countryside. All too soon they drew up beside an imposing and dazzlingly white colonial-styled house. Jane felt quite awed, thanked Tom as he held the door open for her, then stepped back a few paces to view the graceful gabled frontage.

'Tom, do we have to stop here? This is Mr. Saxon's home and I'm supposed to go to the offices.'

'Yes, ma'am, this is Mr. Saxon's home. My instructions were to bring Ma'am here.' He pointed to a row of neat, white-painted, red-roofed buildings some distance away. 'Them be the general offices, but the master's private office is here, if Ma'am will please come this way?'

He accompanied her and stepped back slightly at the wide, shallow steps flanked by tall pillars that led on to a cool, spacious verandah. They faced the heavy, superb oak door that fronted the house. It opened as if a signal had passed and Jane faced a lean pale woman of indeterminate age. Tom touched his cap and retreated the way they had come.

'Miss Wheeler? Please come in. I'm Minna Du Toit, Mr. Grant's housekeeper. He asked me to show you to the study and serve tea, he'll be right with you——'

'Jane, Jane!' A small body hurtled through an open door-way and Jane gasped as the missile contacted her solar plexus with breathtaking force. 'Gee, I'm glad to see you what are you doing here are we going fishing and why aren't you wearing your jeans?'

'Sandra!' Minna Du Toit grabbed the hurricane with steely fingers while Jane bumped against the wall, searching for lost breath.

'Toicky, let me go, that's my friend Jane. You know I told you about her. Jane's come to visit me 'n she's awful pretty in that yellow dress, isn't she just, Toicky?' Fierce hands tried to free Sandy's captivity.

'Hullo, Sandy. I'm glad you like my dress and I'm very pleased to see you, but this isn't a visit. I've come to do some work.' Jane smiled at the excited child and lifted her eyes to catch a peculiar expression on the older woman's face; very fleeting, but the pale eyes had definitely darkened and warmed to some inner emotion.

'It's a very nice dress, Sandy, but that's no way to treat it or your friend. Good morning, Jane, I'm positive you'll need a cup of tea after that attack.' Grant spoke from the doorway that Sandy had hurtled through. He had evidently witnessed the whole scene including Jane's breathless stumble against the wall—clumsy as usual!

'Good morning, Mr. Saxon,' she answered primly, while those wretched butterflies started winging crazily at the sight of broad shoulders and freshly shaved, sun-browned features. His dark hair was damp but sleekly combed and a slight aura of shaving lotion gave impact to the lean, male look of him. Jane pulled herself up tartly; this was no way to begin the day! He was her boss and her insides must be controlled if she intended showing her excellent business acumen.

'Minna, we'll have tea in the study. Sandy, scarper off and finished your breakfast. You may share Jane's break for tea at ten o'clock if she desires your dubious company.'

Sandy meekly allowed 'Toicky' to lead her away. Jane could not resist a wink of assurance at her little friend before turning to follow Grant. His lips quirked slightly, but he made no remark at her gesture. They walked through an Lshaped lounge on deep, autumn-shaded carpeting. The furniture was old-fashioned, its coverings green and the wood shining tamboti. Sun-filter curtains of orangey-yellow filtered the harsh sunlight to a muted glow. Jane sensed atmosphere in this house; it was elegant yet homely and comfortable. Sliding glass doors opened on to the verandah and Grant paused to wait for her, noticed her interest, and a small smile deepened on well-cut lips.

'Sandy can show you the rest of the house later, if you're interested. It's a very old house and has its interesting points. This way, Jane.' Grant led her out on to the verandah to the door of his study. Part of the verandah had been bricked across to accommodate the study. Inside, he showed her to her desk facing a long window. Through this she could see a vista of trees, shrubs and well-kept lawns. Filing cabinets and a larger desk occupied more space and a grand new typewriter rested in splendour on a corner table.

'This will be your desk. I've been here since dawn, clearing the mess left by Miss Ames, an excellent secretary but muddled in her ways. Comes of having marriage on the brain, addles it somewhat. You haven't any such thoughts, Miss Jane?' The question bounced abruptly across the cleared desk.

'Good heavens, no!' she retorted, raising startled eyes to meet the hard, penetrating grey stare.

'Good.' Grant turned and slid open a drawer of the cabinet. A batch of files were dumped on to her desk. 'When you've had your tea, look through this lot and compare the opposite figures to see if they correspond. I've found a few discrepancies in them, due no doubt to Miss Ames's state of mind. We can't allow any margin of error in this business, the whole lot will be scrutinised again. Can do?'

Jane had started to page the top of the pile. 'Of course I can do,' she remarked, faintly nettled. This was small stuff she could do with her eyes closed ... well, not quite, so he needn't be so condescendingly anxious, as if she were a rabbit at the game. Jane sat down without further ado, ignoring the large figure across her desk. Grant stood for a minute longer, studying the shining bent head of his new assistant, then moved to his desk, scraped back his chair and became immersed in the work before him.

Two hours later the scrape of a chair disrupted her concentration. Grant stretched his arms and made a gesture of distaste at the work on his desk. 'I sincerely hope Ames bungles her honeymoon as much as she muddled this lot—it'll serve her right! Teatime, Jane, half an hour to get into the sunshine. Minna will serve it on the lawn. I'll join you presently.' He leafed through her file. 'Good going, girl,' and he walked out across the verandah into the lounge.

Jane stretched likewise and went out and down the side steps that led directly on to the lawn where she had seen Sandy. The housekeeper came across the grass and indicated where she had placed the tea. Jane poured her tea and relaxed on the cushioned, wrought iron chair. Her gaze wondered back to the house; it had been the family home for a long time. Where did Mara fit in . . . ?

'Toicky said I could have tea with you if I brushed my hair and washed my hands.' Sandy held out two small hands for inspection and swung a neat ponytail.

'That's great, Sandy,' Jane approved, and poured for her little companion. The child was in a talkative mood, prattling happily of all the happenings since their last meeting. She took a wisp of tissue paper out of her pocket and opened it carefully, revealing a rainbow butterfly wing found on one of the shrubs. They studied it, two heads close together.

A shadow fell across their heads as Grant leaned over to scrutinise Sandy's find. 'A gossamer-winged spring-azure, at a guess,' he remarked, while his eyes lifted to a more interesting study of the older girl's quite delightful curve of soft but firm cheek. 'We could check, though, I might be wrong. Tea, please, Jane.'

Sandy wrapped her treasure, palmed two sandwiches and munched contentedly, her bright eyes roving from one grown-up to the other. 'Ooh, this is nice, my two bestest friends and Toicky's samwiches.' She wriggled comfortably.

Jane smiled at the odd coupling and surprised a similiar quirk on the man's lips.

'Not long now, Sandy, then your mother will be here as

well. That will be grander still, hmm?' she asked, and stared in amazement as the child opened her eyes wide and choked on a mouthful of bread. Small hands trembled as she put down the cup, spilling half its content.

'Yes—yes, I 'spect so,' she stammered, and Jane glimpsed a wet gleam of tears as the child turned suddenly and streaked across the grass to disappear into the shrubbery.

Amazement struggled with anxiety as Jane turned to Grant. 'Whatever came over her? Oh, gosh, Grant, did I say something to upset Sandy? I thought she knew and would be pleased to talk about her mother—coming soon——' her voice tailed miserably.

Grant ran irritated fingers through his hair. 'Sandy knows Mara is coming, but something upsets her every time we mention her mother. I can't understand what's come over her lately. She gets in this sort of tizzy, clams up and dashes away, just as she did now. Almost as if she's afraid of—something.'

'I'm awfully sorry. Shall I go after her?' Jane rose uncertainly and took a few hesitant steps. Grant stopped her with an abrupt movement of his hand.

'No. Leave her, she gets over these tantrums quickly. Perhaps you could sound her out, after lunch. As her special friend you may be in a position to extract her confidence and find out what's bothering the child.' He straightened out of his chair. 'Time's up, back to the study—the sooner that muddle's cleared up the happier I'll be.'

Jane forced the problem of Sandy's behaviour aside and concentrated on her work. An hour passed and then Grant stretched out of his chair.

'I've finished my bit here. Take an hour off at midday, Minna will provide lunch for you and Sandy. I'll be back some time this afternoon,' he paused at the door. 'If you could go with the child to her room, after lunch, presumably to rest, she might just disclose her problems. Try anyway, you'll be doing me a favour as well.'

Jane nodded willing assent and Grant disappeared down the steps.

After lunch, at which Sandy appeared again, Jane asked

50

her to show her the rest of the house. The child eagerly complied and they made a tour of the rooms. The bedrooms, numbering six, were airy and furnished mostly with beautifully grained local wood. The kitchen was a housewife's dream and two bathrooms sparkled with white tiles and fittings. Grant's room was austere, neat, with a three-quarter bed covered by a tweedy, striped bedspread. A room for one person only ... Sandy hung back when they reached the third bedroom and remarked tersely, 'Mara's room.'

Jane peeped in at the blue and white confection. It was superb; blue wall-to-wall carpeting, paler blue curtains and a white suite. The large bed covered with a blue valanced spread. A very feminine room indeed.

'And now for your room, pal.' Jane turned away from the splendour that dazzled her eyes and clasped Sandy's hand. The child opened her door with a flourish. 'I like my room best and Grant said he'd keep this room for me for ever 'n ever, even when I'm old 'n can't walk any more!'

'Why shouldn't he?' Jane wondered aloud, and duly admired the bright covers on twin beds, the dazzling array of animals that marched across the walls and the pretty pink curtains. 'Can I rest on one of your beds? It looks so comfy, and I do like your room best of all,' she added quite truthfully.

'Even better'n Ma—the blue room?'

'Indeed I do. Here I feel I can toss off my shoes and relax, cosy and comfy.' Jane suited her words to action and stretched out to wiggle her bare toes. Sandy watched her warily for moments and then a relieved sigh blew through her lips. She moved to a dolls' cot and lifted her baby doll carefully and settled on the other bed, the doll nestling in the crook of her arm. She said, 'I wish you were my mom.'

'Why, love?' Jane asked, keeping her voice carefully casual. 'Your mom is beautiful and loves you dearly.'

Sandy eased her 'baby' tenderly. 'She's very pretty and I 'spect she loves me and I did long for her, but,' the small voice tightened curiously, 'but now I don't want to see her, ever again!'

Jane sat up slowly and came to kneel beside the bed where

51

Sandy lay with her face pressed into the pillow.

'Sandy dear, I'm your friend and it hurts me to see you're troubled about something,' she stroked the bright hair soothingly, 'and if you don't want to tell me I don't mind. Sometimes it helps if one can confide in a friend, and I do so want to see you happy all the time.'

A muffled sob broke the silence. 'You are my best friend, but I can't tell anybody that my mother did something to my daddy 'n I'll never forgive her.'

Jane felt her insides twist and tighten at the despair in the small voice. What had happened, what had this child seen or overheard to make her so miserable? She remained outwardly calm and spoke soothingly.

'Never mind, sweetie, you needn't tell me any more if you don't want to, but I am sure you've got something all higgeldy-piggeldy on your mind. Tell you what, you tidy your hair and then you can sit with me in the study while I finish my work. Have you any nice books to read?'

Sandy sat up and brushed the tears away with the back of her hand. 'Can I really sit in the study with you? Grant never allows me into the study.'

Jane wished silently that Sandy would say 'Daddy' instead of 'Grant'. There had been a deep feeling in the child's voice when she so unconsciously gave her secret away, partly, and mentioned 'my daddy'. She said brightly, 'I'm sure he won't mind just this once, if you sit quietly and read. I'll go now—find your books and join me, hmm?' She was probably breaking a strict rule, but didn't care a darn. Grant could blow his top if he wished, but he had asked her to speak to Sandy and even though she had not progressed very far . . .

Jane approached her desk with this thought in mind and came to an abrupt halt. Sandy's trouble was connected with her parents; how could she, a stranger, delve deeper to find the basic cause and then have to confront Grant with her findings? It was evidently a personal thing; she would tell him quite casually about Sandy's animosity towards her mother and suggest he settle his own problems. It would be most embarrassing for herself and Grant would certainly not thank her for baring a possible skeleton in the marital cupboard!

Sandy tiptoed into the study and Jane smiled as she indicated the small table and chair she had carried in from the verandah. The child settled down, her troubles forgotten in her sense of importance at having been admitted into forbidden territory.

At four o'clock Jane corrected the last page. She and Sandy again enjoyed the tea spell under the trees. The child was content to play with Lemmy when Jane walked back to the study. What could she occupy herself with now? Scratch around to find something to do or would that annoy her boss? Her problem was solved by the appearance of Minna.

'Mr. Grant phoned. If you've finished the work he gave you, you may spend your time as you wish. He'll be back to run you home.' The housekeeper turned to depart, but Jane called her back.

'Just a moment, please. Thanks for the message. May I ask in which way I must address you—Miss or Mrs. Du Toit?'

The slight, neat woman took a few steps back into the room and her gaze hovered over Jane's head. 'I'm Mrs. Du Toit. My husband passed away many years ago and I took the post of nanny to Miss Mara in her father's home. When she married she didn't want—Mr. Grant offered to take me as housekeeper and I've been here ever since.' A smile pierced the sternness of her mouth, making her look years younger. 'You may call me Minna if you like. Sandy started the "Toicky", her version of Du Toit, and most everyone has adopted that name now.'

Of course Jane did not belong to this household so she would not be invited to be so familiar. She decided to stick to formality until she and Minna knew each other better. Under the prim manner lurked a friendly though somewhat suspicious soul. She was fiercely loyal to Grant and Jane wondered what her attitude to Mara would be; her cut-off sentence about Mara not wanting her after her marriage sounded hurt and strange, yet she was still under the same roof as her former charge.

Jane tidied her desk, did a quick spot of dusting across the filing cabinets, windowsill and other surfaces, closed the study door and then wandered into the garden. Her heart started an erratic beat as the Land-Rover came to a halt and her tall, grey-eyed boss unfolded lithely. She simply must stop that magnetic charm of his from interfering with her organ of circulation, it was dangerous—and useless. No future in it whatsoever.

A few lengthy strides brought him to her side and the dilapidated hat pushed to the back of dark hair gave him a rakish appearance. His hands lifted slightly and Jane had the curious illusion that he was about to say something quite shattering and that her own hands were lifting without volition to meet his! They weren't doing anything of the sort, they were merely clenched in her pockets, and he did not utter any heart-stopping words. But that illusionary moment was to remain indelibly fixed in her memory.

Grant's hand continued its upward movement to remove his hat and run fingers through heat-dampened hair. 'Hi, Jane, finished that lot? I hope we'll now be able to make sense out of them.' Did she sense sceptic sarcasm, or was she being just too sensitive lately?

'Amuse yourself while I have a quick shower. The eastern water tank gave trouble.' Grant turned away and vaulted three steps with a long-legged stride.

Commonplace greeting and words. Jane lifted rueful shoulders; the man would find everything in order; he evidently didn't regard office girls with high esteem, he was disgruntled with water tank trouble and the fleeting moment was a figment of her imagination. Nothing of world-shattering importance could possibly be said or exchanged between her and this . . . family man.

A soft toot of a car horn brought them back from their stroll. Sandy dashed across the driveway to where Grant was standing beside the car. 'Please, please, Grant, may I come too?' she pleaded sweetly.

'Sure thing, poppet. Run and tell Toicky first.' The tall man smiled at the flurry of heels and turned to Jane. 'The kid imagines she's Miss World when she rides in the back seat. Never in front with me, her chauffeur. Children have wonderful imaginations.'

So have some silly grown-ups, thought Jane as she took her seat. My imagination almost jumped the gong not twenty minutes ago!

A breathless Sandy deposited her small self in the centre of the back seat. 'Thank you,' she said grandly as Grant opened the door for her, and the man bowed politely. 'A pleasure, ma'am.'

Back at the Wheeler home he joined Bart in the pump-house. Jane and Sandy walked into the house to see how 'Operation Knit' was faring. Elizabeth looked up from an intricate pattern and her soft eyes smiled a greeting and rested on Jane with a querying tilt. Her daughter circled her thumb and forefinger in the traditional manner and edged Sandy closer.

'So far so good, Mom. Meet my friend, Sandra Saxon. My mother, Sandy.'

Sandy pressed closer to Jane's body, but managed a shy, 'How do you do, Mrs. Wheeler.'

'Hello, Sandra.' Elizabeth beckoned the child closer. 'Just look at this lovely design. Of course I'm only practising, getting the hang of it, but it's proving quite fascinating to watch it grow.'

Jane laid an affectionate hand on her mother's shoulder. 'How many millions have you and Janet turned out today?'

Elizabeth laughed and put a casual arm around Sandy's waist. Her natural gesture allayed the child's shyness and she too bent forward to study the growing pattern. 'My dear Janey, production nil today. Give us time to conquer this monster and then talk about output!'

Janet called from the verandah, 'Coffee for the working gals!' and greeted Sandy with a comradely hug. 'How's my girl enjoying her holiday?'

'Dinkum, thanks, Auntie Janet,' Sandy answered, completely at home now with her three companions. Elizabeth noticed that the youngster stayed as close as possible to Jane, intent eyes fixed on her vivid face as she gave a quick résumé of her first day of work at the Saxon Estates.

Tony and Mick, expert artists of foodsmelling, arrived on cue, dusty and dishevelled from some mysterious excursion.

They greeted Sandy in the casual, lordly manner that boys have towards mere tender females; but soon bore her off with them. The three females relaxed in their chairs to discuss the day's duties and gossip.

Bart and Grant eventually joined them and Janet invited the big man to stay for supper. He declined, 'Thanks, Janet, not tonight. I have to investigate some trouble at Block Six and that gypsy, Olivier, seems to be the cause of it.' His glance travelled from his hostess to Jane, then to Bart. 'Watch that chap when he comes here and send him off, pronto, when his job's done. Idling is his downfall—see that he parks his ramshackle caravan a good distance from the house.' Again his smoky glance flicked over to Jane.

Bart caught the glance and nodded. 'I know Flip ... I've hired him before, as you know, and my eyes are wide open.'

Grant stood up, prepared to take leave. 'I'm not too happy about it, he's a slippery eel and it's time we all gave him a walking ticket. Jane, walk with me to the car, I've a few instructions to lay out for tomorrow.' Bart was about to accompany him but withdrew, and Jane, obeying her boss's command, walked beside him down the steps.

He briefed her as they walked. 'I won't be with you tomorrow, but will set out the most urgent work for you to tackle. Sorry about that, but I'm sure you'll manage. I have to do a round of the packing sheds and blocks. By the way, how did you fare with Sandy, get any sense out of her?'

The sudden flush on her cheeks irritated Jane and she looked past broad shoulders that were too close for comfort. Grant waited, his eyes curious and then alert as he watched the confusion on her face. 'Come, Jane, out with it,' he requested quietly, and lifted his hand to her shoulder. The grip tightened as she struggled to formulate her reply. 'It can't be as difficult as all that—I can see you've succeeded in getting somewhere with her. Let's have it, and don't try to spare me!'

The flush receded and her cheeks paled miserably as she fixed her eyes on the lower button of his safari jacket. 'Well, I didn't perservere very far, Grant. She did confess that— her mother—did something, and she'll never forgive her,'

Jane stopped and bit on her lower lip.

'Sandy said that she wouldn't forgive Mara for something she—Mara—did? What?' The hard hand gave her shoulder a slight shake.

Jane lifted her head at last. Her own hand came up and she tugged the restraining grip from her shoulder. 'Grant, you're hurting me!' Her lashes lifted and she faced him squarely. 'It's a family matter and I'll not say more or probe any further. Sandy has a great affection for you that, if you treat gently, she'll be willing to discuss, to reveal her problems to you.'

Grant hooked his thumbs into the pockets of his pants and his disturbing grey gaze passed from the girl's face, over her shoulder and into the distance. He remained quite still, an introspective, closed look that made the strong face grim and unapproachable. The silent girl felt twinges of unease ripple down her spine at the hard line of his mouth and it was almost a relief when cool, analytical eyes moved back to her face.

He said softly, 'You know more than you've told me, sweetheart. And you're not going to tell—is that so? Well, I admire your reticence if it's an embarrassing subject. My apologies if I've involved you in a delicate family matter. Say and do no more. I'll attend to Sandy's problems and promise to treat her with the utmost gentleness. Don't look so woe-begone and appealing, it does things to my morale.' Grant raised his hands to circle her throat, moved them slowly to tilt her mouth, and the next moment Jane felt his lips on hers.

Transfixed and silent, she suffered the coolness of his mouth on hers. A shock of awareness replaced the unease that had rippled down her spine only moments before as she felt unaccustomed response on her own warming lips. A current of power, vibrant and devastating, came from the hands that circled her throat and exploded against her mouth . . .

Grant Saxon withdrew his lips and his hands slid down to her shoulders. Wicked steel gleamed in his eyes as he said whisperingly, 'You pack a hidden punch, honey—built-in atomic power, perhaps?'

The flame in her cheeks deepened, the tumult in her pulses receded at the derision in his voice. Jane mastered her senses, thoughts and tongue and stepped back with supreme indolence, ignoring the flags of colour on her cheeks. She smiled sweetly above the angry frustration—or something she could not define—that raged within.

'You don't do too badly yourself ... darling. Do you always allow things to have their way with your morale so easily?' she asked mildly, feeling anything but mild, and brought her hands up expressively. 'Nice tips a girl gets for imparting family secrets!'

Grant's expression changed with thunderous intensity, he put a hand on the car door and said bitingly, 'Nice, did you say? Such a milksop word, my dear. We'll have to grade the family secrets—the bigger the secrets the better the tips. I reckon we've made a damn good start, the future's fast becoming bright and exciting. Do a bit more delving, love, for our mutual pleasure?' He slid behind the wheel, started the motor and leaned across to open the passenger door for Sandy. 'Hop in, poppet. Enjoyed your outing?'

'Yes, Grant. 'Bye, Jane, shall I see you tomorrow?'

Her mind a whirlpool of emotions, Jane had stiffened to rigid control at the audacity of Grant Saxon's treacherous suggestions. Suggestions that belied the thunder on his face. His expression was now blandly taunting as he and Sandy waited for her reply. A longing to strike that taunting look from the dark face and shriek like a banshee almost overcame her. Instead, she said stiffly, woodenly, 'I'll be there, Sandy. I don't chicken out easily. Transport being available.' Her challenging look rested on the man at the wheel.

Grant's face softened into a slow smile. 'Yes, my atom, transport will be available. I reckon you've got what it takes, in more ways than one. Pity you'll be deprived of my company so soon, but,' the sun wrinkles deepened at the corners of his eyes, 'work before pleasure, y'know. 'Bye now.'

Jane watched the dust of the departing car and vowed furiously to bring the driver down from his pinnacle of insufferable ego and audacious self-assurance.

CHAPTER 5

JANE stooped to twist a ripe tomato off its stem; they were quite delicious when eaten straight off the bush. She watched the water coming down between the furrows and looked up to see who was directing its course. The man was leaning on his spade and the early morning sun gleamed in blue eyes that were studying her with insolent admiration. An inexplicable shiver recoiled down the girl's back, but her feet did not falter as she approached. She had to pass him in order to reach the side driveway where her transport would arrive at any moment. Jane loved this early morning walk through the fruit trees and vegetable garden. She bit into the fruit and strolled casually, keeping her eyes on the rows of greenery. Flip Olivier raised a hand to his hat.

'Good morning, miss.'

Jane raised her eyes briefly. 'Good morning, Mr. Olivier.' He could only be the subject of Bart and Grant's discussion two days ago.

'Tomatoes are good this year, hey? Oom Bart told you who I am, then ... Pleased to meet you, Miss Jane. You are liking our part of the country?'

'Very much, thank you.' Jane indicated her desire to walk on. The man hesitated for an insolent moment before stepping aside to allow her passage on the dry strip between the furrows. She turned around out of common courtesy when he spoke again.

'The land is good if a man has water to cultivate, but the seasons are very dry these last few years.'

She nodded and looked towards the horizon. 'They have been, the need for rain is great. My uncle says when that haze starts on the mountains there should be a change in the weather.'

The pale eyes lifted from her face to study the direction of her eyes. 'It looks promising, we must hope for it to come soon.'

A hum of a motor heralded the approach of a vehicle and

Jane smiled at Flip, feeling a small sense of relief at the interruption. He seemed of a mind to hold her in small talk and that nibble of recoil still played on her spine when the hypnotic gaze circled her face and figure. She turned her back and walked quickly around the corner of the verandah, took her bag from the canvas chair where she had deposited it earlier on and waited for the Land-Rover. Tom greeted her with a flash of white teeth and they proceeded to the Saxon Estates.

Grant was not in the office when she walked in from the verandah entrance, which she now used instead of coming through the house. This would be his third day of absence. She had not seen him since the day he had brought her home and taunted her on kissing tips. Her work was laid out every morning, so he obviously hadn't disappeared into the blue. Jane was strangely relieved when he failed to appear; how to treat a boss who kissed, then taunted his new employee? The anger inside her might have exploded with dire results—for him!

Yet, as she prepared for her day's work, Jane felt the loss of his magnetic presence; some strange exhilaration inside her seemed to feel the need to cross swords with this audacious autocrat who played on other's feelings while he waited for an absent wife. She was still determined to topple him from his high and mighty perch, and a slight sense of frustration probably had a hand in her feeling of loss!

The obvious thing to do would be to ignore his manner as she normally would with any other self-assured egotist, she had made short work of them in the past. Except ... that kissing episode, which really meant nothing to her or Grant, had not been exactly repulsive. Be honest now, Jane Wheeler, it was only his mocking and flirtatious ways that riled her considerably. Was she a square to object to married men dickying other girls? Grant had teased that pretty blonde Sister at the mission—had he kissed her as well, and did she raise an objection?

Jane swore softly but decisively under her breath as she looked for the elusive square of Tippex to correct a typing error, determinedly wiping all thoughts of an irritating boss from her mind to concentrate on the letter forming under her usually nimble fingers. At this rate she'd be fired before any perch tilting could be accomplished!

Her mind nagged again when she sat down to lunch with Sandy. Had Grant discovered the skeleton in her little cupboard, or had he disregarded their talk on Sandy's troubles? The child was listless lately, off her appetite and hung round Jane when permitted; had he been too harsh or was she merely missing him—where did he go during the course of the day, and what did he do in the evenings—spend his time in the study or take time off to give her the enjoyment she obviously found in his company? Sandy caught Jane's speculative gaze, answered her thoughts with uncanny timing.

'Grant is so tired when he comes home every night, do you know he's got millions of—what do you call that kind of sheep when they stand against the mountain 'n in the valley they look like lots of grey stones? He's got to ride an awful long way to see them 'n then come back every night to stay with me.'

'Merinos. Millions, Sandy? Where?' Jane asked.

'Well, not 'xactly millions, but 'n awful lot. They're near where the forest begins, the gove'ment Forestry, and it's cool 'n the hills look like bread dough. My next holidays I'm going with him, he promised, for a whole week. There's nice bungalows 'n a swell stream where we can fish 'n swim. Will you come for a ride this afternoon, Jane? You can ride on Dicky, he won't throw you 'cause he's old. Can you ride, Jane?' Sandy pepped up at her own proposition and waited anxiously for her friend's verdict.

'Golly, Sandy, I haven't mounted for years and will most likely fall flat on my face regardless of Dicky's age! What's your pony's name?' Jane side-stepped delicately.

'Sugarbush, 'n he's getting fat because I've been too busy fishing to exercise him. You can come and look at him 'n Dicky and I'm sure you won't fall off. Tony 'n Mick says he's too 'crepit for them.'

Jane laughed. 'Probably for those two hell's angels, but he sounds just right for me!' She channelled their chat away from horses and riding, a sport that had never appealed

61

greatly because she had a slight fear of the large animals and suspected her seat was at fault. 'I've got a pile of work and simply must finish it today, so I'll get cracking and maybe I'll find time to look at your horses before Tom takes me home.'

'I'm cross with Grant,' Sandy stated flatly.

Jane felt her heart constrict at the sudden bald statement and looked silently at the pout of the young mouth.

'I'm really cross because he makes you work all day 'n we can't go fishing.'

'Oh. Sandy dear, I'm sorry about that, but even if I wasn't working here I'd have to work somewhere, so please don't be cross with him. Anyway, I don't work on Saturdays and Sundays. You've still got this week-end and school starts on Tuesday, so let's make a plan.' The constriction lifted and Jane leaned her elbows on the table. 'I suggest you ask Toicky if you may come with me this afternoon. Uncle Bart or I will bring you back in the Combi. We'll go down and do a spot of fishing or swimming and I'm sure Grant won't mind.'

The pout was gone in a flash, an eager face was lifted. 'Oh yes, Toicky'll let me go!'

'Well then, eat all your salad in case she objects on that score.' The housekeeper entered right on cue and Jane decided to do the asking.

'On one condition, miss, Sandy must finish all her food.' One look at the young one emptying her plate fast told of the conspiracy and Minna turned an approving look on Jane. 'You have a way with this one—pity the bribe can't be used thrice daily! Take a rest after lunch, Sandy, if Mr. Grant isn't back by the time Miss Jane leaves I'll tell him where you are.'

'Thank you, Mrs. Du Toit. I'll take good care of her and bring her back. No need for Mr. Saxon to fetch or send for her.'

'Right, miss. It gets a bit lonesome for the wee one.'

'And I'd like to take her out for the day on Saturday if I may——'

'Oh dear, begging your pardon, there's a message for you

62

from Doctor Davies, not to forget he's calling for you on Saturday for the dance. And I don't think it will be suitable to take Sandy on Saturday,' Minna hesitated, suddenly agitated, and Sandy interposed anxiously, her fork halfway to her mouth, 'Why not, Toicky, why not on Saturday?'

'You know perfectly well your mother will arrive either Friday or Saturday, that's why.'

'Oh, hell!' Sandy dropped her fork with a clatter.

'Sandra! That's very impolite and rude!' a shocked Toicky scolded her.

'Well, I mean it. She won't take me fishing 'cause the sun burns her 'n the ants bite her 'n——'

'That's quite enough, young lady. Your mother hasn't seen you for a long time and will want you to stay with her while she's here.'

Sandy remained stubborn. 'She sees me 'n slobbers—I mean kisses me all over and then follows Grant all over the place.'

'Sandy, I'm sure you're wrong about her attentions towards you—and as for following Grant all over the place, that's understandable—isn't it? I mean, she sees so little of him as well.' Jane said, and found a small 'oh, hell!' in her own heart at the thought of Mara's imminent arrival.

A shadow crossed the young face as Sandy said in a subdued way, 'Lemmy says a woman's child is "of her own flesh 'n blood" and Grant isn't, so why does she close the study door 'n won't let me in 'n send me to my room when they sit on the verandah at night, 'n put on her prettiest things—and even so, what she did—did——' a small trembling hand clamped her mouth shut. Jane was at her side in an instant.

'All right, love. Your mother will probably be tired from her long trip, so I'll personally ask Grant if you may spend Saturday with me. I'm going to the club with Peter Davies in the evening, but my whole day will be free to spend with you.' Jane's eyes dared Minna to contradict her.

Minna looked from the challenging brown eyes to the down-bent head and brought her hands upwards in a hopeless gesture. 'Be it your responsibility then, miss,' and turned away muttering a low, 'You don't know nothing yet.'

Jane turned back to speak firmly, hiding her puzzlement at the child's flare-up about Grant (jealousy after all, in a lonely heart?) and the strange way Minna had looked at her. 'Come, Sandy, no more of this. You'll only make yourself ill and then you can't come with me this afternoon. Have your rest now and I'll see you at teatime and we can plan what to do, fishing or swimming, mm?'

'Yes, Jane.' A watery smile played on Sandy's face as she obeyed meekly.

Now she'd embroiled herself, but good! The typewriter rattled to keep with Jane's thoughts; her mind urged caution in dealing with this household while her heart wept for the young one. She was already biased against Mara Saxon, and that wasn't fair; Sandy's mother might be quite a charming person and the very person to still her daughter's strange grudge with a perfectly simple and reasonable explanation (what had she done to 'poor Daddy'?) Children did sometimes behave in an incomprehensible manner, especially an only child. It could be pure and simple jealousy of Mara's way with Grant or vice versa. Or an overheard disagreement between her parents could be built up in her mind to abnormal dimensions and the blame placed on the mother's side alone.

Grant Saxon, for all his clam-like reserve on 'Mara-talk', for all his dickying technique with other females, must be experiencing an inner delight at the return of a wife and wouldn't take kindly to a disgruntled daughter disrupting the happy homecoming!

A painful sensation threaded through Jane's breast as her mind pictured that homecoming ... It had absolutely nothing to do with her, this reunion. She was an outsider looking in, purely and simply that. So why did a mental vow to keep on her guard against something—or someone—persistingly hammer in her mind as she gazed absently out of the window, waiting for the inexplicable pain in her breast to pass?

'Come on, Sandy, last one in is chicken!' Jane poised, lifted her arms and cleaved the waters to their clear depths. Moments later a small body came hurtling down and they surfaced together, gasping at the contact of cold water against warm bodies. Their hair, unrestricted red and brown seaweed, floated and framed their faces as they turned on their backs in pure bliss.

A bliss that was rudely shattered by two brown rockets that landed over and under, jetting sprays of stinging water on to upturned serene faces and causing havoc amongst the mermaids! Tony and Mick laughed with glee as Jane retaliated instantly and the ensuing water battle became hilarious and breathless. The boys were wary of Jane's former judo tactics and also gave thought to Sandy's smallness, so the girls promptly took advantage and had their enemy in full retreat to surrender ignominiously on the grassy bank.

Grant Saxon's eyes darkened as he watched the girl in the pool. They flickered from her hair to bare shoulders and back to long slim legs moving languorously in the clear emerald water. Jane saw the towering figure on the rock ledge and brought her feet down to caress the pebbly bed of the pool. Wet mermaid hair dripped gleaming jewels on to her golden shoulders. She brushed wet tendrils from her eyes and more rare jewels sparkled on her lashes, turning nut-brown eyes to amber, to glow like a panther's eyes.

Her every nerve tautened as they faced each other in silence, his smoky gaze holding her mesmerised. She shook off the fairy net and started to walk out of the water, and the silver jewels sparkled down her back and breast to disappear for ever at her feet. Grant stood a moment longer, as if he too were held in a steel web, before he stepped down and reached for her towel robe.

Wordlessly he held it in readiness and Jane turned gleaming shoulders to be enveloped in its warm softness. 'Water sprite, golden nymph, lead I to thy jewelled palace, for I wouldst fain come willingly, holding thy tender hand, even unto my last breath,' Grant chanted gruffly, and stepped back to grin at the astonished expression in her luminous eyes.

'Quite the romantic, Mr. Saxon? Strange how outer appearances can belie the inner, sensitive being.' Jane put her arms into the robe sleeves and stooped for her cigarette case.

'Absolutely fantastic, Miss Wheeler. You should know. One moment ago a panther looked out of your eyes and now—now there's nothing. Pity, he looked engaging.' He lit her cigarette and the smoke wreathed between them.

'And who could believe in a poetic soul by studying the exterior?' she quipped coolly.

'Study must dig deep to extract the full value—does my rough exterior bother you at all? Take no notice, be the earnest archaeologist, the soul-seeker, and I'll be——'

Jane interrupted hastily, 'Not at all. I was only generalising. We had a whale of a time in the water and Sandy's an absolute eel. Who taught her to swim so well? Didn't Minna tell you that I would see her home? I managed to finish that pile of work you left. You're back early today.' Her tongue wilfully hastened in all directions without coalition on her part and Jane allowed it to take a further plunge. 'Can Sandy spend the day with me on Saturday?'

Grant made the familiar gesture of hooking his thumbs into the pockets of his trousers while his brows lowered quizzically. 'Shall we take it in sequence? I agree the water's terrific. I did. Yes, Minna told me, and also very perceptive of you to notice my early return.' Dark brows drew closer together and Jane waited for the curt reminder that precious Mara would be home. 'Saturday ... yes, I guess she can. But aren't you going to do any shopping, hairdressers and all that jazz, dicky up for the dance?'

'I do my own hair, and have no shopping to do.' Jane hesitated and drew on the cigarette between her fingers. 'I thought her mother might object to her absence so soon after her arrival—I mean——'

'I gather your meaning, but doubt if Mara would mind particularly. She'll be here on Friday and will probably go to town for her beauty treatment, not being so versatile as you in that way. No home touch for a model, only the best professional care.' He watched the swing of damp hair as temper started and help up a belaying hand. 'Now don't go off your rocker, I'm not criticising your abilities, merely stating a fact. Now, where was I? Your action's so provoking ... Sandy has my full consent to visit with you on Saturday.'

'Thank you, Grant.' He would be delighted to have his wife's attention focused on himself without distraction. Jane immediately reproached herself for the mean thought, for she sensed instinctively that Grant was anything but mean or mulish towards Sandy.

'Your aunt invited me to supper, I accepted, so that answers for Sandy's transport home tonight.'

'Oh.' She would have to suffer his aggravating presence all evening. Could she do a bit of quick perch tilting ... or did she really want to do so? His wife would be back soon and all his charm would be channelled in the right direction, leaving no opportunity for side-stepping.

'What a dramatic reaction!' The taunt was back, but he turned away at once.

At the table that evening Grant's paricular charm had a personal touch for everyone but her, or so Jane imagined. Elizabeth was obviously taken in by his attentiveness and the rest were already besotted, so Jane did not attempt a battle that was sure to be a dead loss without support.

She surprised herself by enjoying the evening. Sandy started a hilarious game of telling a tale, exciting or memorable, in each one's life. Sandy had fallen out of a fairly high tree and a passing turkey had broken a dangerous fall by strutting conveniently and innocently under the path of her descent. Imagination ran riot when she described the bird's fright, screams and loss of feathers! Tony and Mick relived the time they had bunked hostel after lights out for a midnight picnic at Tadpole Dam. Unfortunately the party became too boisterous, they were covered in mud, sneaked through an open window and nearly caused a snooping matron a heart attack when she confronted the weird creatures in the bathroom.

Elizabeth recounted her battle against the elements during the floods of Port Elizabeth and Janet created gales of laughter on the agitation of a favourite hen who brought out a clutch of ducklings and watched, with angry, ruffled feathers, her brood sail gaily on the dangerous waters of the pond!

Grant demanded a romantic episode from Jane, but she

67

ignored the remark and said, 'Don't try to skip your turn. Surely you too have a past episode, dangerous or romantic, to relate?'

An uncanny silence suddenly reigned. Laughter crinkles disappeared as Grant's face sobered abruptly. He offered his case to Bart and lit both cigarettes before answering.

'My affairs of the heart are not for tender ears, my big moments lie in the future.' He looked at his watch. 'And it's long past poppet's bedtime. I called in at the Mission, by the way, David Muller sends regards and hopes to see you at the club on Saturday. Are you all coming?'

Bart said, 'Surely. It's the highlight of the community, ladies dressing up and the men's chance to watch the girls go by!'

Janet turned to Grant. 'You'll be there?'

He pushed back his chair and held out a hand for the sleepy child. 'If Mara has her way it's a certainty. How is Olivier doing?'

'All right so far and somewhat subdued ... that other matter settled?' Bart asked in return, and Grant nodded.

Jane forbore to mention her encounter with the man in question; it was of no concern to Grant Saxon, and Olivier had been polite to her, though even now the thought of his pale eyes sent another uncomfortable shiver down her spine.

Man and child gave thanks for the dinner and pinpoints of red rear lights finally vanished in a cloak of darkness.

Friday passed uneventfully except for Jane's uncontained curiosity every time a vehicle was heard in the driveway. And yet, in spite of her curiosity, she hoped fervently to be on her way home before the arrival of Mara Saxon. Grant was not to be seen in the morning, arriving in time for lunch, and later he positively prowled, fiddled absently amongst his papers and then disappeared for long intervals.

Minna thoughtfully kept Sandy in the kitchen, occupationally intent on a baking venture. At afternoon tea the young miss proudly presented a plate of lopsided scones which Jane duly praised. They were really good, though queer-shaped. Grant was not present.

Tom was with him when the Rover pulled up in the late afternoon. Jane settled the cover on her typewriter, scooped up her bag and walked down the steps. Tom moved behind the wheel and Grant stepped aside to lift a casual hand as the vehicle drew away. Jane thought, his mind must be full with the imminent return of a beloved one; obviously no time wasted on attentions to a mere female employee today! She tried hard to divert her thoughts as they drove through entrancing greens, beside sparkling streams ... somehow their appeal did not register and she felt a flattened sense of depression.

The telephone was shrilling the Wheeler code when she entered the house and Peter Davies' voice greeted her as she lifted the receiver.

'Hi, Jane, how's our working gal?'

'Just fine, thanks. How is the great healer of bodies?'

'Cussing and stitching madly. The entire Bantu nation are going through an era of falls, fisticuffs and what-have-you, resulting in broken bones and dislocated anatomies. I swear they do it just to keep this medico exercised, and his thoughts away from a certain charming lass. Still on the subject of this lass, how is she passing her time off, and is Saxon slaving you to death—and did you get my message from Toicky?'

'Yes, I got your message, though I doubt if you will make it with all those bones to grind.'

'Phelange, femurs, pelvis and skulls can do their own knitting tomorrow night—I'll be on your doorstep at the stroke of seven, come floods, 'flu or famine!'

Jane laughed lightheartedly. 'Right, doctor, you'll find me on the second step to the right, arrayed in my best and nestled in the wistaria. Will you recognise me, or should I clamp a red rose between my pearly teeth for identification?'

'I'd recognise you draped in poison ivy, sweet one!' Peter declared with passionate confidence, and Jane laughed again as the receiver positively vibrated in her hand.

'A stinging prospect, not to be considered for one instant. Listen, Peter, my folks are all going as well—wouldn't you rather I meet you at the club, more convenient and time-saving for you?'

'Positively not, my pet. Deprive me of that extra pleasure? Oh dash, I'm being stabbed by steely glares from the boss—'bye now, see you tomorrow.' The line clicked in hasty termination.

Sandra arrived at an early hour the following morning, complete with collapsible fishing rod and a case containing her bathing kit. Jane thanked Tom and invited Sandy to join her in the kitchen and help with the sandwiches for their outing. The aroma of new bread, sizzling bacon and tomatoes made her small nose twitch hungrily, so Jane promptly set another place at the table. Sandy declared that she had been too excited to eat her porridge at home.

Bart had breakfasted and departed, Janet, Elizabeth and the boys were still in the throes of waking up and dressing so the two girls had the kitchen to themselves. Jane buttered hot toast as she ventured the question that had hovered on her lips since the child's arrival.

'It was good of Tom to bring you, now we can get away sooner. Did—did your mother come, yesterday?'

Sandy bit into the luscious buttery toast, savouring it slowly before she answered. 'Mara—Mom came in time for dinner last night 'n she was pleased to see me. She says I look better 'n not so scraggy any more.' She chewed reflectively. 'I'll never be as pretty as her, though, I don't think ... I was very polite 'cause Grant said I should be. He talked to me last night 'n asked if I was troubled about her.'

In the silence that followed Jane asked casually, 'And you told him what was troubling you?'

'No, I didn't, but he was awfully nice and said to trust and tell him when I was good 'n ready, and anyway he 'spected my feet were in the wrong boots 'n I must be sure of my—my—' she hesitated, and Jane supplied, 'facts?'

'That's right, I must be sure before thinking wrong things about anybody. B-but, Jane, I can't tell anybody what I heard 'cause it's awful and——' the young face looked downcast, 'I was sneak-listening.'

'Eavesdropping, Sandy?'

'Yes, and I'm 'shamed, but I did hear that—what I heard.'

Sandy's lips closed tightly.

'Okay, Sandy, you were nice and polite, and that's good, I'm proud of you. We'd better move. The day doesn't wait and it's glorious in the sun and I want to catch a terrific tan today.'

They took the short cut through the vegetable garden and lucerne lanis. Jane felt a familiar crinkle in her spine as Flip Olivier straightened up to watch their progress. He gave her absolute goose-pimples!

The girls had a blissful, uninterrupted day. They swam to their hearts' content and basked on the sun-warmed rocks. Sandy's joy was complete when she landed four small fish and Jane showed grateful appreciation of the large one that obligingly hooked itself on her line when she was inattentive and sleepy with the sun's soporific effect.

The sun was a giant orange ball on the fir-clad hills when they reached home again. Tom timed his return trip neatly and Jane waved cheerfully to her little friend, then dashed into the house to wash her hair and prepare for the night's entertainment.

When she finally walked into the lounge the entire Wheeler clan voiced their approval. The African sun had given her skin a golden glow and the simple yet daring apricot midi shimmered in swirls from her slim waist, showing bare shoulders to perfection. Shining nut-brown hair was drawn up and away from high cheekbones to fall from the top of her head in swirly coils. A single smoky topaz on a fine chain nestled in the visible cleft of softly firm breasts. Matching ear-rings captured the light and reflected in her tawny-brown eyes. Wispy gold sandals completed the enchanting effect.

Peter arrived in his own sleek sports car and Jane's eyes approved the well-groomed look of her escort, while Bart proposed a drink before departure. The doctor, in turn, was mesmerised by the delightful vision that would be his companion for the evening and his normal, easy chatter became slightly erratic ...

The trees encircling the club grounds were festooned with coloured lights and the beautifully kept lawns were edged with masses of geraniums which lent colour to a very scenic setting. A white-clad waiter drew chairs together for the new arrivals and Jane looked inquiringly at Peter; did he want to join the family or had he expected and booked a table for two?

Peter was quite happy to join the family circle.

The band swung into sound in the spacious hall and couples lost no time in enjoying the inviting beat of the drums. Peter danced well, held her lightly, and Jane knew she was going to enjoy his company. They returned to the verandah to find Pat Marais and escort had joined the party. Her partner stood, tall and gangly, obviously a farmer, or so Jane deduced when she felt the hardness of a calloused hand as Pat introduced Julius Davenport. Jane's eyes wandered further afield, but she saw no sign of another tall, lithe figure ... a figure she had been unconsciously seeking since her arrival at this gay gathering.

Janet and Bart decided to try out their 'atrophied' (Bart's word) legs while the others rested. Long drinks sparkling with ice were deftly served by the same waiter who had delegated himself to the special care of their tables.

A movement along the entrance of the verandah distracted her attention. Grant Saxon was walking towards them and her eyes told her he looked wonderfully handsome in his dark suit and immaculately white shirt. Her eyes moved to focus on the woman at his side.

Beautiful became an understated word in describing the titian-haired woman who walked with the haughty grace of a queen ... ravishingly lovely, green eyes emphasised with subtle make-up, Mara Saxon's green wet-look dress showed every sinuous provocative movement of her perfect body. She was openly, coolly aware of her attraction and a long slim hand rested with possessive assurance on the dark-clad arm of her escort.

'Well, shake me down, the goddess appears once more on the scene. Wonder what havoc is brewing this time,' Peter said in Jane's ear.

'Are you immune to havoc, dear doctor?' Jane turned to him in her effort not to stare so blatantly. Her heart mocked;

you've seen enough, Janey . . .

'There are havocs and havocs, sweetie, you being one of the pleasanter ones—but that one is a dangerous, snaky, bedevilled witch and, if I guess rightly, will concentrate her charm on the rocky one at her side!'

'So what, Peter Davies? Is it so unusual? Or are you of the school that believes in marriage swops?' Jane asked sharply, with more heat than she realised, and Peter raised astonished eyebrows.

'Jane! Whatever are you saying, or insinuating?'

'Hello, Jane,' a deep, familiar voice said at her back, and she turned to look up at Grant Saxon.

Peter and Julius stood up politely as Grant drew Mara forward. 'Meet Elizabeth and Jane Wheeler, Mara. Elizabeth is Janet's and Bart's sister-in-law and Jane is her daughter. Two charming ladies, very welcome and an asset to our community.'

Mara Saxon inclined her head in gracious acknowledgement (only an experienced, trained model or a lady of inborn grace could make this gesture without embarrassment.) Jane wouldn't dream of emulating, so she merely smiled at Grant's flattery and then at the beauty at his side. Elizabeth did likewise, although her curiosity was more apparent than her daughter's.

Mara said, 'How nice to have more feminine company in this rough, hard-bitten slice of country. Sandra's quite taken with you, Miss Wheeler, and used pretty persuasive powers on Grant and me to allow her to spend the day with you.' She sighed provokingly. 'I guess it's to be expected, when one is away so much, for a small child to transfer her affections to someone closer and willing to do the childish things that children adore.'

Indignation flooded through Jane. 'We must all be very childish, then,' she riposted, and laughed gaily. 'All my family love fishing, swimming and exploring. Even Grant has joined us and he doesn't strike me as being exactly childish!' Put that in your pipe and smoke it, thought Jane inelegantly.

The green eyes transferred from the smoky topaz on Jane's

breast to the man at her side.

'Sweet of you to allow the girls to charm you away from your precious work, dear Grant. I'll have to learn from them, their ways and wiles, to lure you into doing the things I love to do.' Mara's incredible lashes fanned her cheeks. 'Though they're anything but childish . . .' Her smile remained gracious, but Jane definitely detected a thread of venom interlaced with the sweetness.

Grant's eyes narrowed slightly at the interchange, but he answered laconically, 'When will you realise that I'm quite impervious to guile from the fair sex?'

Says who? Jane's mind questioned impudently. You, Grant Saxon, can dish out guile by the bucket, so what makes you so impervious on the receiving line? Luckily Peter interposed before her indignation found tongue.

'Ha, and another ha! Not even you are infallible or immune, Grant. Not one of us—I've found my weak spot, and revel in my weakness.' His eyes rested on Jane.

Pat suddenly looked nettled and her retort came unexpectedly. 'Your trouble, Pete, is that you're riddled with weak spots, like—like a tea-strainer!'

It was Peter's turn to look exasperated and Jane felt the air vibrate with tension and a forthcoming battle of wits and sarcasm. She stood up and smoothed her apricot skirt. 'Come on, Julius, let's not waste that effort on the part of the band while these two run through the holes of said strainer!'

Grant had to step aside for her to pass and his glance seemed to rest for the first time on her appearance. Grey eyes circled her hair, to bare shoulders to her bosom. A subconscious stream of awareness, or memory, surfaced impetuously as she compared the look in his eyes with that of Olivier and was further shocked to find that it did not repulse her as those pale eyes had done. The feeling down her back was there, but not of repulsion . . . it contained a strange, unholy excitement that made her very aware of her own body and his closeness.

Jane stepped past Grant and took the hand of Julius Davenport.

Other perceptive female eyes watched Grant's scrutiny

and the girl's reaction. Mara kept a smooth smile on her lovely lips and a caressing hand on his arm. 'We're keeping our friends from their enjoyment, darling. Shall we find our table?'

Julius grinned down companionably at Jane as they circled the floor. 'Quite a dish, I'll say! Like a slinky green mamba—dear Mara didn't like your crack about childish things. I watched her eyes turn several shades of green. You know, Jane, I suddenly yearn to invite her out to my place and put her through the ropes—fishing, swimming, riding, climbing, and watch how she comes out at the other end. I also have an uncontrollable urge to find out what unchildish things she loves to do!' Julius closed his eyes in mock ecstasy and Jane's humour was restored by his comical expression.

How dared her own body betray her like that? Grant had a magnetism that attracted greatly, but she was not merely another magnetised steel pin, to be drawn so easily . . . Mara would be, was the recipient, the one who surrendered to the magic of belonging . . . Jane brought her mind back abruptly from the devastating, treacherous trend it was taking. She actually gave a small sigh of relief when she and Julius returned and found that she would be seated with her back to that other table where Grant and Mara were sitting.

Pat and Peter were back on amiable terms, Bart and Janet were talking at another table, the boys were out on the lawn and there was no sign of Elizabeth. Pat started the laughter and hilarity between the four of them when she discoursed on her and Peter's escapades in and out of the Mission. Peter was not slow to follow her lead, and their wily ways with Dr. Muller, more often unsuccessful than otherwise, caused shocked merriment between the two listeners. Peter and Pat looked often at each other for collaboration and Jane thought with certain affection, they were right and good for each other. Under all this wit and sarcastic comebacks something else was blossoming, slowly but surely. Peter's sweet way with her, Jane, was only the attraction to a new face . . . She came out of her matchmaking reverie as Grant politely requested the next dance with her.

CHAPTER 6

'YOU'RE a golden girl tonight, Janey.'

Over the arm that held her she saw Mara dancing with another man. So now that 'glamour girl' was dancing with someone else he dutifully took the opportunity to dance with his employee? Well, his employee had a great urge to dance with her boss, to find out if her spinal trouble was indeed a symptom of his nearness or merely some dreaded disease. She absorbed the feel of his arm, the steel strength of the hand that held hers, the latent vitality of the man's body, and decided she hadn't the qualifications to judge or diagnose the rubber in her bones.

She lifted her eyes from an earnest study of immaculate shirt. 'Apricot, not golden. You colour-blind, boss?'

He gave her a little shake and his voice roughened. 'I am not your boss tonight, and don't think this is a duty dance ... oh yes, your mind is an open book. Apricot or golden, what's the difference, you still look good enough to eat. As luscious as the golden harvest on my trees.'

Open book! Invisible covers were shut in mental haste and Jane queried gravely, 'Round and juicy?'

'Yum.' He matched her gravity.

'Your—girl—is quite beautiful, Grant.'

'My girl?' His eyes flicked her face. 'Meaning Mara?'

'Who else?' Jane countered.

'As you say, who else? Mara always looks chic and beautiful.'

'And I don't.' It was not a question but a flat statement.

Grant brought the hand that was holding hers down under her chin and she was forced to meet his direct gaze.

'No, you don't. That's why it's a pleasure to see you looking so enchanting. A man can't and doesn't want to eat cake every day.'

A mounting flush spread from her neck to ears. Mara had only arrived the day before and already he was passing outrageous remarks to her, Jane! Had she given him cause to believe she was easy prey to loose flattery? Or did he belong to the brigade of compulsive male flirts? Not something special as her betraying heart would believe? Her eyes glowed with amber fire as she said in a small, cold voice, 'Grant Saxon, after this dance is over I'll thank you not to approach me again.'

Grant remained silent and only a slight tightening of his hand over hers gave clue that he had heard. The music stopped and the arm round her waist forced her to walk with him to a side door and out under the stars.

Grant dropped his arm. 'Enlighten my darkness,' he said simply.

Jane knew a moment of puzzlement as she looked at his tall, straight body and direct grey eyes. 'You're being obtuse,' she whispered huskily, 'because you want to stay that way. You're perfectly aware of the reason behind my request.'

'Jane,' Grant put his hands on her shoulders. 'Jane, are you hurt because I said you weren't chic and enchanting every day?'

'No, Mr. Saxon, don't deliberately misunderstand. Enjoy your cake while you have the opportunity, it's not always available.'

Jane felt a sliver of fear as the hands on her shoulders tightened with painful force. His breath was warm on her face as he jeered softly:

'A most profound observation, golden one.' He drew her closer. 'Maybe we can soothe that ruffled, jealous heart with a certain anodyne?' She was drawn inexorably closer and then his mouth got in the way of her furious denial.

The starry heavens became a crazy kaleidoscope and the girl shut her eyes and forced her traitorous body into rigid stiffening control.

Grant Saxon lifted his mouth from her bruised lips. His eyes were black in the starlight and his hands suddenly, caressingly gentle on her back and shoulders.

'Janey, why are you fighting so stubbornly ... I know you're attracted as much as I and I've no intentions of trying to seduce you, sweet and alluring as you are. Why the angry barrier and oblique words? Why, Jane?'

Tears of angry misery made her eyes luminous. Jane knew without doubt that she loved this indiscriminate man. Knew, too, that if she lost control, every nerve in her body and mind would respond joyously and she would forget that he belonged to another!

Her approach choked on heartbreak. 'If you can still ask that then I can't answer. Does conscience or loyalty mean nothing to you? If not, please don't choose me as recipient of your—favours!'

Grant stepped back and with deliberate, ominous restraint lifted his cigarette case from his jacket pocket. He allowed the smoke to wreath past his eyes before he spoke again.

'I can't begin to understand what you're implying, but it sounds highly insulting, my patience is wearing thin, and if you've turned out to be neurotic about romance and such things, my apologies. Though, being obtuse, I failed to sense it. It's not a habit of mine to get so close to a girl and my sense of perception seems to have deserted me.' He looked across her shoulder and his face closed and hardened like a granite image.

Jane whirled to follow his glance and Mara and Julius were within two yards of them. Her heart began a dull beat as she saw the green glitter of the redhead's eyes ... she was still suffering from the shock of Grant's grim onslaught and would now have to bear the brunt of Mara's anger. Had she misconstrued the whole set-up by blaming the wrong party? Was this the reason for Mara's long absences from her home —her husband's dalliance with other girls, despite contradiction that it was not a habit of his?

Mara's mouth wore a thin smile. 'So cool under the stars. Julius and I decided to explore the possibilities, and we find —others are doing likewise.' Julius's eyes widened at the falsity of her words; she had demanded that he accompany her. Mara continued sweetly, 'You don't look as if you've found it very romantic, Jane. Grant told me about his obliging little secretary. Has he been lecturing you? He's so obsessed with the affairs of the estate. You look quite sweet when your feathers are ruffled, dear.'

'How right you are, Mrs. Saxon. We were in the midst of

solving an enormous, universal problem. But it usually dwindles to petty proportions when faced squarely, have you noticed? Grant will grasp my point when he stops being—obtuse.' The lowered dark brow touched Jane with strange fear. She walked to Julius's side, masking her apprehension under an appealing smile.

Julius drew her hand through his arm. 'Nothing romantic about our little walk either. Mara's found what she was looking for.' He disregarded the icy look from green eyes at his failure to back her reason for coming out, and smiled at Jane. 'Enough fresh air? Come and dance with me.'

'A pleasure, Julius.' Jane held her head high as they walked, arm in arm, across the velvety lawn.

Her apricot skirt whirled gracefully as he executed complicated, expert turns, and she lifted her eyes once, to meet Grant's mocking smile across her partner's shoulder. Mara's gleaming head nestled against his cheek, she was taller than Jane (her head only reached his heart). After that, someone suggested champagne and Jane imbibed with uninhibited gaiety. She was frothy and gay, laughed a lot and her dazzling wit became as sparkling as the 'bubbly', and if it was slightly forced only Elizabeth sensed this and wondered briefly what was boiling in that young breast.

Grant leaned nonchalantly against a verandah post, Mara at his side, Julius in earnest conversation with them. Jane was too far away to hear what was being discussed, but a sidelong glance showed Grant's gesture of consent and Mara's dazzling smile bestowed evenly between the two men. The cacophonous music and chatter blasted her ears, her nerves jumped in the pit of her stomach and she felt weary and deflated with her attempts to mask her emotions. The champagne brought a throb to her head and she wished desperately to be alone, anywhere in the soft cloak of darkness, in absolute solitude. To examine the burst of knowledge that had come to her when Grant had held her under the stars; torture herself with this new, blinding torment. This she wanted to do with almost sadistic urgency, having the curious illusion that in doing so she could exorcise the love that

79

rioted in her heart, kill it stone dead before it became overwhelming, completely and slavishly insuperable.

Julius Davenport rejoined them with a satisfied glint in his eyes and Jane studied him with some trepidation when he threw her a conspiratorial wink before disclosing his plans; they were all invited to spend the Sunday at his home. His grandmother would welcome the company; she was in her seventies, hale and hearty except for troublesome arthritis in her hip which kept her from visiting too often. She dearly loved company, so would they all come, gladden her heart and enjoy themselves?

The Wheeler family accepted the invitation. David said he would take over morning duties and allow his two assistants the day off.

Julius whispered in Jane's ear, 'I'm starting my campaign on the queenly Mara.'

She felt exasperation rise and whispered back furiously, 'Leave her alone, Julius. You'll only cause trouble and I think there's enough of that in the Saxons' life. Anyway, I don't want to come. I've had my day in the sun and all this—I'm tired and completely——'

He interjected rudely but with a humorous twist to his mouth, 'Shush, sweet one. I'm merely going to crack that case of superiority complex ever so slightly; under that glamour and scheming red head must be something worthwhile ... And you simply must come and visit my grandmother, she and I would appreciate it greatly.'

'Why don't you leave Grant to crack his own way to her worth?'

'My good deed,' Julius grinned, 'help him and enjoy myself into the bargain! Will you come, Jane?'

She felt dispirited and wanted to go home, away from the intrigue that seemed to be affecting everyone. 'Yes, I'll come, Julius.'

Peter said, 'What are you two conspiring? Jane, you're looking pale. Say the word and I'll take you home.'

'Thanks, Peter. That overdose of bubbly's finally catching up with my liver and I'm suffering in consequence. Do you mind?'

'Not at all. I've had enough as well.' He collected her beaded bag and wrap and Jane waved a casual hand at the circle and walked away quickly, before any objections could be voiced.

An insistent tapping on her bedroom door brought Jane out of a heavy sleep and her travelling clock showed just after six o'clock. Oh, bother! It was Sunday, why couldn't she be left just for one morning to sleep on and on? Her heavy spirit lifted a dark head to remind her of the promised jaunt to Julius Davenport's homestead. She had taken one of her mother's sleeping pills the night before, or rather, in the early hours. Taken because Jane suddenly feared the outcome of that inner insistence to torment her heart in solitude. She knew with painful conviction that nothing in the world could exorcise the unwelcome love that had entered her unwary heart. A number of times she had believed herself to be in love, but when it hit you like this then you instantly recognised the gold from the dross.

And of what earthly, or heavenly, use would this remarkable knowledge be to her? Absolutely, hurtingly and hopelessly none whatsoever.

Her decision to stay at home (primarily because Grant Saxon would be there) was overruled by an unsympathetic family and she eventually subsided listlessly on to the back seat of the Combi next to two horribly boisterous boys. The magnificent scenery on the Sabie road failed to arouse her normal enthusiasm; this was part of the Summit Route that he had mentioned and she would never travel it with him, as promised.

The Davenport home was built in the old tradition, with modern additions and appliances discreetly blending. The wide stoep, or verandah, overlooked a sloping lawn and the pool nestled in a hollow surrounded by indigenous shrubs and trees. Jane aroused herself to take note only when Elizabeth drew her attention to the intensity of varied greens and wild natural beauty of a carefully planned landscape.

Mrs. Davenport sat in an old, comfortable chair on the

verandah. Julius, incongruously clad in wildly coloured Bermuda shorts and blue T-shirt, looked fit and brown as he ambled down the steps to greet his guests. Pat and Peter were already there and voiced their longing for the tea that was being held back to await the lazy laggards, so Julius decided not to prolong the torture. Fresh tea could be made for the Saxons if and when they arrived. Tony and Mick hastily greeted the old lady and their host, then made a beeline for the pool. Thirst being quenched satisfactorily, the adults followed suit with the exception of Jane, who chose to laze in a deck-chair and visit Mrs. Davenport. Pat declared she was being chicken after her night out and Jane lazily agreed, closing her eyelids serenely against their jeers.

The two of them got on well and chatted companionably, and then Julius's grandmother took Jane into her bedroom and opened a heavy stinkwood chest. With reverent hands she lifted a beautiful crocheted bedspread which nestled in tissue and sprinkled with aromatic camphor. The wondrous work of love and art had been handed down to each succeeding generation and now awaited the future wife of Julius.

'And my wicked grandson will soon reach his forties and still hasn't found a girl to suit him. He'd better make haste, for I'm determined to hold a grandchild—I mean a great-grandchild in my old arms,' she smiled mischievously, 'and I'm getting mighty weary of waiting, being selfishly eager to meet up again with my dear departed in the delightful hereafter! Come, help me fold this again, my old ears are still good and I can hear a car, must be Grant. I haven't seen young Sandy for over a year now——'

Jane followed slowly and stood beside her to watch Grant, Mara and Sandy walked down to the pool. Mara appeared self-possessed in a short towelling wrap and the man beside her, in light safari suit, strode with indolent, loose-limbed grace. Sandy flung her own small beach coat off her shoulders as she reached the edge of the pool, hesitated a moment while she obviously looked around for her friend; the watching girl saw Elizabeth wave towards the house and all three new arrivals turned. Sandy waved madly and Grant started to walk back alone. He would naturally be coming to greet

Mrs. Davenport ... Jane thought desperately for a way of escape.

'Mrs. Davenport,' she gripped the arm nearest her, 'I don't want to speak to Grant Saxon, not just yet—don't waste time asking why, just give me an out, please, darling?'

Darling Mrs. D. took one quick look at the troubled brown eyes of her companion and said, 'Go through the house and find the back door, to the left of the house is a row of fig trees, the pigsties are beyond them. See if Mama Pig's not squashing her young litter. There's also a new clutch of chicks just come out ... that's all I can do, dear.'

'Mrs. D., you're an absolute doll—thanks!' Without a backward glance Jane disappeared into the cool haven of the house.

She found the downy yellow chicks and fondled them one by one while their ruffled mother scolded loudly. Jane left them and walked on. Mama Pig lay contentedly on her side while the little ones, twelve of them, fought hungrily at the exposed milk bar. Finally they all found a place and Jane leaned on the low stone wall, listening to little grunts of satisfaction and watched the tiny fore-paws kneading swollen udders to excite the flow of milk. She leaned over perilously to see where the out-of-tune squealing came from, the sow moved her hindquarters, and Jane saw the thirteenth piglet, squashed under a heavy haunch!

Without further thought she jumped over the wall and approached the family, talking soothingly to the sow. A quick heave and the squashed, angry one was clear, unhurt except for his hungry feelings. But now things began to happen ... Mama thought this red-shirted human was doing the hurting and came clumsily to her feet, scattering babies right and left, and they in turn voiced their disapproval in no uncertain terms! Jane stepped back from the advancing menace, her foot skidded in a puddle and she found herself sitting neatly wedged in a trough of swill.

A tall shadow moved on the wall. Sandy and Grant Saxon were studying her in equal astonishment.

The child's control was not so great as the man's and a high giggle escaped. 'We heard the row and came to see—oh,

Jane, what are you doing in there?' Her giggle exploded in convulsed laughter.

Through clenched teeth Jane said, 'I'm watching the pigs,' and eyed them haughtily. She was firmly jammed and was not going to let anyone be entertained by her struggle to extricate herself. Damn him, oh, damn him to hell—and Sandra could join him there for being so inquisitive!

Grant bent down and leaned laconic elbows on the wall. 'I grant you the other pool is a bit crowded and sympathise with your wish to be alone, dear Janey, but not with your alternative choice,' he said.

'Go to hell, Grant Saxon!' Jane hissed between pearly teeth.

'Language, dear, in front of the child too!' he reproached, softly taunting.

'And take her with you!' she riposted in cold fury.

'Oh, Jane, don't be cross, but you do look funny. Are you hurted?' Sandy's laughter subsided at the look on her friend's face.

Jane forbore to answer and turned her had to watch the wretched sow, cursing inwardly at the cause of her embarrassment; she would have let the piglet suffocate gladly if she had but known the outcome of her kindly rescue.

'Need any help, Miss Wheeler? You look slightly stuck——' Grant began conversationally, but stopped as furious nut-brown eyes stabbed him.

'I'll thank you to leave. Go away!' Wilfully her voice betrayed her too, coming in a husky croak. Grant moved behind her back, leaned his long length down and slid two hands between her upper arms and body; a quick heave and she was out and up. He steadied her while she found her footing. The swill runnelled down her jeans and squelched into her shoes. Jane kept her back to him when he released her, fully aware of the odorous picture her posterior presented.

'Thanks,' she said bitterly.

'Sandy, show Jane to the outside shower and bring her bathing suit and wrap ... and some nice scented soap,' Grant added thoughtfully.

Jane turned her head to watch his receding back; there was a definite quiver to the broad shoulders! She stamped her foot in sheer frustration and her shoe squelched back happily.

Sandy complied promptly and sympathetically, then waited outside the roughly built workers' shower while Jane soaped herself thoroughly with the 'scented' soap. Feeling sorry for her outburst towards the child, Jane made amends by recounting her rescue of one piglet which resulted in her predicament. Sandy passed in her towel and swimwear and when Jane emerged she saw a maid soaking her odorous clothes in a laundry tub. The maid smiled shyly when Jane thanked her and promised to have them dry and ironed 'jus' now'.

Sandy skipped back to the pool and Jane walked over to Mrs. Davenport and told her about the smelly climax of her attempt to keep out of Grant's way. The old lady tried to keep a sober face, but the twinkle in her eye could not be denied.

'Grant didn't tell me. He ambled past with the assurance that the pigs were fine, that you and they were on very cosy terms! I'm sorry I couldn't keep him here with me, but Sandy demanded to find out what the fuss was about and he decided to accompany her. I'll have to give you that particular piglet as a memento of the furore he caused!'

'Thanks for the kind thought, but I never want to see him again, and if you leave him on my doorstep I'll promptly strangle him,' Jane threatened.

There was much cavorting in the water when Jane's reluctant feet finally brought her to the pool's edge. With the exception of two: Mara lay on her back, dark glasses protecting her eyes and the brief white bikini accentuating the lines of her slim loveliness. Grant, darkly tanned in blue trunks and smoking on the far side, had evidently just emerged, his hair and skin glistened wetly.

Jane greeted Mara briefly and a slender hand lifted in acknowledgement. She scanned the upturned face with a quick sweep of lowered lashes and found no signs of derision or mocking smile and concluded that Grant had not tattled, as yet, about her adventure. He was biding his time, waiting for a suitable moment, no doubt. She didn't dare to glance at him but shed her wrap to stand poised, young and clean-limbed, before executing a smooth cleavage into the water.

Everyone had tired of water battles, for which Jane was thankful, being in no mood for that sort of thing, and soon they climbed out one by one, leaving her to wallow in the silken, cool water on her own. She was very aware of the tall figure standing at the far end and stayed at her end, floating with her eyes closed.

It came as a shock when she felt a rippling movement at her side and opened her eyes to find him floating alongside. Jane immediately made for the edge and rested her arms on the warm slate, allowing her feet to sink down. Grant followed promptly, did likewise with his arm close to hers.

'Your hair floats and resembles seaweed, and you're a slick chick in the water. Feeling more aromatic now?'

A searing look was her answer, but it seemed to have no burning effect on the man's tough hide or stony feelings. An imperceptible pause followed before Grant continued conversationally, 'That unfinished business last night—I'm still trying to figure out what you were doing your nut about and why it took such an insulting trend.'

Jane interlocked her fingers tightly. 'Leave it be, Grant. Call it a silly episode, anything you want to, but forget it. I apologise for any insult, apologise for whatever you think needs an apology.'

His direct glance held genuine curiosity. 'Haven't you been kissed before and enjoyed it without behaving like an outraged innocent?'

'I have, I'm no innocent, and it's still no concern of yours. If you can't or won't figure it out—my attitude—on your own, then I can't help any by going into details.' His nearness brought a breathlessness to her words.

'For heaven's sake, child, what details? I can only conclude that you've formed some nasty hallucinations about me or, another alternative, I revolt you in some way.'

'Oh, heavens!' Jane wondered if he had a blind spot in his make-up; there was genuine puzzlement apparent. If he only knew how opposite to revulsion were her feelings towards him, how eagerly she would have co-operated if he were of single status! She turned her head away, silently mute.

Grant studied her closed face for a moment longer, then impatiently ran his fingers through his wet hair, expelled deeply and said, 'Very well, Jane, I'll not trouble you further. If you persist in being obstinate about this, there's no point in persuasion and it becomes rather boring,' he slipped under water and a slight rippling on the surface showed his progress to the other end. A tightening of muscles in brown arms as he lifted himself out of the pool and then walked to where Mara watched and smiled invitingly.

Jane couldn't isolate herself any longer from the party on the lawn and forced her body to obey good manners by walking round on the warm slates to join them. Bart, Janet and Elizabeth had left, to dress and sit with Mrs. Davenport. Mara now prepared to follow suit.

She stood up and smoothed her hands sensually over the satin skin of her arms. 'I've had enough of the sun, my skin blisters easily.'

Julius barred her way. 'But you haven't even been in the water, darling.'

'That's for the birds, and I do feel rather worn out from my late night.' Her glance played lightly on Grant's upturned face.

'We all had a good late night ... getting too old to play?' Julius taunted.

'Oh, let up, Julius. Julius, put me down.' He had suddenly lifted her in strong arms and was striding towards the pool.

'Put me down, Julius, don't act so juvenile!' Her voice seemed to dwindle on the last word and only her tormentor saw the sudden terror in her eyes. Mara Saxon was afraid of water!

Grant said, 'She can't swim, Julius.'

'Well, I'll be damned! What price all those lovely swimwear adverts? The sooner she starts learning the better and it'll be my pleasure to teach you, young woman!' Julius lowered her to her feet and tugged playfully at the coil of hair on her neck.

Mara moved away irritably and her mask of sophistication dropped for an instant as she glared at him, knowing that his action had exposed her one weak spot. All John's and Grant's attempts to teach her had failed miserably; she was absolutely terrified to enter water over four feet in depth. So now this swim-mad party knew she couldn't swim and, to lose face in front of others, even though it was only that dippy Peter and Pat and Grant's sulky secretary (what was she doing out under the stars with Grant, last night?), and the tiny look of contempt that had come into Julius' eyes when he put her down ... she was used to admiration in all men's eyes ... to lose face was one of the major crimes in her book and jet-set circle!

As if he knew what was going on in her mind, Grant said casually, 'It's no crime not to be able to swim, Mara.'

'Thanks, Grant.' Mara fluttered her eyes gratefully. Julius bent down to pick up his shirt and said sharply, 'Not a crime but a necessity, don't you think? Fortunately Sandy can swim like a fish, so probably won't need your help some day, but you might just topple from one of your poses and land in deep waters!' He glanced at his watch. 'I reckon we should have a light lunch and start on our walk, as planned.'

Pat explained to Jane about the proposed walk. The younger people were going up the mountain and Bart, Janet, Elizabeth and Mrs. D. would take the car later and meet them at a designated spot for a picnic tea.

Jane's clothes were clean and ironed and quite 'aromatic'. Sandy was the soul of discretion, merely winking gravely when Jane appeared in her jeans and shirt. Had Grant warned the child or was it her own finer feelings for her friend's pride? Thoughtful, if it was he, but she would reserve judgement in case Grant was waiting to burst the bubble himself!

Mara's wish to come later with the car was downed in chorus, and her face was quite sulky when they finally set off. She kept shaking her wispy sandals and made good use of Grant's willing arm. It became obvious that she was holding them all back and soon the boys, Sandy and Jane lost patience and forged ahead. Pat, Julius and Peter caught up with them and Jane looked back to see Mara sitting on a rock while Grant knelt at her feet, shaking the offending grit out of a sandal.

They walked and climbed for about half a mile when Julius stopped with a shrug of irritation. 'I'm going back to relieve Grant, his patience must be wearing thin. I'll carry the flipping girl, if necessary!' He turned on his heel and disappeared down the incline of trees and jutting rocks.

After negotiating a stiff, rocky climb which shortened even the breath of the very young, a sharp drop stopped them on the brink of a clear stream that cascaded down to misty, green depths.

Jane stood on the lip of the gorge. She stood alone, a remote figurehead carved by the wind that whipped her hair into a silken pennant and moulded her shirt to slender firmness.

Her nerves signalled his approach before her ears registered the firm stride and crackling of leaves. She knew instinctively that it was Grant, even before she heard him warn Sandy to be careful. Jane turned her head and saw fires of anger in wood-smoke eyes.

His voice was steel as he gripped her arm and pulled her back roughly. 'Get back at once and stay with the party. Don't you recognise danger? A slight lift of the wind could put you off balance, dizziness could plunge you to the bottom of this gorge ... if you haven't the sense, at least Peter or the boys should know better!' His face was granite-hard and pale.

Jane stepped further back and the iron hold on her arm slackened. Her heart started knocking unevenly as his words brought home the danger and her unthinking foolishness. She drew a jagged breath and whispered contritely, 'I'm sorry, Grant, I really had no fear—d-didn't realise——'

'At least you could think of others, their feelings if something should happen to one of the party.'

Jane went a trifle pale at the cynical contempt in the rough voice. He might as well say outright that only she could cause catastrophe, it was there in his tone. She suddenly resented his attitude and the colour crept back into her cheeks; after all, she had apologised most contritely.

'Did your—Mara give you a bad time? If so, don't work your spleen off on me. I'm sure I was quite safe until you frightened the living daylights out of me.' Dark brows drew together and she added hastily but offhandedly, 'I'll be most careful as from now, no need to go jump down the boys' throats.'

Grant Saxon's eyes narrowed. 'You're the sort that positively invites a man to shake you till every bone in your body rattles, Jane Wheeler!' he gritted, and turned abruptly.

Jane took the child's hand and followed slowly. Sandy said thoughtfully, 'I wonder why ever'body's so cross today. Mara is cross 'cause her feet hurt, you're cross with Grant all the time and h-he's not nice today.'

Jane stopped impulsively and put her arm around the small shoulders.

'Sandy dear, I'm a real misery today and I know it. Thank you for not telling anyone about my mishap this morning. I—I guess that's why I'm out of sorts. It's very humiliating to be found in a pig's trough, particularly by Grant. I wouldn't have minded if it was only you—it must have been very funny—my sense of humour seems to have deserted me.'

Sandy returned her smile. 'You're not a misery, Jane, but ... since Mara came ...' the young voice hesitated and Jane interposed quietly, 'Why don't you call them Mummy and Daddy? I'm sure they would love——'

'But my daddy is dead, Jane.'

CHAPTER 7

QUIETLY spoken words, which took a full moment to register, then coursed through her body with shocking rigidity. Jane fought the threatening lockjaw and paralysis of nerve centres.

'Sandy,' she whispered at last, 'whom—what are you—what did you s-say?'

The child's eyes were lowered, and missed her companion's distress. 'Ever'body knows my daddy's gone to h-heaven. When my—Mara was driving his car, there was 'n accident 'n my daddy got killed and Toicky 'n Grant said he's gone to heaven.' The slight shoulders trembled in Jane's arms. 'I think it's her fault 'cause she rowed with Daddy a lot, so God took him away from us. I was good 'n loved him awfully, so why did God punish me too, Jane?'

Troubled eyes looked up trustingly and Jane sought desperately to collect shocked wits, to find the right answer.

'God is good, Sandy, never forget that. Th-there must be a reason for taking your daddy. He didn't mean to hurt you or your mother and I'm sure He wasn't punishing her. He n-needed your daddy too——' She stopped, at loss for words or comfort. The tumultuous shock she had just experienced left her bereft of sane thought.

'I never called my daddy John, but my mother likes me to call her Mara.' A small chin lifted bravely. 'I'm going to ask her 'bout the accident 'n if she was under the influence and rowing with my daddy.'

'Who told you that?' Jane asked urgently, through a second upsurge of emotion.

'Nobody. I heard Flip say to this other man, down by the hedge, that "madam was under the influence 'n they had this accident" and the other man said "boozed up again 'n fighting", 'n I knowed they were talking about—Mara. I think I'd rather ask Grant 'cause I'm frightened to ask her, 'n I think maybe Flip is 'n awful liar. Jane, will you come with me when I ask him? I feel all wobbly inside, but I'd like to know 'cause he said people must always be fair to ever'one.'

'He's quite right, and I'll come with you,' Jane suddenly remembered the night at the Mission when Grant had discussed a fault in the steering with David and felt justified in continuing, 'You'll find that things are not at all as you were led to imagine. Not today though, darling, because we're visiting the Davenports—after work, tomorrow,' a swift thought crowded out shock; maybe, after today's contretemps, she wouldn't have a job! 'Come now, the others must be waiting, we still have to walk to the road to meet the car for our tea.'

Well, she had committed herself, would have to keep her promise to be with her young friend, when she confronted Grant or Mara with her important question. She hoped fervently that they were in a position to settle Sandy's troubled doubts. Grant had told David that the fault had been in the car, not the other. The 'other' being Mara, a woman incapable of driving safely?

They teamed up with the rest of the party before she could assimilate her own shock at hearing that Grant was not Sandy's father after all. Julius and Mara had caught up as well and the lady was evidently in a furious temper, not quite so immaculate now, her hair tied back with a piece of string, extracted handily from Julius' pocket, her fair skin deeply flushed from sun and exertion. Julius was carrying out his plan with vengeance. Jane felt a quiver of sympathy for Mara run through her.

Her mind and thoughts were a tangled mess; however hard she struggled to find the pattern, the worse became the skeins. Jane walked mechanically, only answering when addressed directly, her feet finding their way blindly.

Not one of her family had contradicted her when she had coupled Grant and Mara as Sandy's parents; Pat had mentioned John's accident and said that when Mara came back, she would have her way; Bart had described Mara; Sandy always mentioned Grant by name; everybody took for granted that Mara would accompany Grant to the club dance and not once had he disputed their right to take it for granted; Mara had her own room in the Saxon household. In fact, she was mistress of the house but not married to the master of the Estate.

What an almighty misconception she, Jane, had been labouring under—and suffering!

And, her heart shrivelled, insulting a perfectly innocent man. Dear God, no wonder Grant Saxon, after asking her to clarify her insulting remarks, had become angry, contemptuous and bored. She, who loved so desperately, had killed all chances of reciprocation by repulsing his advances with highly insulting advice. She had even told him to go to hell!

Oh, why, through all that had been said and transpired, hadn't anyone been more explicit on the relationship of the two Saxons?

Simply because they were not to guess that she didn't know—oh, damnation!

Jane must have cried out aloud because Peter asked solicitously, 'What now, Jane?'

'I banged my knee, Peter,' she lied brazenly.

'There's a doctor in the trek, love,' he enlightened softly. She grimaced at him and continued on her way. 'Never known such a grumpy, silent party—can only be last night's left-overs,' he muttered.

She stopped at the road edge and looked back. Grant was still at Mara's side. Something was irregular about the situation—Mara had a perfect right to live in her late husband's home (with her brother-in-law?). Now that Jane had their relationship in perspective, she recalled snips of gossip and hints: that Mara had her claws bared for Grant, that he had loved someone who had let him down ... It could only be Mara, and he still loved her. If her conjectures were facts, why hadn't he married? A suitable time had passed since the death of his brother: was there a governing law against a man marrying his brother's wife?

And why did he bother to flatter her, Jane, and kiss the way he kissed her last night? She had watched him tease Pat. Did he kiss her as well, because he couldn't have the one he really wanted?

Her intent gaze had settled on the man uppermost in her thoughts. A dark eyebrow raised as he intercepted her inward preoccupation.

'Seeing ghosts, Miss Wheeler?'

'No, Mr. Saxon. Lost visions, that's all.' Julius called and Jane turned away before Grant could delve deeper.

The car was parked in a shadowy bay scooped out of the side of the towering mountain. A coloured driver had driven the roomy station-wagon. Janet and Elizabeth were setting out tea and scones on a folding table.

Mara drew attention as she started to count the newcomers aloud.

'Janet, Elizabeth, Mrs. Davenport and Bart, plus driver. That makes five. There's room for me, for the return trip. I flatly refuse to walk back, and don't ever invite me on a big walk again, it's for the birds and——'

'Childish and juvenile?' asked Julius sweetly.

'As for you, Julius Davenport,' a graceful body whirled to face the old lady, 'your grandson, Mrs. D., is quite uncivilised, he handled me like a—a sack of maize, an absolute boor and—and——'

'Patient, long-suffering, and perfectly charming!' concluded Mrs. D.'s grandson, his smile dazzling.

'Shut up!' Fury made her fiery. 'May I accompany you back, Mrs. Davenport?'

'Surely, my dear,' said that lady equably.

'Chicken!' sneered Julius, but did not pursue his taunt.

'You see, Jane, everybody's mad today,' Sandy whispered.

Jane nodded complete agreement. She was the maddest, most miserably mad of the lot.

Peace reigned while tea and scones disappeared down thirsty throats. Jane desired a lift back as well, but in the face of the jeers that had met Mara's demand, she stifled her own request. There wouldn't be room anyway.

Her step was not so buoyant as they set off on the return trip. Peter and the boys seemed to be the only fit ones left. She, Pat and Sandy stayed together, followed by Julius and Grant. The trail back, on a different route, was steeper and required concentration, for which mercy Jane was thankful. It kept her mind away from the startling disclosures that Sandy's amazing words had revealed.

Mara had freshened up considerably by the time a tired group reached the homestead. She walked down the steps to Grant, who held Sandy's hand in his, and bent down solicitously.

'My poor little girl, is she worn out? I'm an unthinking beast, I should have let you come in the car as well. I think we should leave soon, Grant.'

A bit late, thought Jane cattily, to act the anxious mother now, Mrs. *John* Saxon. And felt a ripple of pure jealousy at the cosy trio they made.

The trees were throwing tall shadows, they were a long way from their respective homes, so all decided to take their leave. They thanked host and hostess, with the exception of Mara, who pointedly thanked Mrs. D. very sweetly and ignored Julius. He smiled nonchalantly at a back view of an exaggerated mannequin glide to Grant's car.

Grant spoke to Jane briefly. 'Tom will call at the usual time.'

She nodded her head and followed the boys into the back seat of the Combi.

Jane lay back and folded both arms under her head to gaze unseeingly at the stars that winked impishly through her open bedroom window. Her recent findings were still too new and raw to share; she herself didn't quite know what it was all about and inner turmoil was an absolute kaleidoscopic mess. She sighed deeply, moved one hand to switch off the bedside lamp, cuddled both hands under her cheek like a tired child and closed her eyes. A pathetic plea flew from her heart to brain, to dispel that persistent image of wood-smoke eyes smudged into a strong, dark face; to let her rest peacefully through the long night. Tomorrow would come and Jane Wheeler must face the gigantic task of sorting out the upheaval, unwanted and sudden, that threatened her placid existence.

Sleep hovered over the troubled young face, took pity and lowered its gentle cloak . . .

The hastily fashioned Psyche-knot of nut-brown hair wobbled slightly as Jane lifted a proud chin when she entered Grant Saxon's study on Monday morning. He glanced up with an absent smile of greeting.

'The returns for that last shipment came in on Saturday—check and file them, Jane. I must take you down to the packing sheds soon so that you can have or form a clearer notion of what's going on—easier for you.' His eyes focused absently on her tilted chin.

Which instantly made her feel absurd and quivery. 'Good morning, yes, Mr. Saxon—Grant.'

The smile became slightly pronounced, more sardonic at her obvious hesitation. 'The week-end—er—interlude, with all mishaps had passed safely, I assume, no broken bones, regrets or vengeful aftermath?' Grant's fist thumped the papers before him, giving her not a chance to reply, even if she could (which was most unlikely). 'Good, and so to work, my young rebel, to the slave-wheel once more!'

'Yes, boss,' said Jane, grateful for his light manner yet bristling instantly at the knowing, sardonic smile on his lips. The bristling helped to settle emotions that had stirred at the sight of him sitting there, dark, rugged and heartbreakingly distant. And quite openly referring to her mishap at the Davenports', no regrets for the attempted flirtation. An interlude to slide over amusedly. He would never know how much more it meant; to discover he was not a married man after she had shown her contempt even while feeling his potent attraction. Her seemingly neurotic manner had surely dispelled any loving thoughts, if there ever had been any such towards her. And above all, not forgetting—Mara.

Jane lowered wistful eyes from the down-bent head of her boss and shuffled the papers on her desk.

An hour passed in comparative silence with an occasional crackling of paper. Jane's interest in the work at hand quickened and she gave an involuntary sound of disagreement when she came across an error of calculation in a final total. Grant looked up immediately, a deep frown of concentration furrowing his brow. 'Let's see, Jane.'

She picked up the offending paper and walked over to his desk to stand beside him, putting the missive down for his inspection.

'Show me what and where.'

Jane leaned over, unthinkingly placed her one hand on his shoulder while she guided his quick eyes with a finger of her free hand. Her hand blanked part of the figures and Grant moved it aside to look for himself. He retained her hand in his while they both mentally toted again. A tingle feathering up her arm diverted Jane's eyes and her glance shifted to the tip of his ear.

Mara chose that moment to drift in unannounced.

'Moral support because of a great deficit or merely—moral deficit?' Her dulcet tones floated across the study to startle Jane and Grant equally. Her wintry smile rested on the other girl's hands, one on the man's shoulder, the other nestling in his clasp.

Grant dropped the hand in his, to reach for a pen. Jane straightened abruptly from what could easily be misrepresented as a cosy pose.

'Morning, Jane dear. Please don't let me interrupt your—session—with your boss. Grant, Sandy's being tiresome, insists on riding her precious Sugarbush this morning. Is it safe? I'm simply not up to haring around with her.' Mara was superbly cool and chic in a willow-green catsuit. A green band circled her hair and the shoulder-length fall was flicked up to perfection, magnolia skin showing no bad effects of the previous day.

The girl at Grant's side felt that she, in comparison, suggested everything her name implied. Plain Jane. Here before her was someone who could exploit her finest points and beauty to the utmost. Experience had taught her to tone down or highlight with subtle finesse. Jane's skin glowed with natural, healthy sheen, her only make-up a pearly lipstick, but she felt like a naïve amateur compared to the artistry of this one.

Grant ignored or was unaware of Mara's sarcastic comment on Jane's proximity. His eyes approved the picture of languid grace she presented but were blind to the sparkle of venom that flashed for an instant in green depths before the woman shifted her eyes from the girl to the man.

'Sandy's perfectly safe with Sugarbush. Lemmy always rides with her and she won't wilfully do anything foolish,' he smiled at his sister-in-law, 'and I can't see you being much help if any rescuing's to be done.'

Mara smiled back, her movements deliberately evocative. 'You do know me so well, darling. I'm no dashing lifesaver. We'll leave Sandy to her own devices. Can I help here, or is your little secretary quite efficient in every way?' She laid stress sweetly but surely on 'every'.

Jane had moved back to her own desk, eyes lowered

studiously on the papers before her. Under that bland mask she was fighting an incredibly brutal, pagan urge to clutch the heavy paperweight and hurl it straight between those insufferable green eyes, to shatter that mask of beauty and superiority!

'I've no complaints. Jane is every man's dream of the perfect—secretary.' Grant's smile showed sudden wicked awareness of Mara's allusion to the cosy scene she had witnessed. 'Thanks for the offer, but we're coping very well. Entertain yourself elsewhere and we'll join you for tea later.'

Her dismissal was evident in the way he bent over the figures that Jane had brought to him. Mara's eyes swept critically over the other girl before she made an indolent exit.

'Bully for you, boss!' Jane commended silently while a little warmth circled her cold heart. She insisted on having her tea in the study because she became genuinely immersed in her work and had no inclination to watch the sorceress manipulate her willing victim. Grant did not insist, as he usually did, that she have a fresh air break. Jane felt that this was sure indication that he had changed—since Mara's arrival. The pattern was changing, even Sandy failed to appear for the tea break that she adored sharing with her new friend.

Lunch was as usual, except that Mara and Grant did most of the conversing, Sandy and Jane the quiet listeners, where before they had been spontaneous and cheerful in exchange of confidences.

And so the pattern of days proceeded. Jane became withdrawn and recoiled inwardly at any attempt on Grant's part to put their association back on its former natural, friendly basis. He sensed her withdrawal and gradually ceased trying, became just her terse, businesslike, matter-of-fact boss. Just that and no more. Mara found many pretexts for drifting in and out of the study or merely sat out under the trees, reading, varnishing her nails or boredly watching Sandy at play. She livened considerably when Grant appeared and ignored Jane with the indifference of mistress towards menial. Jane seethed, but managed to subdue her feelings, quietly pursued her duties with serene composure. Grant Saxon was her boss, not Mara, and he paid well. She also tried hard to squash an inner conviction that she stayed on because it kept her close to him and her sadistic heart delighted in self-torture; there would be no difficulty in finding employment elsewhere, just as lucrative. Her mind considered seriously, but the rest of her rejected immediate action.

One afternoon Tom anxiously requested her to wait while he replaced a defective fanbelt. Jane assured him that there was no special cause for her to hurry home and started to walk down a shrub-lined path towards a grove of aromatic gum trees. The air hummed with bees in the tree-tops; gum-tree honey surpassed in flavour any other she had tasted. A taste of honey ... on her lips, unforgettable, one night not so long ago, never to taste again ... that was sweeter. Now unobtainable through her own stupidity.

Sandy ran down and joined her and they walked in companionable silence.

'Jane,' Sandy's hand in hers tugged an invitation to sit beside her on a gnarled stump, 'Jane, you know, we've got no further with my nature book 'n Christmas is nearly here 'n I've collected lots of wings and ferns 'n wild flowers. I do so want to complete a book to give to Grant for a present. You're always so busy,' large eyes pleaded, 'will you help me? You promised. I've got it all set out in my room, but I don't know how to place 'n name them by myself.'

Jane remembered her promise to the child and wanted to help, but the very thought of an evening in the house of Grant Saxon sent her nerves into quivering crescendo. For the sake of her pleading friend she would have to steel herself to remain one evening with Sandy in her room, while the child's mother disported her charm on a certain person under the same roof perhaps on that cosy swinging couch, a mere thickness of wall away. Why couldn't *she* help her daughter? She did absolutely nothing constructive around the house, unless being attractively at hand to delight the master could be construed as construction ... Jane shivered at the ugly change in herself; her thoughts and mind had developed a wicked will of their own, ruled by a rearing green head!

'Let's find out how long Tom will be, maybe we can make a start now and finish off another evening.' Jane took Sandy's hand and they started back at a fast clip. Grant appeared around the corner of the house. Sandy saw him and suddenly stood stock-still, her hand jerking Jane to a stop as well.

'Jane,' the name came on a slight gasp, 'you're with me now. I'm feeling brave, so let's ask him—about Daddy!'

The hand holding hers tightened painfully. 'No! Not now, Sandy, please.'

Sandy's voice drifted loudly in sudden appeal. 'Please, you promised!'

Grant's head turned, he stopped for a moment and then diverted his course towards them.

Sandy's hand tightened nervously and Jane felt her own back go rigid while every nerve protested at the child's nervous determination. The man came to a stop, two yards away, surveyed the unsure stance of both girls and his thumbs automatically hitched into his trouser pockets. 'What's happened now?'

Jane unlocked stiff lips. 'I—I—nothing's wrong, nothing has h-happened. Sandy wants——' she was unable to proceed and Sandy interposed stutteringly, 'It's something I w-want to ask you. Have you got time to listen and—and can we sit down, please—my legs feel funny.' She plonked down on the grass as if her legs had indeed become fluid. 'It's about my—daddy.'

Grey, probing eyes lifted from the small figure to Jane's stiff stance, circled swiftly to the house. A calculating dark-browed estimation of distance, possibly to see if Mara was visible or within earshot. Long legs folded as he haunched down on his heels.

'Okay, poppet, but before you ask, may I let you in on a secret? It's this; I've wanted very much to talk to someone, most of all to you, about John, your dad, and I'm so glad that you've decided to do so of your own free will. Sit down, Jane, you're in on this and, I suspect, the open sesame.'

Jane refrained from a cold reminder that it was he who had asked her to delve into the cause of Sandy's misery. Instead she too sank silently on to the soft grass. Sandy sensed her perturbation and instinctive defence came in her words. 'Grant, please don't mind if Jane stays with me. She's made me brave 'nuff to ask you about—things.'

His eyes crinkled slightly at the corners as he noted the swift fall of Jane's lashes, veiling her eyes. 'Okay, kid, I accept your bodyguard. Shoot away.'

Sandra cast a nervous glance towards the house, looked back at Grant and gained confidence from his level, steady gaze. She said, with sweet determination, 'I know Daddy died in a car accident when Mara—Mommy was driving. Was she—was it really all her fault, Grant?'

If Grant received a severe jolt at her unexpected question the only indication was a sudden deep pucker of dark brows. Jane gave him full marks for control, there was no doubt in her mind that he had not expected this to be the cause of Sandy's display of misery and strange outbursts. She saw enlightenment dawn and compassion darken the wood-smoke eyes as he realised what agony of mind this small soul had endured. A brown hand came up in a slow, familiar gesture to brush back an unruly lock of hair. Jane had learned to recognise that simple action as a sign of deep thought, an aid to solving certain problems. Was every familiar gesture always going to affect her heart this way?

Grant answered with loving firmness. 'Sandy, I'm frightfully sorry that I didn't realise long ago, before you had to draw courage to ask this, that you may have overheard that particular version of the—accident. It's quite evident now that you heard certain gossip which spread, untruthfully, before anyone was aware of the true facts.' He paused long enough to lift a small hand that trembled amongst the grass blades into the firm clasp of his warm hands, continued with slow deliberation, 'Your father's death was caused by some fault—something wrong in the steering system of the car. Your mother happened to be driving at the time and was in no way responsible for the accident whatever you may have heard to the contrary. The car went through a bridge railing. Mara was—lucky—but your daddy—John, he didn't suffer, darling, God took him straight away. Do you understand, poppet?'

Sandy's eyes showed a glimmer of tears, but they held her uncle's gaze with steadfast faith. 'Yes. I knowed you wouldn't ever lie to me, and I'm glad my daddy didn't suffer.' She swallowed bravely. 'I'm also glad m-my mother wasn't hurted.'

The quiet silence enveloped three people and their thoughts. The man watched the small down-bent head while he stroked the fingers in his hand, one by one. Their silent listener felt her heart turn with sympathy and burned to have the right to lay her hands on each beloved head in wordless consolation . . .

A sigh escaped the big man. 'If only my poppet had asked me, or your mom, right away, all this heartbreak would have been spared, darling. Tell me, anything else worrying you?'

Jane's breast swelled at the pure, grave concern for his brother's child. Sandy lifted her head and said, equally gravely, 'Yes, Grant. Now I'm worried 'n 'shamed of all the bad things that was in my head about—Mara.'

Grant put a comforting hand on her shoulder. 'Well now, it's all over, and you can make amends by showing your mother in all sorts of ways that you love her. How about starting right away by calling her Mummy, instead of Mara?'

Sandy nestled into the pressure of his palm, but uncertainty showed in her eyes. 'Jane said the same at the picnic, but she likes me to say Mara 'n I don't think it'd please her awfully for me to call her Mom. Should I 'fess to her about my bad thoughts and—'n ask for—forgiveness?' The very thought of this darkened her eyes with apprehension and Grant's discerning comfort came quickly.

'No, Sandy. It wasn't your fault, you can't be blamed for any bad thoughts. They were put there by silly gossip and it'll only upset her again, after all this time. Call her as you've done in the past if she wishes it and just be your natural sweet self, and everything'll work normally. I'm sure your friend will agree.' His deep gaze lifted to the quiet girl at Sandy's side. 'Not so, Jane?'

Jane had been silently applauding his handling of the situation, his forbearance in not questioning the source of twisted information, also regretting that he should have to be the recipient and consoler while the mother got off scot-free. A little girl who was afraid to turn to her own mother . . . His question caught her completely off guard, she was tongue-tied as the blue-grey eyes suddenly speared her.

Her eyes fled from his and she looked towards the house. Mara was walking down the steps with studied, indolent grace. She had most certainly noticed their huddle on the grass but was not aware of its grave cause and decisions. Jane stood up and brushed wisps of grass off her skirt. Her tongue unknotted at last.

'I certainly agree, nothing more should be said to anyone. I'm only sorry that Sandy didn't speak sooner. To labour under such misapprehension must have been simply awful—and lonely.'

Grant straightened up as well and held a helping hand to Sandy. 'We all do, at some time or other—and find our particular island of loneliness. Sandy braved the storm before it became too late. So few have that courage.' He spoke almost indifferently, his gaze held by the woman walking towards them.

Jane also watched Mara while her heart echoed agreement. Her boat was surely wrecked on her particular island. And she dared not brave the storm; she would never receive compassionate treatment. Scorn would be her reward, derisive contempt at her temerity in hoping that she could get to first base ever—while there was Mara—his first love. And last?

Grant stood beside her, but they were miles apart, because of her ignorance. Perhaps, in spite of Mara, something sweet might have budded if she had known the true set-up; she had felt that he was attracted. Her insults had withered the **bud and drawn** taunts instead of tenderness. Past events had baffled her completely and now she felt sick, incredulous lump in the pit of her stomach as she saw appreciation lighten grey eyes as he watched Sandy's mother.

Stop! Stop deluding yourself, Jane Wheeler. You were a pleasing interlude in the interval of waiting. That star-studded night that blasted the truth to you meant very little to Grant Saxon!

CHAPTER 8

'It's a promise, Sandy, I'll finish the pressing and complete your nature book.' Jane squeezed the small hand in hers.

' 'n you promise to write?' Sandy gave a small excited skip beside the car and turned to watch Mara and Grant descend the terrace steps. 'I'm going to be extra good at school 'n then she'll be proud of me. That'll make up for my wickedness, won't it, Jane?' she voiced her plea and resolution in a small hurried whisper. Jane leaned down with a secret affirmative to both questions, then withdrew her hand and stepped back to allow Mara's farewell to her daughter.

'Sorry I'm not well enough to accompany you and Grant, sweetie, but truly my head feels like a carpenter's shop with every hammer banging.' Mara stooped and kissed Sandy's cheek. 'Be a good girl and I may come and see you the week-end after next.' She stood back while the child settled into the front seat of the car. 'Really, Grant, Tom or one of your other drivers could have taken her.'

Jane cast a swift glance at Grant before she turned and made her way back to the house. His face had a grim set this morning; something had upset the master of the house. She had received terse instructions for the day and now she heard him reply to Mara abruptly.

'I have every intention of conveying Sandy personally. I hope your hammer shop will close shortly. Goodbye now.' His tone was threaded sarcasm. The car swooped away in a scatter of gravel.

Jane worked solidly all morning. The silence was only broken by Minna with her tea and a remark that Mara was confined to her room, having taken pills for her headache. Lunch was quiet and solitary, Jane missed Sandy and kept glancing at Grant's empty chair. She tried hard to dispel the quivers of loneliness and despair that persisted and did not linger at the table, but walked briskly twice round the shrubbery before returning to her desk. Later in the afternoon she saw Mara strolling to the garage, dressed in casual slacks and sweater with a gay bandanna holding back her luxuriant hair. Five minutes later her sports car swept out of the drive and disappeared from view. Jane concluded that her headache was gone and she fancied a run to pass the time until Grant returned.

Tom was waiting for her; she had worked later than usual and the shadows had lengthened considerably, flamingo pink flared across the western sky as they wended home.

'There's Ma'am's car!' Tom exclaimed as they negotiated a wooded curve.

'Slow down, Tom, she may be having trouble with her car,' Jane advised, and in the same instant recognised the man leaning negligently against the side of the car. Flip Olivier! Why in heaven's name had Mara stopped on this deserted section of road, and why was that man adopting such a familiar pose? Mara made a sudden movement, sliding her arms off the steering wheel as she watched the Land-Rover slowing to a stop beside her car. Olivier straightened up with a defiant deliberateness. Tom slipped from his seat and touched his cap.

'Anything wrong with your car, ma'am?'

Mara's eyes glittered greenly and a queer lilt made her voice strange. 'Not now. This—gentlemen—fixed things. I'm on my way—not to panic.' She engaged gears and shot away so fast that Olivier had to leap back to avoid flying particles of sand.

He recovered and watched the departing car for malevolent moments before switching his gaze to the occupants of the stationary vehicle. Tom reseated himself and Olivier sauntered round to where Jane was sitting in complete surprise at Mara's abrupt departure.

'Some woman, that,' he indicated, and smiled at Jane.

'You're running late today, miss?' One foot raised laconically to rest on the footboard.

'What happened to Mrs. Saxon's car?' Jane lifted her chin and stiffened inwardly at the look in those pale eyes.

'Just a slight—adjustment. I'm good at that sort of thing.' His eyes were openly gloating at some inward thought. Jane passed a signal, Tom nodded and pressed the starter. 'Much obliged, Mr. Olivier,' she said distantly, and for the second time that gentleman had to step back fast!

'Him not good, missy,' Tom ventured after they had travelled some distance. 'Mrs. Mara be careful and not stop for such a man, begging your pardon, missy.'

'You're right, Tom, I'll tell her. Maybe he happened to be on the spot to help her when she was stuck. Luckily it was just some small adjustment.' Jane hid her own disquiet at the encounter. She could still envisage the glitter of green eyes and wondered what had passed to bring that strange breathlessness to Mara's brief exchange, and felt relief at Tom's timely arrival to put a stop to any mischief or intention of mischief. His polite warning made it quite clear that Tom was fully cognizant of the man's reputation. She would say no more now but would drop a word in Mara's ear at the first opportunity; she might well be ignorant of Olivier's disreputable ways. That gloating look in his eyes meant trouble for somebody! Her thoughts turned to Grant; he had chastised Olivier only recently; it was quite possible that he harboured revenge, and what better way than through Grant's household . . . Jane shivered suddenly, inexplicably.

The homestead was unusually quiet. Bart, Janet and Elizabeth had taken the boys back to school. Jane felt thankful for the quiet peace of an empty house; her mind was so muddled lately that she couldn't concentrate wholeheartedly on family fun or discussions—a quiet evening would prove blissful. Jane leaned back in the swing seat on the verandah and relaxed to the healing touch of nature, allowing her mind to blank out troubling thoughts. It was the only tonic; all the man-made medicine in the world couldn't cure the invasion of peace of mind and body . . . let what come later, she would find strength to cope. If leaving this heavenly portion of Africa was her only choice she would do so, even if her heart stayed for ever, and wander far to other countries ... the panacea lay in work, wearying mind and body to numbness.

A restful night coupled with an upward surge of spirits made her jump out of bed with the old alacrity. The morning was bright with promise and Jane felt lighthearted as though infused with new young life and the joy of being alive to greet a new day, whatever it might hold.

She was seated at her desk when Grant entered the study and her smile of greeting was filled with such warmth that the big man's sure step faltered momentarily. He returned her greeting with a look of wonder in smoky grey eyes, and the questioning focus remained on her bent head and fanned eyelashes as she studied the paper in front of her.

Jane felt his glance and traitorous colour crept upwards. She was thankful that she had left her hair hanging loose and shining because the tips of her ears were burning to a crisp. He simply had that effect on her. She surreptitiously fumbled at her skirt, closing the gap that lay open over her legs, expecting sarcasm to erupt any moment.

Nothing happened and she dared a quick look. Grant was frowning over a letter on top of the pile of post. She relaxed, drew the typewriter into position and waited for instructions. Without volition her fingers played lightly on the keys 'I love you—love you, darling——

'Stop that, for crying out loud, Jane! It's maddening on the nerves.'

'Sorry.' Jane stopped immediately and wondered what would happen to his nerves if he could hear the words of the classic her fingers were following. Minna came in with the tea tray.

'Mister Grant, Mara asks that you see her after tea. Her head's not so good.'

'Very well, Minna. She's supposed to accompany me to Sabie today—tell her I'll be along.' Minna nodded and left the study.

Jane stood up to pour the tea, her spirits unaccountably drooping. She carried his towards the desk and was stopped

107

in her tracks.

'Stand quite still, Jane Wheeler!' Grant's command immobilised her into petrified marble. A dancing tempest smouldered in grey eyes as he surveyed her, from swinging nut-brown hair to slim stockinged legs and neat shoes. She stood there with posed cup, one dainty ankle and foot forward, eyes large and luminous. His eyes lifted back to her face and wonder flickered in smoky eyes.

'Nifty get-up,' he mused thoughtfully. 'But I think I should warn you—your skirt's come undone. I'll turn discreetly while you make the necessary adjustment.'

Jane was released from her trance. She stepped forward, cautiously placed the cup on his desk. A moment longer and it would have landed on the carpet. She emphasised deliberately, 'I'm so glad you approve. It's the in thing for office girls nowadays. Don't let the skirt worry you, boss.' Said skirt swung away to reveal neat pants and shapely legs as she whirled back to her deck. Those same legs felt mighty shaky as Jane sat down. And then she felt uncontrollable laughter well in her throat . . . his look was that of a fascinated rabbit confronted by a sinuous snake.

'Well!' A deep breath was expelled from well-cut lips. Grant reached forward to take his cup and the view from under her desk made his hand waver uncertainly. His eyes were raised piously. 'How can any boss be expected to work under duress?' he asked the ceiling.

'Nothing to it, Mr. Saxon,' his secretary intoned with maddening composure.

Grant put down the empty cup and strode to the door. 'Now I must confront another vision, most certainly clad in the latest slumberwear. It's too much to bear. What's going to happen to my morale?'

Jane reached for a cigarette and smoked thoughtfully; she had to wait for further instructions. Ten minutes passed and he was back again. 'Did you find out, and how's your morale?' she asked curiously.

'Ravishing, m'dear, absolutely stunning.' Grant kissed his finger-tips delicately and irrepressible laughter shook the girl at the sight of a manly figure making like a couturier. Grant joined her merriment with a deep chuckle.

A breathless joy impeded her heartbeats. She wanted to whisper urgently; dearest one, I love your carefree chuckle, please laugh for ever with me, I do love you so very much. But it would most certainly wipe that smile away for ever if voiced aloud...

Grant's amusement settled into a smile. 'You should laugh more often, Janey, it's attractive and becomes you.'

Almost an echo of the whisper in her heart ... except for the loving part. She composed her features, clamped a lid on the protesting whisper and said, 'Well, you're still in one piece, so let's get cracking so's I can earn my keep.'

'Who's the boss here?' Grant grunted, and walked to the window. 'You, Miss Wheeler, will come with me today on a business trip. We leave within half an hour. Mara is unable to accompany me, I need feminine support, so that'll be your chore for today, I'll list your duties on the way. And,' he turned suddenly to catch her look of utter surprise, 'you're dressed for the part, fortunately!'

Jane controlled her surprise and began to feel distinctly nettled. Dear smart Mara was unable to oblige, so Jane Wheeler was a passable second best? She opened rosy lips ...

'Second choice very often turns out the better. I should have asked you to accompany me in the first place as you have a better grasp of what will be required as my accomplice. Mara offered, and you've been rather sullen lately, so it never occurred to me to invite you along with us.'

Jane closed her mouth tightly; the man was psychic in his choice of words; second best, sullen, was she? Her mouth opened again. Grant leaned over her desk. 'Darling, don't look like a fish. That was a compliment, however obscure it may seem to you. I'll put a call through to your mum, advising her you'll be late home tonight.'

Jane watched his receding back. Mara must really have a bad headache if she was willing to forgo this trip with him, or did the thought of some hard work at the other end deter her? That was a cattish conclusion, Jane scolded herself, and spared a moment of sympathy for the ailing Mara, forgotten almost instantly as she considered that, although she was second best, this was going to be *her* day with him. Possibly not alone all day; the drive there and back; that alone she would savour and absorb into pages of memory; for the time when she was no longer near, no longer able to see or hear, respectively, his smoky-grey eyes, tanned, strong features and deep voice. Jane reminded herself that, on awakening, she had felt this day would be special; take it as it comes and blast the consequences, the aftermath—the gods may never smile again!

Only then did she begin to think of the duties entailed and how her substituting would affect Mara if Grant had told her that he would take Jane instead. Oh, please, don't let her headache disappear within the next few minutes, Jane pleaded, crossing her fingers at the wickedness of thought.

'Ready, Jane?' Grant's figure filled the doorway.

'Yes, Grant.' She controlled an urge to snatch her bag lest he detect the haste to be away before her wicked thought came home to roost. Grant opened the car door for her, then walked leisurely to the other side and climbed behind the wheel. He took a notebook out of his pocket, studied a listed column of figures while the girl at his side interlocked her fingers and watched the front door of the house, expecting it to open any moment to reveal the figure of Mara, dressed for travel.

At last he deigned to press the starter and they were away!

Grant's hands were firm on the wheel, the car purred powerfully as he negotiated the curves, sharp declines and hills. Jane found the lush scenery wonderful, but her eyes turned again and again to the strong brown hands that manipulated so skilfully. The urge to touch them, to feel the vibrant power course through her own fingers predominated, became almost an obsession. She forced her eyes back to the passing countryside. It was vaguely familiar; she recognised certain landmarks and realised they were nearing the Davenport farm. Jane remembered that day, her lack of interest in the route—colour rose in her cheeks at remembered happenings.

Grant's amused gaze flicked over her warm cheeks. 'Care to stop for tea? The old lady will be pleased to see you again, if only to satisfy your anxiety about the progress of a certain little animal rescued under dashing circumstances,' he jibed softly.

Indignation deepened the tawny brown eyes that lifted to meet his cool, innocent gaze. 'Grant Saxon, I don't want to know—I never want to see——' The retort died on her lips as Jane recalled that neither he or Sandy had taunted her or disclosed their hilarious knowledge of her smelly predicament. A projected vision of the incident floated across her inner eye and the humorous, the comical view as seen by an outsider effectively stilled further retort and tilted her lips delightfully. Surprise lifted Grant's eyebrows as she continued, 'I guess it was screamingly funny, I haven't thanked you and Sandy for not broadcasting—for not making fun of me. It was most humiliating at the time, but I can see the comical side now.'

'Comical, I agree, but,' Grant added musingly, 'you looked quite adorable apart from the absolute hate sparking your eyes to yellow fire. Disintegrating, what! Hotter than the place to which you wished us——'

'Any girl would feel that way,' Jane interposed spiritedly. 'Especially if her predicament's discovered by the very one who——' She bit her tongue sharply.

'The very one who ... what, Jane?' The insidious query was repeated when she did not answer and drummed against her ears hypnotically.

Her treacherous tongue vindicated itself ambiguously, 'The one who's my boss, of course!' Her breath expelled in little bubbles as a gimlet eye returned to the road.

'Oh.' Grant turned the car through white gates. 'I never thought you set such store in your boss's regard. Here we are, and there's Julius and horse ... he's a great guy, don't you think?'

Jane's 'Wonderful!' came with such relieved gusto that a surprised eyebrow was raised again. Grant made no further comment, for Julius was striding towards them. The car came to a stop and he stood ready to open the door for Jane.

Tea was a very pleasant interlude and Jane felt immensely

cheered by the warmth of Mrs. Davenport's welcome.

Back in the car they said their goodbyes to Julius. He leaned down to speak to Grant through Jane's side window. 'I'll be down your way in a day or two—got a spare bed?'

'Surely,' Grant smiled.

He pointed out places of interest as the powerful car ate the miles and explained the reason for wanting a female companion. Mr. Dixon had come up from Johannesburg for the interview, and his wife and daughter would be with him. 'I expect this interview to be of some length, so would appreciate it if you'll entertain the ladies. Dixon mentioned his wife particularly wished to visit a well-known citrus estate in that locality. Your knowledge, gleaned from working with me, should make it interesting for the two women and for you, gaining insight, so to speak, from a personal tour.' Grant smiled at some hidden thought. 'I would never have suggested that Mara take them, she hates walking ... just as well you're with me. The car is at your disposal, to drive there and back. Inside the gates is where the walking starts.'

'I don't know anything about citrus except book work, and that's no help! And you're asking me to drive this car—she's far too powerful, my driving abilities are of the Mini standard, and that's gone rusty with disuse—I mean my ability to drive, not the Mini——' Jane was hardly coherent with nervous anticipation of having to entertain two slick women from the golden city *plus* driving this monster, with two pairs of sophisticated eyes watching her every move—*and* what she knew about oranges, apart from drinking the juice, was anybody's guess!

Grant pulled her up abruptly.

'Nothing to it, once a driver always, etc., so stop dithering. A personnel officer will accompany your party through the estate, all you have to do is to look knowledgeable and charming. Not very much to that?'

'Oh no, Mr. Saxon!' Jane disclaimed sarcastically. Her trepidation returned as they drew up in front of the hotel.

Her anxiety was misplaced. The Dixons were unassuming and friendly. Grant knew the family from previous meetings and all three showed their approval of his feminine com-

112

panion by drawing Jane instantly into their warm circle, and, she was secretly amused and relieved, it was she who was being entertained, not the reverse. A meaningful look passed between the older couple when Grant asked Jane solicitously if she would like to freshen up after the long hot drive. Heavens, she thought, they've convinced themselves that I'm 'promised' to Grant Saxon!

To confirm her suspicions, just for fun, Jane smiled so sweetly and lovingly at Grant that he stopped in the middle of some ordinary remark and, poor unsuspecting man, couldn't remember where he had left off and had to start all over again.

After a leisurely lunch, Grant walked the three ladies to his car, winked intimately at Jane's nervous concentration as he indicated points to remember about this monster she'd be tackling single-handed. Her sullen glare at him was misconstrued as sultry by two occupants and he played right into their dreams by patting his 'promised' tenderly on her cheek—also proof that he was aware of their turn of thought and deliberately playing up. Jane's glance would have withered a lesser man, she felt like biting the hand that patted!

'She's a wonderful girl—I mean driver, I have every confidence in my Jane. So competent,' he remarked fondly—to step back hurriedly as the monster lurched forward in slender 'competent' hands.

'Oh, my, this does take me back to my young days!' Mrs. Dixon settled back complacently from the sudden departure.

They arrived at the offices of the citrus estate in one piece with Jane's discovery that this was no monster after all, just a purring tiger, easily controlled. She patted the boot gratefully, in passing, to join the party. The tour proved of considerable interest and the official allotted them most charming.

When they got back a smiling waiter passed on his message, 'Mr. Saxon would take pleasure if the ladies would join them in the cocktail lounge.' Jane thanked him with a return message; they would do so within ten minutes. Over cocktails, Grant regretted they could not accept the Dixons' invitation to dinner; they had a long run home, and he wanted to detour slightly to show Jane some fantastic scenery and the waiter had already been instructed to pack a hamper. Both men seemed highly satisfied with the outcome of their conference. The family would return to Johannesburg on the morrow.

Their farewells were cordial, with a pressing invitation to Grant and Jane to call on at their home when visiting Johannesburg.

Although the sun was casting long shadows, it was still hot and Jane opened her window fully to catch some cooler air. Grant guided the car with one hand while fumbling to loosen his tie with the other. His companion watched his efforts for a moment, then leaned over, removed the tie and undid the top two buttons of a still immaculate shirt. Grant smiled his thanks and ran a quick, clinical eye over her flushed face. Flushed from heat, unusual imbibing of drinks at that hour, and mostly from the little service she had just rendered; it had brought her very close for a few moments and his masculine magnetism did things to her!

They passed a sign indicating a garage one kilometer ahead and, without a word, Grant turned into the driveway and stopped the car.

'There's a ladies' toilet. Pop in and take off your skirt— I've noticed it's detachable—and your stockings and shoes. You'll feel mighty cooler then.'

Jane sat looking at him and a brown hand nudged her not ungently.

'Come on, girl, don't gawk. The road's long and I want to show you something of interest,' Grant urged.

It took her exactly seven minutes to follow instructions plus tying up her hair into a ponytail with the lace extracted from her shoe. Back in the car her modest feeling soon disappeared as Grant gave but a cursory glance of approval before turning his attention exclusively on driving. She actually blessed him silently for his thoughtful suggestion (or was it an order?). An hour passed, with Grant's deep voice coming at intervals, telling her about the deal with Papa Dixon and the outcome, a very satisfactory market for forest pines. Finally, a grunt of confirmation and he turned the car

114

on to a subsidiary road, pointed at a sign on the grass verge.

God's Window.

Jane straightened in her seat with sudden excitement, eyes wide in wonder as they ascended under a canopy of breeze-stirred sentinels. A dappled hush of green, sprinkled with rosy overtones of a setting sun. Up and up they rose, by twists and turns between verdant greenery, with glimpses of blue sky resembling magical, faerie lakes. Grant brought the car to a smooth stop on a tiny open plateau. He led Jane by her hand up the last ascent and her breath caught at the sheer wonder of the scene that met her eyes.

They were surely gazing from a heavenly window, down, down at a world spread before enraptured eyes; to the right a red fragment of sun cast the most wondrous magic over misty blue valleys and gorges, to pagan artistry on pinnacles and escarpment. To the left, mile upon mile of untamed, wooded land stretched to the far reaches of hazy lowveld. The sheer magnetism of far, unexplored depths at her very feet, a world cloaked with beauty and mystery and an eternal peace, tugged at the girl's heart and made her step forward involuntarily.

A firm hand gripped hers, safely and surely. 'Careful, child, one more step and the valley will claim you for ever. Over there, in the distance and beyond, further than the eyes can see, is the vast lowveld. The road that way leads past Bourke's Luck and the Potholes, Blyde River Canyon and nature reserve, through the Strydom Tunnel and on to Tzaneen and points further north. Beit Bridge and Rhodesia——' Grant stopped. The hand in his was trembling and large brown eyes were caught in a mist of doe-like agony.

Only it wasn't agony. The overwhelming scene, the solitariness of just the two of them, his hand holding hers with gentle strength and his voice speaking huskily as if, he too, sensed an All-powerful Closeness. It was a hypnotised ecstasy and just too much for Jane. The next moment she pressed her face against an immaculate shirt and wept with deep, sobbing gulps.

Grant's free arm lifted to encircle her slim waist. The

warmth of his arm, right where she longed to have it, stopped her sobbing for a rending moment, and then the very nearness of his warm body reduced her to further misery.

Grant stood perfectly still and silent, a rock of timeless patience. Gradually the slim shoulders stopped shaking and Jane started to feel quite appalled at what she was doing. With perfect timing a large white hanky was thrust into her questing hand and a voice in her ear jibed softly:

'Janey, Janey, who would ever dream a tomboy with long nut-brown hair could turn out to be such a softie?' His lips touched the top of the head resting against his chest and nearly precipitated another display of tears. Jane turned in his arms and scrubbed her eyes and nose with a crumpled handkerchief. Her being cried out silently, willing him to say, 'I love you, Janey with the long brown hair and soft heart.'

Then he would find out how swiftly a long-haired tomboy could become soft, urgent and very feminine!

Grant said, 'My navel's playing tunes on my backbone, let's open our Pandora box and discover what the boy packed for our delectation. I'm starving—come on, softie.' He removed his arm from her waist and gripped the nape of her neck to propel her gently back to the car.

Jane stood like a bare-footed, chastised little girl, her back to him while he extracted basket and rug from the depths of the car. Grant spread the rug on tufted, springy grass, straightened up and stood with feet slightly apart, his hands on lithe hips, and regarded the drooped head, stiff back and long bare legs tapering from rounded hips to bare feet. A smile hovered for a fleeting moment as he watched one slim foot come to rest across the top of the other, as a small shy child would do. Some vagrant thought wiped away the smile and the man made a hopeless, negative motion towards the stiff back.

'Come now, Jane, not to worry if the make-up's slightly rainwashed. I can bear it, being more concerned with my stomach. Here's the flask and cups, do your thing.' He lowered on to the rug. 'I'm beginning to feel sorry I brought you here, had no idea it would affect you so wetly——'

Her body turned with a rush and Jane sank to her knees before him, grasping the handle of the basket until her knuckles shone white. Dew-wet eyes glowed with amber fire and parted lips showed pearly teeth in a gay smile although a usually firm chin wobbled only a little bit.

'Don't every say that again, Grant. Or ever regret bringing me here; it was only with you that I could ever have had this glimpse of heaven, and I shall never forget it, to my last dying breath!' Jane spoke huskily, fervently, drew a deep breath and said softly, 'Thank you, Grant Saxon.' She sat down then, crossed her legs and drew the basket closer. The cups were set down with care and over the pouring of tea she added, as an afterthought, 'I'm not a bit sorry about that disgusting flow of tears either.'

Grant watched every movement and a full minute passed by before he lifted his hand to delve into the basket. They ate and drunk in silence. Jane's eyes darted in exploration; of trees, foliage, bird twittering, rosy clouds, everywhere, with one exception; the man sitting opposite her.

Grant offered her a cigarette, leaned forward to light it. Her eyes rested on the steady hand and a sharp movement made her ponytail swing. She smiled brightly, 'Thanks.'

He lay flat on his back and closed his eyes, only lifting an arm to draw deeply on the cigarette between his fingers. Jane dared to look at him then. His lithe length, strong tanned arms in sharp contrast to white, rolled-up sleeves. High cheekbones, with fabulous Irish lashes fanning them darkly, mouth in repose still firm yet faintly vulnerable. His whisper startled her considerably.

'Why "only with me", Jane? Anyone could have shown you this place. It's here for ever, you know.'

'Well,' she hadn't meant to reveal that little bit, so her cover-up had better be good, 'I—I meant that coming here— with you—and my silly crying fit—well, I couldn't do that with just anybody. I mean——'

'I get your meaning loud and clear. You feel safe with me, whereas another chap would take advantage of a perfect set-up. You're quite delectable in shorts; why safe with me? Have you forgotten another time and place, when you were kissed very thoroughly by this safe person? We're very much alone, and your—wild—ways are most intriguing.' Grant lifted his eyelids to squint through his lashes.

Jane shivered as though a bite of cold air had touched her spine.

'You're my boss—and who would do or even think anything wrong in this beautiful spot?'

His sudden laugh blasted the silence. 'What wild reasoning! Bosses are human, exceptionally human, from the jokes I've heard, and this place is ideally romantic. And the way you turned to me, love, you can count yourself lucky I didn't lift you then and there, to carry you to some leafy bower and ...' he lifted his head to observe her hands clamped to her ears. 'Very well, we'll leave the rest to your colourful imagination!'

Jane was on her feet. 'Please don't trample with careless feet. May I pack now, it's getting late.'

Grant stepped over the basket and gripped her shoulders. 'Forgive me, I can't help imagining what some bounder could do to a trusting little atom such as you. Be more careful, will you?'

'Yes, Grant,' Jane said, then continued with irrepressible spirit, 'Not forgetting my judo ... I could throw even you now, with the greatest of ease.'

Her eyes held such unconscious appeal, with that bit of daredevilry lurking behind the innocence, that the grip on her shoulders tightened roughly and Grant spoke quietly, distinctly. 'You may well have to use it within the next few seconds. I'm going to kiss you and if you're a sensible girl you'll co-operate, because I've been so good and deserve it, not so?'

The air became suddenly charged as a dark head bent lower and Jane felt cool, seeking lips on hers. Famous judo tactics were forgotten as her face lifted, of its own accord, her lips responded with heart-leaping urgency to the sweetest kiss ever given, and taken, in that Window of the Universe.

Grant lifted his mouth and looked for a long moment at the mouth he had kissed.

'I shall never forget this time and place either, Janey. Come on, let's go.'

Jane lifted her bag (And the girl, Grant Saxon, how long will she remain in your memory?) and disappeared into the undergrowth, to walk back minutes later with skirt, shoes and stockings suitably adjusted. A quizzical eyebrow was answered with a smile, 'The air is much cooler now.'

CHAPTER 9

MARA dislodged herself from the edge of Grant's desk and sauntered over to stand behind Jane. She watched nimble fingers on the typewriter, stifled a yawn and walked round to the front of the desk. Well, here it comes, thought Jane, and she was so right . . .

Grant had not appeared this morning and Mara had prowled the study for the last ten minutes. Jane's 'good morning' raised a curt query on his absence. Jane didn't know his whereabouts and said so. She worked composedly under the other woman's lengthy scrutiny, but could feel tension building.

'Got back pretty late last night.' It came as a statement. Jane said, 'Mmm' and looked over her typewriter at the fingers drumming on her desk.

'I phoned last night and Dixon obligingly informed me that Mr. Saxon and his *girl-friend* had left before sunset. Have trouble?'

Jane's fingers paused on the keys. 'No. We stopped for a hamper supper.'

'How nice for you . . . quite a lengthy supper. Grant's an exciting man to share supper with on a moonlight night.' The slight laugh that followed had suggestive venom.

Too true! Jane said aloud, 'I agree. My boss is interesting and charming,' she met the green eyes with a clear, direct gaze, 'no matter whether morning, noon or night. What we working girls dub a real nice gentleman to work for,' and continued her typing.

Mara's fist drummed on the desk. 'Stop acting holier-than-thou, and stop that hammering!' Jane finished the paragraph and dropped her hands.

'Mrs. Saxon, my boss left me a pile of work, so I'll have to "hammer" even if it disturbs you. I suggest you speak to Mr. Saxon if you're interested in his business trip.'

'Why, you——' Mara's beauty was marred by a sneer. 'Mr. Saxon, is it? How businesslike—was it like that yesterday? Minna tells me you were wearing a snazzy hotpants job, and wasn't it just too, too handy that I had a headache and you all dressed for the occasion? Shouldn't you stay smart and stylish every day, just in case another occasion arises?' Her disparaging glance raked over Jane's simple cotton attire.

Complete amazement was tinged with a slight feeling of guilt as Jane dwelt on her emotional episode at that lovely place. Not planned, just a happening, but the fact remained and her cheeks coloured at Mara's onslaught. To Jane it would remain an everlasting memory, but to others it would be regarded in a different light, according to their level.

Her silence seemed to infuriate the woman across her desk. 'I've noticed your cow-eyed looks at Grant and attempts to draw his notice. He kissed you that night at the club, I know very well what a girl looks like when she's been kissed—and—Grant told me——' Jane's indrawn breath told Mara what she hadn't known, only guessed. 'Now get this straight,' she leaned forward so that every nuance of her message would register. 'Grant was mine long before John tempted me away. Only after our marriage I discovered that Grant was the one who held the purse strings and have regretted it ever since. Grant still loves me, his silly sense of decency is all that's holding him back. It will pass, I'm working on it. You'll never make first base—he likes kissing girls, but make no mistake, I'm the one Grant Saxon will marry!'

'Are you quite, quite sure of that, witch?'

Mara turned very pale and wheeled round with a gasp. Julius Davenport walked into the room, to stand beside her, his eyes on Jane. She sat, quite stunned by Mara's cold-blooded message.

Julius leaned forward, both hands on the desk. 'Don't upset yourself, Jane, this woman's brain is addled. I heard that bit about John and it makes me sick to my stomach; what will it do to Grant, if he finds out how mercenary she was, and still is?' He turned and gripped Mara's arm, hard. 'He believes you loved John and God help you if he ever hears otherwise. And stop pestering Jane, or I'll personally put a large spoke in your wheel——'

'You wouldn't dare ... Grant loves me and wouldn't believe you!' Mara wrenched her arm from his hard grasp. Unperturbed, Julius lowered it to encircle her waist.

'Don't ever dare me, lass. My great weakness is the inability to refuse a dare. Now, offer tea to your guest, like a nice girl——'

'Make that all round, Mara, tell Minna I'm back, and we have a guest who'll spend the night.' Cold grey eyes surveyed the scene. 'I don't mind a little amour myself, but why choose my study? Julius, I presume you will be spending the night?'

Julius dropped his arm laconically. 'Surely. I'm not one to let grass grow under my feet—and that, old man, answers both your questions.' His smile was bland and friendly.

Jane could hardly believe it was the same grim Julius of a moment ago. Nor could she believe her eyes as a transformed redhead walked to Grant's side and smiled back at Julius.

'You know, darling, I really don't think we should encourage this naughty man to visit. He's so—impetuous—as you noticed.'

Grant moved to his desk and sat down. Grey, enigmatic eyes glimmered through the rising smoke of his cigarette. 'You're welcome any time, Julius, and you, Mara, should know by now, how to handle impetuous cobbers.'

'Of course, dear,' said Mara in an astonishingly mild tone. 'I'll see about the tea.'

'I've actually brought those papers for you to scrutinise, Grant. You promised to look them over before I did anything rash, and time is of the essence,' Julius explained his presence.

'I'll be here for about an hour, sorting this lot out and helping Jane with the day's logging,' a clefted dimple showed unexpectedly. 'Entertain Mara and—have your tea. I'll be with you shortly.'

'Right!' Julius beamed, unabashed, and walked out of the study.

'Morning, Jane.'

'Good morning, Grant.' Jane slipped a clean sheet in the typewriter and closed her mind to the ordeal and scene she had just endured. But two sentences persisted insidiously, like a black fog, in the cracks of her mind; he kissed you at the club—and Grant told me ... he likes kissing girls, but I'm the one he will marry.

Men who kiss and tell. He'll laugh with Mara—'You see, love, it was ridiculously funny, she simply fell weeping into my arms, so what could I do, etc....' If he did tell about the night at the club, why shouldn't he repeat this far more amusing episode? Oh no, she could not believe Grant was like that. Mara had made it up or seen them when she and Julius had appeared so suddenly. Jane had come to work this morning, reconciled to hug the memory of 'her day' close to her heart. Determined, too, to establish a firm, friendly basis with her boss. The sweet taste of yesterday, his thoughtfulness, cynical humour, teasing—and then one kiss taken and given without thought to further liberties; these were hers to savour whenever she was alone or lonely. He'll forget, or vaguely remember a girl and a promise, 'I shall never forget this time and place either, Janey.'

Mara had spoilt the sweet taste by her degrading insinuations. Jane squared her shoulders resolutely, there *was* nothing to be ashamed of, and no treacherous female was going to trample or bully her! She swung the carriage fiercely.

'Anything wrong, Miss Wheeler?'

'No. This darn thing is too slow. Why you didn't invest in an electric job in the first place I'm damned if I know!'

'Stone the lizards, we are in a blasphemous mood this morning! Please, miss, I'll order one right away, thank you ma'am. Was Mara the early nigger in your woodpile? How come she's scouting so early—not industriously minded,

122

that's for sure.'

How right you are ... *mischief* minded aptly described Mara's early scout!

That hidden thought made Jane say with some asperity, 'You needn't be so facetious. I'll manage with this derelict, *and* I referred Mrs. Saxon to you. She's *very* interested in how you spent the day, and especially half the night!'

'Shall I confess all, do you think?' Grant asked softly.

'Don't you usually do that?' Her eyes met his squarely across the room.

'Do you always believe everything you're told?' he countered with uncanny sixth sense.

'I'm not concerned, either way.'

'Very cheeky, this morning. I like my gals cheeky. Now, to tell or not to tell? I'll not tell,' Grant decided.

'Bully for you!' Jane muttered nastily.

He studied her with critical concern. 'When a girl backchats her boss in this manner it's a sure indication that she needs a change.' Jane felt a cold chill down her spine. 'You may have this afternoon and tomorrow off. Yesterday seems to have affected you badly.'

'Understatement of the decade!' came out sotto voce.

'I beg your pardon?'

'Oh, nothing, Mr. Saxon!' This time her voice cracked on a high note.

'You are in a vile mood, sweetheart,' Grant decided belatedly.

Jane kept her lips tightly shut while her mind screamed, 'I'm not your sweetheart nor ever will be—how vile would you feel if someone attacked you the way your beloved did me—and oh, my darling, I do love you so desperately, and do you really kiss all the girls, and may you never find out that she married your brother for the money he didn't have. Perhaps it would be better, because then you would discover her true worth and turn to Miss "second best" on the rebound—and shut up, Jane Wheeler, you maniac!'

Minna brought the tea. Jane did the necessary in stiff silence, which nearly disintegrated when she put Grant's cup on his desk. He looked up and gave her a grave wink ...

She set to work as if her life depended on it and looked up in surprise when Minna put her head in the doorway to announce that lunch was waiting. Grant had long since left the office. She had a good mind to skip lunch, since she was officially off for the rest of the day. Tom would be having his break now; Jane wondered if Grant had given instructions to take her home. Well, she wouldn't appear cowardly, face them for lunch with her chin in the air. Thank goodness for Julius's presence; he was a dear, and Jane had a notion that, for all her scorn and for some reason, Mara acted just a little afraid of him.

She was briefly amused at Mara's pretty chaffing of Grant about his late homecoming the previous night. She ignored Jane and spoke to Julius only when absolutely necessary. He was completely unconcerned, directing his full attention on Jane. This, after a time, seemed to pique Mara; her dislike of him was evident, but, dog-in-the-manger, she wanted all the male attention.

Grant said, 'Tom is at your disposal when you're ready to leave, Jane. Have a good rest this afternoon and tomorrow.'

'How thoughtful you are, Grant! You do spoil your staff. I wouldn't have been so clapped after one little day's journey. Pity I had such a bad head and let you down so badly— I hope it didn't affect your business adversely.' Mara accepted his offer of a cigarette.

'On the contrary, all went exceptionally well. Jane was the right sort for the Dixon family and she did some legwork on the citrus estate which I doubt you could have accomplished, my dear Mara.' Grant leaned back and blew smoke rings.

'Legwork?' Mara laughed. 'I do believe Jane revealed quite some limb in the delectable outfit Minna tells me she was wearing.'

'Quite a bit, and, as you say, delectable,' Grant returned blandly.

'Most distracting for the poor little guide. Did he fall hard, or don't they provide guides any more?' Spots of colour high on her cheeks showed that Grant's needling was prickling. Mara looked directly at Jane.

Jane said clearly, 'As a matter of fact he did. A most

124

charming man, tall and handsome. So persistent, but understandably regretful when I had to whisper that I was already spoken for.'

'Oh, is that why Mrs. Dixon referred to the "girl-friend" so romantically?'

'When did you speak to Mrs. Dixon?' Grant asked abruptly.

Mara lost her poise for a moment. 'I—I phoned through—darling. Worried, you know. It was late, and one does begin to worry.'

'You need never worry your beautiful head about me. I'm grown up now and perfectly able to help myself.'

'To what, darling?' Mara countered sweetly.

'One-track mind the dear, sweet, nice-minded girlie,' Julius observed, and stood to hold Jane's chair.

'I would like to take you home, Jane, if you don't mind. It's a short run and a visit with Bart and Janet would be pleasurable. May I?'

'Thank you, I'd like that,' Jane smiled, and turned to Grant. 'Thank you too, boss, for the time off.'

'What are you doing this afternoon, Grant?' Mara asked.

'Completion of labour sheets. I suggest you go with Julius, it's boring for you here alone.'

'No, thanks, I can entertain myself. We could take a run to the club this evening, hmm?'

'Can do.' Grant was noncommittal.

'That will be great,' Julius counted in with superb disregard of Mara's green glare. 'How about it? Want to make a foursome, Jane?'

'No, thanks, I'll catch up on neglected chores and stay with the family. My mother and I are almost strangers lately!'

'Sorry about that, but suit yourself, lass.' Grant and Mara made no comment, so Julius took Jane's arm and led her to the door.

'Stop me if I'm interfering, love, what was Mara so fussed about when I walked in this morning?' Julius asked as they walked along.

Jane hooked thumbs into the pockets of her jeans, in unconscious imitation of Grant when thinking. 'She was ferreting the reason for our late return last night.'

'Did you enlighten her?'

'I referred her to Grant. For your information, we made a detour to God's Window and—stayed longer than planned.'

'Hmm,' Julius accepted this in a small silence, then said, 'That wasn't all she wanted. How did John's name crop up?'

Jane's lips twisted mirthlessly. 'You heard her. I was informed in no uncertain terms that Grant Saxon was her property, before she—married his brother—and I must refrain from making cow's eyes and—angling for him.'

A hand on her arm halted her rapid stride. 'Jane, stop me if this is an imposition, but, seeing you've confided so far— are you in love with Grant?'

Jane stood quite still under his disconcerting scrutiny. At last she raised her lowered lashes and Julius read the answer in amber brown eyes.

'Grant belongs to Mara.' Her lips trembled and pearly teeth clamped hard on her lower lip.

Julius said sharply, 'He does not! Not yet. Now I'll exchange a secret with you. Grant is not going to belong to her any more, because I'm going to make her my woman. I know all her faults and she's not everybody's idea of the ideal woman, but I happen to fancy that redhead for a wife!'

Jane gasped, became dumbfounded as she stared at her companion. The set of his jaw finally convinced her that Julius was in earnest.

'But, Julius,' she exclaimed at last, 'what about Grant? You can't do that to him! Anyway, they're in love with each other—and I'm not belittling you, Julius, but nobody will succeed in taking what belongs to Grant Saxon. Mara said he was only waiting for a decent period to elapse before— proposing.'

'Who says!' Julius interrupted rudely. 'My grasping, greedy redhead doesn't know the meaning of love. I've known her for a long time, but I was too poor to be noticed while the Saxon wealth was floating before her beautiful eyes. Granted, she and Grant were close before she suddenly

126

upped and married John. If he's a man, as you so fervently declare, in complete command of any situation, why did Grant allow her to slip through his fingers? Because he loved his brother more and believed Mara reciprocated John's love for her? Which you and I know now to be a mercenary love, on her side. John worshipped her. He was an idealist, Grant the realist and the one to build the estate to what it is today. Quite a shock for our heroine, to discover that the *younger* brother held the purse strings! John was not financially embarrassed, and Grant was overly generous, but—well, that was the set-up. The present position is this: if Grant wants Mara he'd better get cracking, because I'm going to do my damnedest to take her for myself; dangle my own acquired wealth most illuminatingly and show her what a dazzling, charming catch I am. In fact, by hook or crook. And believe me, from the day she becomes my wife I'll shape and pound her into the finest wife any man could wish for. I like my women pretty, but I prefer them, at least a wife, to be a housewifely, loving and obedient female!' His eyes sparkled as Julius paused for breath. 'All's fair in love and war!'

Amazement struggled with a certain amusement and affection for his determined air and became mixed with angry sympathy for Grant's relinquishment of sweetheart to loved brother. But he was free now to claim, if he still desired Mara. She was waiting to fall into Grant's arms!

'Are you going to warn Grant of your intentions? He is a friend of yours, I gather?'

Julius grinned. 'Not I! Surprise is the element of success in my venture.'

'How low can one get? I'll make it my business to warn him!'

'Equally, how high-minded can one get? Grant will draw the ace if it's so ordained. In the meantime this bod can try a bit of cardsharping. Anyway, why spoil your own pitch? Don't be a doormat, get in some fast bowling for your own side, sweetie, you'll be helping poor Julius at the same time. Grant isn't the kissing kind, but by jove, Mara and I saw you in a fine clinch under the stars, at the club, and if you didn't take advantage of a little frolic at Providence's window then you're soft in the head!'

Mingling through her mixed emotions and his mad suggestions in mixed metaphors, one warm fact emerged clearly: Mara had lied about Grant telling her of the episode at the club and Julius had stated positively that Grant was not the kissing kind. Where one lie started others could follow ...

Jane stared absently into Julius's eyes as she considered this aspect.

'Aha, I see the wicked struggling with the righteous.' Julius came close and hugged Jane hard. 'I could almost go for you myself when you look at me like that ... if I wasn't "spoken for", so to say. Something did happen yesterday.' He felt her stiffen in his arms. 'I'll respect your silence, but I'm going to use you and it'll cut both ways. We'll make those two so jealous, and wanta bet we both land with aces?'

Jane struggled free. 'You're mad, Julius Davenport!'

'Yes, Jane Wheeler. Crazy enough to try any lowdown trick. Come on, it's time to depart and plan my mode of attack.' Julius grabbed a slender hand, started off with long, quick strides which forced his victim to abstain from angry protestations.

His verve for the impending attack bubbled over into practising on Janet and Liza. Julius lifted them in turn with a smacking kiss of farewell and chased Jane twice round his car before blocking her nimble feet with a long-legged leap in the opposite direction of her flight.

'See you tomorrow, my beauteous collaborator!'

Jane washed her hair and joined her mother and aunt.

'You'll have all the girls in the neighbourhood gunning for you,' teased Elizabeth. 'A day and almost half the night out with your boss, Julius hugging you in the lucerne *and* Peter coming to take you out tonight. Pat's coming to keep an eye on things ... all eligible bachelors, and you must hog the lot!'

'Well, a girl can't work all the time.' Jane drooped wearily, then demanded sharply, 'What about Peter taking me out?'

Elizabeth looked contrite. 'Sorry, Jane, you were late last night, I didn't see you this morning and Julius's visit made

128

me forget. Peter is coming to take you out. I think he mentioned the club, and Pat promptly invited herself. I accepted on your behalf.'

'To the club?' Mara's suggestion to Grant flashed through her mind. 'No. I'm not going.'

'Why, Jane, have you made other plans?'

'I just don't feel like it, that's why!' Temper made her blood rise, she whirled to the door. 'I'll phone Peter, right now——'

'The telephone is out of order,' Janet said mildly.

'Oh, damnation!' wailed Jane.

'Oh dear, I am sorry.' Elizabeth clasped her hands together and looked so distressed at her daughter's reaction that Jane curbed her blood pressure and managed a weak smile.

'I did so look forward to an early night. Perhaps they'll be content to spend the evening here. I'd like that.'

'Peter said something about visiting a patient in that vicinity, love, making it a round trip, so to speak. Combining duty with pleasure were his words, I recall now.'

'Oh, Mother, since when have you become so—so vague? If they're coming all this way to pick me up. I'll just have to go,' Jane said helplessly.

Janet intervened briskly, 'It won't do you any harm and you needn't make a late night of it. You're not working tomorrow so you can sleep late for a change. Get dressed, my girl, you can't go in jeans, supper will be ready soon.'

Jane was waiting on the verandah when Peter swooped up the drive. He looked freshly vigorous in tan slacks, open-necked shirt and sporty cravat. Pat was neatly cute in cotton sun dress, Jane in a patterned dress in autumn shades.

'Thanks for accepting my second-hand invitation, beautiful. I knew if I got Liza to accept on your behalf you wouldn't be able to wiggle out. Excuse the drag—she insisted on coming, and when Pat looks so beseeching a leech has nothing on her!'

'I'm glad you hung on, Pat, it's more fun this way.' Jane cheered away the desolate droop of pretty lips, and Peter threw her a 'spoil-sport' look.

'Is that what you think of me? Haven't you heard of two's

company, three's a crowd?' he demanded morosely.

'Peter dear, how was I to know you yearned for a two-some?' Pat showed wide-eyed innocence. She turned to Jane and whispered, 'I had to come, to protect you from a wolf. Don't be deceived by appearances, take it from one who knows.'

'Yes, nurse.' Jane smiled across at Peter's cocked ear. 'She's only saying she's so wild about you, she can't bear to let you out of her sight.'

'You traitor!' Pat hissed. 'Don't expect a helping hand when you land in deep waters, I'll revel in delicious revenge at your struggles.'

Peter passed cigarettes and they smoked and chatted on the trip to the club. He stopped at the side of the building. 'I'll see you lassies settled, then pop in to my patient, he's the caretaker and lives in that cottage peeping through the trees.'

'Can't we wait in the car?' Jane hesitated beside the car.

Pat nudged her back. 'And waste drinking time? C'mon, it's quite in order for girls to enter without escort. We can pass the time ogling other women's chaps and causing feminine havoc.'

'Watch it, you alcoholic siren!' Peter armed them up the steps and seated the two girls on the deserted verandah. The waiter appeared, Peter ordered their respective drinks, a Cinzano on the rocks for Jane and vodka for Pat. Piped music and chatter came from the interior cocktail bar.

'Stay put, don't move, I'll be back in two shakes.'

'Don't kill him off in your haste, dear doctor,' Pat offered Peter's departing back.

The Mission nurse leaned back and studied her companion with open frankness. 'How is the job going, and how's Grant and Mara?'

'The job's fine, thanks. I've got the day off, tomorrow. Grant and——' Jane stopped as a familiar feminine laugh reached her sensitive ears. 'Grant and Mara are well, Sandy is back at school. I think they're here with Julius, who's visiting for day or two. He seems rather keen on Mara.'

'Is that so?' Pat rested her elbows on the table. 'How blind can a man get ... what's the matter, Jane, you're looking pale around the gills?'

'Don't be silly—this drink—I gulped too fast, hit my inside like a charge of dynamite!' Jane prevaricated, and breathed deeply to control a thudding race in her chest. She wished desperately for Peter to return before someone appeared and found them sitting alone. Pat was eyeing her strangely so she spoke with forced calm. 'Just fancy, Pat, until last Sunday I was under the impression that Grant was Sandy's father.'

'What!' Pat looked her amazement. 'You thought she wasn't John's child?'

'No, no, I was—I thought Mara and Grant were married, to each other.'

'Goodness, it must have been a shock!' Amazement turned to curiosity. 'You're in their house daily, Jane, couldn't you see if they were on—intimate terms—like husband and wife?'

Jane flushed and twisted the glass in her hands. 'Mara has her own bedroom, and I stop work at five—I'm not there at night. Grant is very busy during the day and Mara wanders around, and calls him "darling"—I'm merely telling you this to prove how easily a person can be mistaken.'

'Your mistaken impression may well be rectified if Mara has her way and persuades Grant to take the plunge. They were close before she suddenly showed preference for John; he was a fine man, make no mistake, but I have my own personal suspicions of why Mara acted on that preference. Later, she couldn't show open regret because Grant was very fond, attached to his brother and has high ideals concerning wifely behaviour; Mara had to toe the line because she daren't lose face, to disillusion the one she really favoured.'

Silence ensued. Jane put the glass down, rubbed the tips of her fingers along the edge of the table. 'I know that now. I told Julius not to interfere, not to—hurt Grant—all over again. He's determined to woo Mara——'

'He doesn't stand a chance if Grant truly wants her for his wife.' Pat confirmed Julius's own words.

'Julius is fully aware of that but prepared to try his damnedest and has declared intentions of using me to further his interests.'

'How?'

'By trying to make her jealous—he says it might help us both to achieve our hearts'——' Jane stopped abruptly.

'Well, well ... that's how the land lies?' Pat's quick mind read the conclusion. 'Are you going to connive?'

'I am not!' A slim hand closed convulsively as Julius spoke to Mara in the doorway leading to the verandah.

'Much cooler here, and not a soul to contaminate the fresh air.'

'I'm not a fresh air fiend and—oh, not quite deserted, take note.' Mara inclined her head and Julius turned, dropped his hand from her arm and sauntered to the occupied table.

'Two angels disguised as mortals, luck is smiling at me tonight.' He grasped the empty chair in front of him, pulled it back and turned to meet Mara's haughty green stare. 'Come, sweet one, join the heavenly harem and proceed to entertain my lonely heart suitably.'

'I'm sure the *angels* have their reasons for coming here unaccompanied. Stop spoiling their pitch, Julius.' The innuendo was unmistakably insulting.

A smile remained on the man's lips, but his eyes were very cold as he replaced the chair. 'My apologies for the distress that remark may cause, angels.'

'Hello, Mara, Julius.' Peter bounded up the steps, stopped to study the redhead clinically. 'State of rigor mortis? Join us in a spot of medicinal.'

Julius said, 'Thanks, Peter—later, if the angels permit. Right now Mara needs fresh air. Her head feels very ... stuffy.'

Peter watched the stiff figure being led firmly down the steps, into the gloom of shrubbery. He sat down slowly. 'What gives?'

Pat opened her mouth ... Jane forestalled her. 'Nothing, Peter. As Julius said, Mara isn't feeling too good. The—smoke in there affected her, she'll be all right and won't need your medical attention. We need you—look, our glasses are empty.'

Peter nailed them in turn with alert appraisal. 'Okay, I get the message. Waiter!'

'How is your patient?' Jane asked.

'He'll live. Speak to me, Pat, silence doesn't become you ... a slight case of lockjaw?'

'Lockjaw be damned!' Pat exclaimed. 'Can you believe it, that——'

'That drink you had, Pat. You gulped it too fast, remember?' Jane interposed swiftly.

'Yeah? Oh, sure, it took my breath away, I remember. Now lockjaw, or tetanus, is caused by invasion of bacillus entering through wounds, multiplying to secrete poison which travels along lymphatic vessels—something about nerves—to the spinal cord. Symptoms, some days after injury, spasms and stiffness of jaws ... if untreated is fatal. Prophylactic dose of anti-tetanus serum should be injected, deep wounds thoroughly cleansed; skilled nursing required to feed patient without precipitating attacks——' a deep breath, Pat continued hypnotically, 'bacilli normally present in intestines of horses and other animals. Wounds or injury on roads should be treated by doctor——'

'I prefer a silent Pat,' Jane reckoned, while Peter gaped in awed wonder.

'The treatment is to prevent bacilli gaining foothold in wounds ... dead, damaged tissue must be cut away and antiseptic applied.' The little nurse waited modestly for acclaim.

Wonder turned to beaming satisfaction on the doctor's face. 'And I often despaired, wondered if my teachings ever penetrated! Jane, I feel the most extraordinary symptoms attacking me for this wonder protégée. Do you think marriage is the prescribed prophylactic dose?'

'I do,' Jane advised.

'No other cure?' he pleaded.

'No other known cure,' Jane contradicted gravely.

'Will you marry me, protégée?'

'I will,' said Patricia Marais promptly.

Doctor Davies coughed as if he had an obstruction in his oesophagus.

'Yippee!' he croaked on an expiring note.

Complete silence reigned. The waiter placed the order and backed away with puzzlement screwed comically on his face.

Jane raised her glass slowly.

'Congratulations,' she whispered.

Grant Saxon cleared the doorway in time to behold an exalted nurse drain her glass, throw it over her shoulder on to the grass verge beyond the verandah wall and emit an excited 'Yoicks!'

He came to a standstill within a yard of their table, to study the scene at closer range: Jane and Peter regarding each other blankly, Pat leaning back with eyes closed in rapture. She opened one eye slightly, saw him and murmured, 'He's proposed.'

'Accepted?' Grey eyes were fixed on Jane.

'Most promptly.' Jane raised her head to meet the smoky, intent stare. 'Congratulations are acceptable.'

'Congratulations,' Grant gritted huskily.

Pat opened her eyes fully at his tone and saw him hypnotising Jane. 'You don't have to sound so grim, and you should be looking at *me*. After all, I'm the one that was proposed to!' she stated ungrammatically.

Peter found tongue. 'Oh, God, what have I done ... clobber me, pal, clobber me hard!'

Grant drew a chair and sat down with unusual care. 'Accept the inevitable, Doctor. It happens, sooner or later.'

Jane found herself unable to resist saying, 'What will it be with you, sooner or later?'

'My dear Jane, fate has not revealed her plans, which is most probably fortunate for my peace of mind. But I am considering,' his narrowed gaze held hers levelly, 'some problems, peculiar problems to solve, which will make it later, no doubt.' He beckoned to the waiter and ordered iced champagne.

Jane tore her eyes away and looked towards the shrubbery. His problem could only be certain formalities to observe, before marrying his brother's widow. She unclenched her fists, forcing her hands to relax on her lap.

Pat took Peter's hand in hers and stroked the top of sensitive fingers, cajoling a weak smile to his lips. 'You have five minutes to retract, before the champagne arrives, darling.' She was in perfect earnest.

Doctor Davies looked long and hard into the eyes of his medical assistant.

'Do you know,' he said thoughtfully, 'I don't think I want to retract anything . . . Have you seen the pool by moonlight lately, Patricia? Come, let me show you, it's a beautiful sight.'

'Yes, dear, but not via the shrubbery, it's occupied.' They left Jane and Grant without apology.

'Someone else romantically minded in the shrubbery?' Grant asked, uninterestedly, and continued without waiting for a reply, much to her relief. 'For a moment there, I thought it was to you the good man had proposed marriage. 'I'm relieved it's not so.'

'Why are you relieved?' Jane asked quietly.

'He's not the man for you. Secondly, I wouldn't want to train another secretary.'

'Indeed? Can your superior knowledge describe the man for me?' Jane felt nettles rising at his bland superciliousness.

'Give me your hand, *chérie*,' Grant leaned over to take her hand in his, palm upwards. 'A very pretty hand, I declare,' a questing forefinger traced the lines and Jane felt a shock of awareness tingle up her arm and jerked her hand. 'Steady now, I can't read your future if you wriggle so much. Yes, there he is, tall, dark and handsome . . . very elegant, with flashing eyes. The very man to suit your personality. Davies would have been too—juvenile—for you. This one I see in your hand will be demanding, brave, fierce and will cherish unto eternity. Not a bad guy at all,' he mused, 'the sort I would approve of, if I were your mother. I advise you to start a trousseau immediately—he's already hanging on your lifeline.'

'Oh, Mr. Seer, how clever! Can you foresee the extent of my family as well?' Jane was deliberately scornful, to cover a feeling that his mocking description described himself . . . excepting the cherishing bit.

'Family? Now, let me see—here's one, a girl with nut-brown hair like her mother, and a boy with a flashing eyes . . . can't see the colour. My stars! there's little feet pattering all over your fingers, I can't keep track of 'em all. Poor Jane,

135

you'll become so weary of love and its consequences that, at the early age of seventy, I see a mug of poisoned ale being rammed down the old man's gullet. He expires dutifully, at last you're free to throw that maternity rag over the wall— but what is this? A stranger picks it up and returns it, bows over and kisses your pretty wrinkled hand, a greater love is born—and you start all over again!'

'At seventy?' Jane's laughter bubbled irresistibly.

'A very young seventy,' Grant consoled, his lips curved disarmingly.

A movement across her shoulder caught his eyes. Jane followed his gaze and her laughter subsided as they both watched Julius and Mara walking slowly, deep in conversation. Jane turned back to find Grant still watching with narrowed, enigmatic eyes, absolutely unreadable.

Pat and Peter met up with the couple and ascended the steps together. Julius hesitated a moment when he saw Grant sitting with Jane, held Mara back to say something in undertones, then walked to the table still holding her arm. Peter seated Pat and drew two more chairs. The waiter appeared with a bottle of champagne nestling in a bucket of ice, and glasses.

'Somebody celebrating something?' Julius inquired, quick eyes darting speculatively to Jane. Did he think, or hope, she was 'conniving' faster than sound? Her brown eyes scorned negatively.

'Spot on, Julius, however did you guess? Pat and I have decided to take the plunge.' Peter waited for the pop of the cork.

Grant unwound with ease, stood while the others settled in chairs and the glasses were filled. He lifted his own glass. 'To Peter and Patricia, may their engagement be happy and their marriage everlasting.'

Mara voiced a forced 'Congratulations' and studied the amber liquid in her glass. Her green gaze rested on Grant at intervals and Jane guessed she was trying to read his reaction to her disappearance with Julius. He gave no indication of any feeling in the matter and Jane marvelled at his superb control. Nothing disturbed his equilibrium; any other man would surely show signs of anger, or contempt, towards one of them. Grant must be very sure of himself, or sure of Mara's loyalty.

Well, Jane sighed, that's how love should be, but she wished it hadn't been Julius, knowing he was going to do his utmost to woo Mara away from Grant. That would prove trying for Mara and Grant would be very angry, when he found out, angry enough to sever a good friendship. Somebody was going to be hurt in the process and, looking at Grant's disturbing nonchalance, she suspected it would be Julius.

Grant requested a dance with Pat and Julius beckoned Jane. Peter took his cue and they drifted on to the small dance floor in the cocktail lounge. The piped music was soothing and a few couples swayed languidly.

Jane whispered, 'Julius, you looked very cross when you dragged Mara into the shrubbery ... how come she came back so subdued? What did you do to her, beat her?'

'I have a way with me, poppet. Women cringe when I lay down the law. I won't bore you with details except that I had a little hellion on my hands when I remarked, quite amiably, that girls who pass such remarks to others only cheapen themselves, the common trait reveals its true self. Oh boy,' Julius' eyes sparkled reminiscently, 'I almost had to hog-tie the filly, to prevent her from clawing out my eyes! After she quietened down I apologised for the rough handling and said there were other ways a girl of her spirit could vent surplus energy. A woman's inborn curiosity got the upper hand, so I propounded with great fervour on the most beautiful Arab stallion in Southern Africa. I owned that stallion; I glowed, I shivered ecstatically when dwelling on his finer points. Mara wanted to know what that had to do with her surplus energy. She used to be a fine rider. I don't know when last she mounted a steed, but her interest was aroused. I deplored the fact that Sheik, that's my stallion, wasn't getting the exercise he needed and her mettlesome spirit (no, darling, I didn't say meddlesome) would match his perfectly, she would look queenly superb mounted on such an animal. An open invitation was delivered with great courtesy, with

137

an offhand, veiled hint that, being stinking rich, I wouldn't put it past myself to offer Sheik as a gift to one who could match his pride and beauty.' Julius crossed two fingers against his partner's back.

'You beast, Julius Davenport!' Jane hissed, aghast at his temerity.

Grant lifted an eyebrow beside them. He had heard her exclamation quite clearly. Julius tightened his hold, kissed the top of Jane's head and said, 'Quite beautiful, when she's angry,' and whirled into an intricate step.

'If you insist on doublecrossing Grant with your beastly bribes I'm going to warn him!'

'My sweet girl, if Mara is open to bribery then she's not worthy of any man's love. Think of all the misery curtailed if he finds out now, and not too late. Warn him if you consider it necessary, but remember, you weren't present at the actual bribery; Grant heard your outburst, and you'll feel mighty foolish if he interprets your warning as jealousy, of my little stroll with Mara in the dark.'

'And I thought you were a nice simple farmer when I first met you!'

'Not so much of the simple, darling, but rather definitely nice,' Julius summed up placidly.

Without leaving the floor they changed partners, Peter claiming his new fiancée and Julius bowing Jane over to Grant. They moved in silence to dreamy music and Jane savoured the steel feel of his arms and male nearness.

'Julius is tall and, some would say, handsome,' Grant said thoughtfully, above her ear.

'So are you,' Jane quipped tartly.

'Thanks, Jane.' He looked surprised. 'How is your palm going to work that one out?'

'You're the teller of fortunes.'

'Well, there seems to be an influx of handsome men in your life. Don't fall for all of them and hope for the best, just because your palm says so.'

'Oh dear, if this influx swarms around me, how will I know which is the brave, fierce one who will cherish unto being poisoned by my wrinkled hand?' Jane looked appealingly confused, even though her heart clamoured that she was in the arms of the only one, right now.

'When *he* touches you, your palm will tingle warningly,' Grant prophesied. And was stunningly ignorant of how very right he was!

CHAPTER 10

A BENIGN sun sent forth busy rays to sweep away morning mists from the eyes of another glorious day. Jane stood, barefooted, at her open window and watched silky, sulky puffs of candyfloss disperse reluctantly from the meadows to huddle defiantly in shadowed foothills, a last veiled resort against inexorable golden brooms. She felt a rise of youthful resilience warm her mind and body at nature's eternal promise.

An invigorating shower and hearty breakfast started a satisfactory morning, gossiping with Liza and Janet, catching up on her mending and just faffing around the house. She started a walk through the fruit and vegetable garden, but retreated when she saw Olivier busy in their midst; an encounter with him was not to her liking. Uncle Bart had mentioned that this would be his last day of work, he would be moving on. Jane's thoughts dwelt on this man, Flip Olivier. His way of life, roving, working for others with no fixed abode or family to call his own; he was good with earth and growing things; did he ever yearn for a place of his own, a wife and children, to which and whom he could work for and find comfort? A nomad existence sounded exciting, but it could be very lonely.

Two hours after lunch Jane announced her intention of walking to the river for a dip. Janet warned her not to wander too far and offered the company of a young coloured maid.

Jane promised and laughed at her offering. 'My darling Aunt, I'm a natural in the bush, so don't panic. I've yet to get lost and snakes slide backwards at sight of me. One can't get lost here, with the hills, river and orchards as positive landmarks!'

She drifted in the cool, clear water for some time and basked on a warm rock like a lazy rock rabbit. Back in shorts, shirt and sandals she decided a small exploration would be fun, keeping the river obediently in sight. A few specimens of interesting leaves and ferns were stowed in her haversack for future study with Sandy's nature book in mind. After supper she would embroider the linen cover she had cut that morning for the book. The ground alongside the river was damp with the close jostling of willow saplings, berry bushes, grass and stray gums and pines. Halfway down the bank she noticed a peculiar jutting root, most realistically resembling a cheeky elf with a fantastic red nose. Jane went down on her knees and her seeking fingers were intent on investigating a possible breaking point when a sudden loud nicker startled her. Unbalanced, she slid forward on her stomach and started her downward journey. A waterlogged root obligingly met her wild grab and saved a mud-smeared victim from deep waters . . . by the time she topped the bank, back-sliding, crawling, clawing her way up, she was a sorry mess with a newly acquired bloody scratch from elbow to wrist!

A short distance away she spotted the cause of her downfall. The horse was tethered and nickered again, eyeing her with bright sympathy and apology. Jane walked slowly towards him, wondering to whom he belonged and what the unknown rider was about in this silent neck of the woods. The river bank was lower here, the water shallower. She spoke softly to the animal while bathing her arm in the cool stream. On the brink of stepping in to wash her legs she suddenly stood quite still . . . a distinct, feminine cry . . . not bird or beast? Again the sound reached her intent ears; not a cry but a female voice scolding—or frightened!

Jane moved softly and swiftly up a rise of pine trees, her feet cushioned on a blanket of fallen pine needles, to stop warily while her eyes travelled down the shallow clearing in front of her. A gipsy-like caravan nestled in the grassy hollow—a woman in riding clothes was leaning against the gaudy side, scolding the man facing her. Jane's breath escaped in amazed recognition.

Flip Olivier and Mara Saxon!

The man made a rough gesture, his voice carrying on the clear air.

'So why do you come here if not for a bit of jolly? You knew my pad was parked here. Chickening out—scared, Mrs. Saxon?' His laugh was ugly.

Jane started her silent approach while her mind could only register amazement at his attitude and Mara's presence. She watched him take a closer step as Mara raised the stock in her hand, to whip it brutally from her grip.

'Oh no, baby, you don't!' Mara pressed against the side of the caravan at the fury in his voice. 'Your great brother-in-law has already insulted me enough, do you think I'm going to let his woman beat me as well! You killed your husband because you're too fond of swigging——'

'That will be all today, Mr. Olivier!' Jane's command cut across his tirade.

Flip Olivier whirled to face the slight girl walking towards him, the stock upraised threateningly—to lower it as she passed him unafraid, to join Mara.

'Well,' he sneered, 'the birds're gathering like homing pigeons today!'

Jane ignored him. 'All right, Mara?'

'Yes—I didn't expect——'

'Didn't expect, my foot! What you come her for, where nobody ever comes? You stopped your swanky car the other day to speak to me and I told you my pad was here—and lied to this bird about me fixing your car. And you, Miss High and Mighty, can't even pass the time of day with a lowdown gardener——' he pushed Mara aside roughly to lay his hands against the boards on either side of Jane's shoulders, imprisoning her effectively. 'You're free with your kisses, and that's no lie. I saw you at the club with Saxon and I saw Davenport hugging you in the lucerne. The way I figure, how's about my share, huh?'

The insinuation and venom enraged Jane to icy flash-points of anger.

141

'I'll give you five seconds to remove your arms.' Her acid contempt hazed the air between them. 'I'm waiting.'

'I'll do that for the price of one kiss—not being the greedy sort. One kiss and I figure you'll come back for more, baby.'

Grant Saxon lengthened his silent stride down the opposite side of the glen. Mara took a step closer to Olivier. 'Leave her, you——'

'Shut up. What about it, girl?'

Jane wasted no more time. With swift accuracy her knee lifted sharply and, while pain exploded from his lips, she turned to grip his arm with sure knowledge of her next move.

Grant lifted the man off the ground where his slim adversary had hurled him, head over heels! Jane felt a rigid shiver up her spine at Grant's savage, strangling grip and steely jaw.

She spoke with deceptive calm even though, flowing wildly through her breast, came a savagery to meet and meld with primeval delight at sweet conquest of evil. 'Let him go, Grant, he's not worthy of anger, just a spineless rat.'

His eyes cold dangerous ice, Grant shook Olivier in a steely grip.

'You two—has he touched—harmed either of you?'

'No. Didn't have time,' Jane assured him laconically, stilling the erratic beating in her breast.

The man in his hard grasp was still grunting with pain. Grant flung him contemptuously against the wheel of the caravan. 'Olivier, hear me. Report to Sergeant Mason within the next two hours. I'm allowing you that much time to report and leave this vicinity. If you haven't done so I'll sign a warrant for your arrest in connection with assault on helpless women. Two hours. The Sergeant will be waiting because I'll advise him of your coming.'

Jane beckoned Mara and started walking back the way she had come. 'Just keep your mouth shut and let me do the talking,' she advised softly.

'What—what are you going to tell Grant?' a pale-faced Mara hissed.

Jane stepped carefully on the carpet of pine needles. 'I

won't give you away,' she answered shortly. They turned then to face the grim man, side by side.

Grant watched them in silence, hands on hips.

'I'm waiting.'

Keeping her fingers crossed in apology to a listening, shocked Providence, Jane outshone the proverbial trooper. 'We—Mara and I met at the swimming hole and—decided to investigate up the river. We didn't know about the caravan until we walked slap bang into it.'

'You can't see it from here, granted. Topping that rise it hits you in the eye immediately. Why didn't you turn back then?' Grant demanded sharply.

'We——' she turned to Mara questioningly. 'Oh yes, we were talking and watching our feet. Snakes, you know.'

Grant raised a sceptical eyebrow. 'Only a woman could be so blind! Did you walk while Mara rode?'

Oh, heavens, the horse! 'She—er——'

Grant interrupted, 'Did you ride while Jane walked?' His eyes were on Mara and Jane held her breath. Did Mara know there wasn't room for a rider in that tangle of branches?

Mara brushed back a strand of hair. 'I led him.' And Jane coughed delicately to hide her expelled relief. Mara must have come off the road and led her horse right across the clearing, judging from his tethered position. Grant's horse or car must be on or near the road. Had Mara deliberately moved the horse to an unseen position?

'Why didn't you leave him at the pool?'

'Because there's a way out on to the road which is nearer home,' Mara said unthinkingly, and Jane recoiled in horror at the gleam in smoky eyes.

She breached the chasm hastily. 'Olivier told us before he started getting stroppy.' His lips tightened grimly and Jane grabbed her throbbing arm. 'Ouch, this scrape stings! That was a bad fall when I slipped down the river bank, wasn't it, Mara?'

'Real nasty. It should be taken care of.' Mara managed her cue and Jane laughed out loud, in sheer relief.

'We weren't really two helpless women, Grant. Mara had her stock and I—other means, as you noticed!'

Grant stepped closer to scrutinise her arm. 'This must be attended to at once. Mara, lead your horse the way you came ... follow her, Jane, I'll be right back.' He turned on his heel and walked in the direction of the glen.

'I'll lead the way.' Jane showed Mara where she had slipped. 'We're sunk if he questions Olivier. He's gone back for his horse, I suppose.'

The redhead bit her lip and walked behind Jane, the horse followed meekly. 'What possessed me to be so damned inquisitive!' she exploded, as they followed the river.

Jane kept silent. Only Mara herself could find the answer to that and she, Jane, was mostly preoccupied with a bad vision of Grant questioning Olivier. The lies she had told! Her instinct, probably misguided, to protect Mara had lead to deep deceit which would sink further into morass, Grant, being no one's fool, would ferret until one of them fell into the web of their own making. Now she was in the act of making a further fool of herself as she turned to Mara.

'Mara, if Grant does find out we weren't together, I'll say I was with Olivier and you came to my rescue. Understand? No matter what that man tells him, we stick to that. We'll reason further and say because he hates Grant he'll say that it was you.'

Genuine wonder was in green eyes as Mara asked, 'Why are you doing this for me?'

Even if Jane could have answered, which she doubted, there was not time, for over Mara's shoulder she saw Grant close behind them. They crossed below the pool and waited for him. He dropped the reins of his horse and studied the two girls.

'Found a more plausible tale to tell, perhaps nearer to the truth?' Two hearts dropped in unison, but his glance at Jane held only curious wonder. 'You sure have a knack of muddling into the most awkward situations!'

Jane's face flamed at the reminder of her past encounters with him. 'Don't I just!'

A smile tugged his lips. 'That was an awesome judo trick you played on him ... his painful silence when I passed by for my horse proved it! Why did he pick on you?'

144

Mara looked bravely pathetic as she stepped to Jane's side. 'He got—fresh—with me and grabbed my stock and—turned on Jane when she wanted to help me.'

Grant's level gaze shuttered from one face to another. 'I have a queer notion that I'm being shacked. There's more to this ... have either of you more to tell, not only for your own sakes but for the safety of other girls, helpless girls who can't defend themselves. Sergeant Mason can deal——'

'Nothing at all!' Jane's immense relief that he had not questioned Olivier and that they had no further reason for lies was only slightly tinged with guilty sympathy for other girls who could not handle Olivier the way she had done. Her gaze flicked to Mara; what might have happened to her if she, Jane, had not appeared on the scene? She had been frightened and that cove had acted mighty nasty ... Grant interrupted her queasy thoughts.

'Very well, we'll ride back to Bart's house.' He legged easily on to his horse and held out a hand to Jane. 'Up you get, in front.'

She allowed him to seat her, his one arm circling her waist. Every time she had been in an awkward situation this strong arm about her waist had been available. Here it was again, warm around her waist, awakening the fluttering wings in her insides, his chest hard against her back, his breath lifting tendrils of hair to tickle her left ear. Agony and bliss made a strange mixture—another golden opportunity not to waste. Jane closed her eyes and absorbed the comfort and male aura that enfolded her.

Jane turned her head sharply, and watched Mara galloping ahead. Grant maintained the silence to the homestead.

Exclamations of concern came from Elizabeth when she saw the muddied state of her offspring and the girl had quite a time of it, trying to reassure her mother that all was well, under the raking eyes of Grant Saxon. Jane took thankful advantage when her aunt shooed her off to a hot, cleansing bath. Janet positively ordered Mara and Grant to stay for supper.

Mara was tidying herself in Jane's room when she returned from the bathroom. The redhead made as if to leave, but

Jane invited her to stay. Mara sat down and silence ensued while Jane dressed, and moved aside for her to brush her hair and apply a pale lipstick.

'Please make use of these, and there's powder, if you wish.' Jane smiled tentatively offering meagre make-up. 'It's not up to your standard, but any make-up makes a girl feel less defenceless.'

'Thanks,' Mara accepted stiffly. Jane waited in silence.

Mara turned at last. 'Thanks,' she repeated.

'Pleasure. You look better now, not so pale.'

Lovely lips twisted in a ghost of a smile; Mara was finding it hard. 'I mean, not only for the make-up but—thanks for what you did.'

'You would have done likewise,' Jane accepted casually.

'Do you really believe that ... and would you ever find yourself in such a situation?' Mara asked obliquely.

'Never mind, it's safely past!' and Jane held up crossed fingers with a hopeful grin.

After supper they settled on the verandah in the cool half-light and conversation flitted desultorily. 'Where's Julius?' Mara asked. Jane thought she looked more attractive without heavy eye make-up, more natural and rather pale, as if she still suffered from shock.

'He left after you suddenly decided to ride off on your own,' Grant answered. 'For some obscure reason, justified after the event, he seemed worried about you and would have followed. I stopped him. He left later than he intended and, his concern rubbing somewhat, I decided to ride out and meet you. Did you two have a tiff?'

'A slight altercation,' Mara began loftily, then continued hotly, 'I hate that man, stallion and all!'

'Stallion?' Grant showed surprise at her outburst.

'He suggests I ride Sheik in the contest, next month.'

'He's a fine animal, Mara, and you would have to practise like fury to come up to scratch. Julius is very proud of Sheik, he must have confidence in your prowess——'

'Well, I'm not going to accept. It's too far to go backwards and forwards every day, I'm not staying there—and I'm going back to Johannesburg soon. A big fashion do between

146

the houses—I've already accepted a contract.'

The silence was electric.

Grant asked softly, heavily, 'You're going back to your profession?'

'My usual procedure, isn't it?' Her eyes were intent on him, oblivious to company. 'What would you have me do—any suggestions?'

'Plenty!' The violence of reply startled them all. 'That place is not good for you. There's never been a dire need, financially, for my brother's wife to display herself to all and sundry. You'll not go back to pollution while there's a solid roof right here in clean, pure country air!'

Mara smiled suddenly, fondly and wisely, as if some inner knowledge had proved satisfactory. 'Dear Grant, let's not embarrass everyone with our problems. We can discuss your —proposition—cosily at home, hmm?'

'Very well.' His lithe body came upright and he held out a hand to aid her from the deep wicker chair. 'Watch that arm, Jane, for infection. Bart, we can still use the horses——'

'No, I insist. Janet and I will run you home as arranged. The horses are taken care of and bedded for the night. Send those chaps with Tom tomorrow morning to ride them back.'

'Right.' Grant retained Mara's hand in his. ''Night, Elizabeth, Jane.'

Mother and daughter stayed on the verandah. The sound of the motor died in the distance.

'Enjoy your outing last night?' Elizabeth asked.

Jane came out of her reverie with a hand to her mouth. 'Oh, Mum, with all our gossiping this morning I forgot the latest news. Peter and Pat are going to be married, he proposed to her last night.' She recounted the events that led to the proposal.

Elizabeth agreed that they were well suited. 'I bet Pat was equally surprised when her medical malarkey achieved the desired effect! Seems to me there's more mischief in the air. Grant was very vehement about Mara not going back to Johannesburg. She's certainly angling for a proposal and the silly man may do just that, if only to keep her settled.'

'Mum, one doesn't take such a big step just to keep the

147

other settled! There surely must be love as well, on both sides!'

'Mara doesn't strike me as the sort to bother or give her all for love. No, she's too mercenary. Grant is a good catch any way you look at it, and Mara will get older, as is inevitable, and in her profession you're *out* once the first wrinkle shows, so she'll want a well feathered nest in advance.'

'She's well provided for, Grant mentioned that. She doesn't have to marry for security,' Jane protested.

'Some people are like that, the more they've got, the more they want.'

For some obscure reason Jane wanted to defend the girl who had insulted her on two occasions within two days; in the study and again at the club. A girl, a woman who felt curiosity and excitement in a man like Flip Olivier; certain women were attracted to the animal aura of men like him. Surely not the well-bred widow of a gentle man, who had everything her heart desired, with one exception ... and that, too, would shortly be hers, to possess and cherish. Cherish him, Mara Saxon, for I would that I could be in your shoes ...

'No, I don't think Mara is like that. Remember, they were —sweethearts—before she married John and—and Grant— oh, Mother, talk about something else.'

The sudden appeal shook Elizabeth considerably. 'My child, how I wish I could help. You do love him, and it hurts desperately, inside?'

Jane rubbed her upper arms, as if seeking comfort. 'Silly of me, but beyond my control, nothing can take it away. Even if I go to the other end of earth it will always be him. If, I mean when they marry I shall have to go—I couldn't bear——' She broke off painfully.

'We'll do that, darling.' Elizabeth did not question or probe.

Doctor Muller studied the chart handed to him by his harried assistant. His eyes moved steadfastly down the formidable list.

'Hmm—quite redoubtable.'

148

'Yes, sir, we're running short of antibiotics at this rate.' Peter ran impatient fingers through his hair.

'I've put an urgent footnote to the supply order, Peter, and the call to Pretoria should be coming through any moment. Our biggest trouble is shortage of staff since those three nurses contracted the virus. I don't like the way it's spreading right under our noses.'

'No, sir. But here we can take precautionary measures—it's the virulent spread in the district that's troubling me.'

David agreed. 'Davenports' housemaid was brought in yesterday and I've just had a call from Julius ... his grandmother is poorly. She's not one to complain, but he's worried; characteristic pains, headache, aching limbs, sore throat. The tendency of pneumonia follow-up could be fatal to elderly patients. I'll take a run out there and check. She must have someone in constant attendance.' He rubbed his chin reflectively.

Peter said, 'Most of the women in the district have their own household to attend but have offered to help whichever way they can, Pat is busy now, mapping out a plan for the free ones to tour around, spotting possible cases. Mara is on the loose—a bit of forceful persuasion from Grant may help.'

'It might,' David agreed sceptically, and reached for the ringing telephone. 'Dr. Muller here.'

'David, Jessop has just called here, diagnosed 'flu as you suspected.' Julius sounded very worried.

'How is she?'

'Not too good. Jessop gave an injection and left the necessary stuff. He can't supply a nurse for intensive care—this thing has become widespread—can you help?'

'I'm sorry, Julius, three of our nurses are down and Peter and I have been racking our brains. I suggest you contact Grant for two healthy young women, Jane and Mara, either of whom could help you. A sensible person is all you need, not necessarily trained, and you can stand over them, whip and all, to see that doctors' instructions are carried out implicitly. I'll be on call if Jessop is unavailable.'

'Jane or Mara? Yes, well, if you're sure there's no one else. My neighbour's with Gran, but she has her duties at home and can't be here all the time.'

'Try Grant,' David urged the worried man.

'Thanks, I will.' The telephone clicked.

Tom handed a note to Jane on his arrival. She slit the envelope with mixed feelings; Mara and her complicity had been revealed and this was her walking ticket. No man would continue to employ a deceiving, lying girl as confidential secretary. The note was from Grant:

'Jane: Would you pack a case of clothes, preferably overalls, and be prepared to stay indefinitely? I'm up to my eyeballs with an invasion of influenza amongst the workers and Minna's down as well. Can do? Grant.'

A relieved sigh escaped even as she pondered his predicament. It must be bad if Grant wanted her indefinitely. For a painful minute she wondered why things conspired to draw her closer than she wished and then asked herself if that was truth; what was her desire, which was the greater agony—to be closer or to avoid contact?

She put the note into her pocket with a decisive movement. He needed her now and she was his to command. She instructed Tom to find himself a cup of coffee and whirled into the house to pack.

The study being deserted when she arrived, she instructed Tom to leave her case on the verandah and walked through the house to the kitchen. A slightly dishevelled Mara invited her to a cup of coffee and cigarette. Jane poured her coffee and sat down on the opposite side of the kitchen table, glancing round at the disorder of Minna's normally spotless domain. Mara inhaled sharp puffs of smoke.

'So what, I haven't a clue where to start, and Grant just disappeared.'

'Have you and he had breakfast, and how is Minna?' asked Jane.

'Grant made toast and coffee and told me to help myself. He gave Minna some pills, she's sleeping, and that wretched maid, Polly, hasn't turned up yet. Now I'm supposed to make jelly and cook up barley water for Minna—he didn't even wait to tell me where the stuff is, never mind how to make it!' Mara's cigarette glowed fiercely.

Jane put the cup down and leaned her hands flat on the table. 'You can make a bed and dust? Well, do that and I'll pop in to Minna to see if all's well. Then I'll do the jelly, barley and clean up here. Polly will come in due course if she's not ill too, and so will Grant. By then we'll be ready for further instructions. Okay?'

When the big man walked through the open kitchen door later on he was met by the usual sparkle of shining cleanliness plus a delectable fragrance of peppercorn and bay leaves in the steak and kidney simmering on the stove. Cups were set in readiness for tea.

'Good work, Jane,' he said gratefully.

'Good morning, Grant.'

'Now, I'd appreciate for you two girls to be on call in case we can't manage. I'll try to find help with the household chores, we may need you in the sick bay. Seven employees are down with 'flu and more show symptoms. The mission is crowded—I'll phone David and find out what the chances are of moving them. We must put a stop to spreading infection. Both of you must take precautions when attending Minna——' the telephone stopped further instructions.

He came back with set lips. 'Sandy is coming home, in fact she'll be here any moment; the schools have closed for the duration of what could well be an epidemic, and Angus McDonald called for his children at four this morning. He took upon himself to bring Sandy, being neighbourly and a sensible man.'

Almost on cue, a car stopped in the drive and Sandy jumped straight into Jane's arms. Angus, lean and freckled, was rueful when he heard he had brought the child from 'the fat to the fire'. Grant assured him he would have fetched her anyway, she was as safe here as conditions permitted. He thanked Angus for his forethought in saving himself from a long trip. A quick cup of coffee and the McDonald clan were away home.

Sandy clung to Jane's hand after a quick, perfunctory greeting to Mara and Grant, and was gravely concerned over her darling Toicky. Mara kept glancing at her small daughter, who seemed to prefer Jane to her relatives. Sudden perceptiveness made her aside to Grant anxious. 'Isn't Sandy rather flushed, Grant?'

Jane's keen ears heard; she had noticed the flushed face but had passed it off as excitement at coming home so unexpectedly. Now she took a closer look and casually passed her hand across Sandy's forehead, brushing back the russet hair. Sandy sneezed explosively into her hand. ''Scuse me, Jane, the dust's made my throat sore 'n it was very hot. Can we go fishing tomorrow?'

Three adults exchanged glances over her excited head. Mara said, 'Come along, Sandy, I've got a nice pink pill for that sneeze, you can take it and lie on your bed for today and then it will clear away.'

'*All day* in bed by *myself* on such a—a grand day!' Sandy stamped a small foot, utterly unlike her normal, happy self.

Mara consoled, 'I'll sit with you, dear,' with a slight edge of irritation. The child sensed it immediately and her warm hand clutched Jane's hand spasmodically.

'Jane must—Jane can sit with me, then I'll be good—I promise . . .'

Grant said firmly, 'Very well, Jane can sit with you for just a little while. The office is closed today, but Jane has come to help with the sick people. So be a good girl and help us by following instructions.'

Jane walked with the youngster to her room and helped her undress. She became calmer in her bed and asked for her favourite books. While they chatted Jane's thoughts hovered back to the expression on Mara's face when Sandy insisted on Jane's company; a strange mixture of relief and injured ego . . . she hoped Sandy's preference would not further the enmity Mara had shown towards herself. So far there had been no insulting remarks this morning, there hadn't been time! Since the Olivier episode Mara was more subdued; maybe the shock of Grant appearing so suddenly on the scene had jerked her to a semblance of normality.

Jane heard the telephone in the lounge ring demandingly. It stopped and Grant's answering voice was muffled by distance. Shortly after the call, the raised tones of Mara's angry voice came clearly through the open door of Sandy's room.

'I absolutely refuse—I can't stand the man, he's a rough-neck and I detest him!' Even her footsteps sounded angry as she walked towards her room.

'There's no one else. You will go and pull your weight in this crisis.' Grant passed her door and entered Sandy's room. 'Give poppet this capsule now, Jane, another in three hours' time.' Mara's bedroom door slammed hard and his eyebrows drew grimly. 'Julius has asked for help—his grandmother has caught this wretched thing.'

Jane was concerned. 'She's an absolute darling—oh, I do hope she has the stamina to fight the virus.'

'Doctor Jessop called there, gave her an injection and capsules, but Julius needs a woman to tend her and the only available one seems to be Mara.'

'You're sending Mara? Can she—I mean, I could go. I know——'

Mara stood at the door of Sandy's room, in a flaming temper that made her wild and beautiful and her teeth actually gritted as she cut across at Jane.

'You know what, Jane Wheeler?—do tell! That I'm incapable of caring for the sick and you're more capable and superior? I can look after Minna, Sandy or Mrs. D. just as well as any nit!' She turned to Grant. 'She can go and I'll stay here.'

Sandy's eyes grew large at the display of temper and words. 'No, Jane, please don't go away,' she pleaded urgently.

'That's enough.' The tall man stepped forward with a firm hand on Mara's arm to guide her back to her room. 'Pack your things. Julius will be here at noon and you will accompany him, to care for Mrs. Davenport to the best of your ability. Upsetting the child is not going to do her good.'

Mara's voice lowered to a wheedling tone, but Jane heard her say, quite clearly, 'You may not know it, darling, but your *capable* Jane is quite gone on Julius. So why spoil her fun? You saw how eagerly she offered to go in my place, and Sandy will soon settle down with me when she's gone.'

Jane gasped at the audacious lie and held her breath. A short space of silence followed, and then Grant said, evenly,

153

'Sandy needs Jane at present. Julius needs a woman to help, not make love, so any selfish desires or grand passions can be suppressed for the duration of the illness. I'm needed at the sick bay, no more tantrums or arguments, be ready for Julius!' His footsteps faded and stillness descended.

Jane was in the dining-room, deep in thought, wondering if a place should be set for Julius when Mara walked in.

She said, elaborately casual, 'That remark about you and Julius—I thought it might persuade Grant to send you, instead of me. No go, nothing works when Saxon's mind is made up. I hate the thought of going——' She evidently meant this explanation sufficient apology.

Jane bit back a hot retort and concentrated on placing the cutlery. There had been enough rumpus without prolonging this particular subject.

'I'm setting a place for Julius.'

'I couldn't care less. You have my full collaboration to shove poison in his salad.' Mara studied a fingernail. 'You're probably dying for us to depart, so that you can have Grant to yourself.'

'Don't be an idiot, Mara!' Jane retorted spiritedly. 'There's work to be done, remember? The world doesn't start and end with larking around with some male.'

'Keep it that way, with this particular male,' Mara advised mildly, and seated herself with a magazine.

The noon Highveld news was on the air. Four new cases of influenza were reported in Kiepersol, a batch of nurses were on their way from Pretoria to relieve the overworked Nelspruit staff.

The Davenport car rolled into the driveway. Grant unwound from the passenger seat, Julius from behind the wheel, and the two men vaulted the steps and entered the lounge.

They sat down to lunch and Grant and Julius discussed the whys and wherefores of measures taken to combat further outbreaks of influenza. Taken by itself, with all the antibiotics available, it was not the danger; that lay in carelessness of the victims contracting pneumonia. The consequent shortage of man-power put extra responsibilities on the shoulders of the healthy ones. Julius turned suddenly to Jane.

'Still love me, honey?' His eyes slid to Grant. 'How about a swap, cobber?'

Wood-smoke eyes darkened as Grant studied the astonishing blush on Jane's cheeks. Mara's colour rose as well, at Julius's obvious preference of company. A 'dog-in-the-manger' assumption that, though she herself did not want to go, the idea that *anyone* should show preference to another was something that shook her ego badly.

'Grant would prefer that, but Sandy's taken such a shine to Jane that we felt it's best to humour her.' Her green eyes dared Grant to deny it.

'I thought you wanted a nurse for Gran?' Grant's cynical look circled to Julius. He ignored Mara's remark.

'Indeed I do, but she does sleep, at times.' Julius, unperturbed, gazed at Jane's flaming cheeks and her open, astonished lips.

'Well, Jane, if there was a choice, which would you prefer?' Grant's deep voice reached out with mocking, maddening coolness.

Jane tore her eyes from the cool steel of his gaze and flicked Julius a sweetly venomous smile. She said, 'Someone—I can't think who, mentioned that passions and selfish desires should be suppressed for the duration.'

'Is that so?' Julius looked surprised and perturbed. 'That can only mean that when this emergency's overcome there'll be a lovely epidemic of suppressed desires catching fire all over the countryside!'

'Picture the holocaust,' Grant said dryly.

'Hot and beautiful! Oh well, dreams aside, I think we should be pushing off, Mara.'

Jane pushed back her chair. 'And I must take Minna and Sandy some baked custard—it's capsule time as well. Good-bye, Mara, Julius ... give Mrs. D. my love and wishes for a speedy recovery.'

'She'll recover with remarkable speed if I have any say in

the matter!' Mara stalked to the bedroom for some last-minute toiletry.

Grant came in late that evening, tired and grim-faced, and told Jane, at supper-table, that they were fortunate in having provided for just such an emergency, having a sick bay and well-stocked medical supplies.

After supper he disappeared in the direction of the office. Jane gave Polly a hand with the dishes, then settled Sandy and Minna for the night. Jane walked through the quiet house. On the verandah, she heard her typewriter clicking erratically in the study. She walked softly to the open door and watched Grant's clumsy efforts. Amusement touched her lips as he, aware of her presence, became more frustrated and banged the wrong keys. Finally he stopped completely to glare at her with dark-fringed Irish eyes. Jane moved to stand beside him, changing her amusement to a superior smile.

'Move over, boss, let someone who knows do the job.' She nudged his shoulder none too gently and he moved with meek alacrity, to watch his efficient secretary in grateful awe as she inserted a clean sheet and ran her eyes over his notes ... The last line typed, Jane looked up in time to see him stealthily slipping roughly scrawled paper on the opposite side to the one she had just completed.

'Oh—do you mind, Jane? Here's another one, it's got to be posted tomorrow—rather urgent, you know. You must be tired and it's an imposition, but——'

'Give, it won't take long when one can use all one's fingers. Go smoke your pipe, you're holding me up.' Jane took the paper without looking up and so missed the strange expression that flitted across the man's face: Fortunately, for it might have demoralised her to the extent of complete inefficiency!

She addressed and stamped the envelopes, covered her machine and walked out, to sit on the low wall of the verandah to join Grant, her head resting against a supporting pillar. The soft night breeze lifted her hair with caressing fingers while starshine gave her face the purity of marble and amber eyes a glistening, mysterious depth.

The minutes ticked by ... (his arms were encircling her body, his warm breath was mingling with hers, he was speaking soft words of love, words that her heart longed to hear.)

'Jane, wake up, you'll fall off your perch. Jane!' She came out of her beautiful world as his hand touched her shoulder and his admonition reached her ears. Her legs lowered off the wall and her body came upright as she lifted eyes that were clouded with dreams. Grant put his hands on her arms.

'Jane, wake up. You look like a bewitched high priestess.' He shook her gently. 'Snap out of it, girl, you make me feel peculiar—are you all right?'

Her eyes focused as dreams departed, forcing back reality.

'Sorry, Grant—my mind seems to have left my body for a space of time. So peaceful and beautiful.' Jane stepped back, out of the clasp of his hands. 'Didn't you feel something, a space of time suspended in eternity?'

'I looked at you and you were cast in marble—as if indeed your soul had left your body, and I felt an urgent need to call you back.' Grant shrugged broad shoulders as if he felt an entangling web. 'Don't go all psychic on me, Jane. It gives me eerie shivers—I think we're both tired. But a cup of hot tea would go down well before staggering off to bed.'

Jane said, through lips that had stiffened to meet reality, 'That shivery feeling was in anticipation of again rescuing my clumsy self from another fall, this time from the wall.'

Grant looked curiously at her. 'You were dreaming—did Julius match your ideals?'

'Julius?' Jane looked dazed.

'A girl usually dreams about the one nearest her heart.'

'Now, how could you guess that, not being a girl?' she hedged, unable to meet his statement with honesty. Let him believe anything about her and Julius, it mattered not a scrap to him of whom she dreamed. 'You've been reading too many romantic novels, boss,' she quipped flippantly.

'Did you dream about him, Jane?' Grant ignored her flippancy.

'No, I hadn't got that far—when you woke me.' That wasn't a lie, she comforted herself; Julius might just possibly have come into her dream later, as best man! She turned

157

away sharply. 'I'll make the tea.'

Grant shut the study door and followed her to the kitchen. He sat on the edge of the table, and remained there when she finally handed him a cup of strong tea.

'I'll take mine to bed, Grant. I love sipping tea in bed, one of my many vices. Good night.'

'Good night, Jane. Pleasant continuation of dreams,' he called after her.

She steadied the cup in her hand while words tumbled inside; your humour would fade pretty quick, Grant Saxon, if you knew how close I came tonight, when I opened my eyes to see you so near, to throw myself in your arms and confess how deeply I love you. That in my golden dream world there was only you—you—you.

Only you, dearest Grant ... Jane drifted into tired sleep.

CHAPTER 11

'I've brought your early morning vice, ma'am.' Jane opened her eyes, saw him at the foot of her bed, tray in hand. Her hair tumbled back as she leapt out of bed, to jump back instantly as she awoke fully to embarrassed awareness of her flimsy shortie-pyjamas.

He laughed and walked to the door. 'I'll leave you to drink without offending modest instincts.'

Jane waited for his footsteps to recede to a safe distance before jumping out of bed. The next half hour whirled by in a flurry as she showered, dressed in her neat mauve overall, brushed shining nut-brown hair into a severe bun on the nape of her neck admonished Sandy to stay put while she flew to Minna's room, to apologise contritely for being so late.

Minna smiled weakly. 'I really am sorry to cause all this extra work for you. I'm feeling much better today, only a bit shaky. Perhaps if I get up——'

'Nothing doing, my good woman!' Jane drew the curtains and turned to fluff the pillows. 'We'll see what Grant says—he may allow you to sit in that cosy chair, later. You're not to worry about the work, we're coping and it's a break for me, really, from office work. You're certainly more efficient and I'll run fast enough for advice if snags crop up, Mrs. Du Toit.'

'You may call me Minna—Jane—if I may call you by your first name. You're being very good to me.'

Jane smiled at her and went off to see to her breakfast.

Breakfast over, she started on the bedrooms. In Grant's room she hesitated a full minute to allow her eyes to roam the room, taking in the neat austerity of bachelordom. Jane ran the duster over wardrobe doors, dressing-table and stopped at the bedside table-cum-desk. Slowly she lifted the framed photograph.

So this was John Saxon. He looked down at the upturned face of his wife with complete adoration. Slightly fairer than his brother, the lineament of his features showed distinct traces of an aesthetic dreamer. Mara gazed back at him with a small smile on her lips, glamorously photogenic.

Studying him closely, Jane's heart ached for the remaining brother, motherless and fatherless, and now the grief of losing a beloved brother. 'Dear Grant, may you find the comfort that is God-given, and may *she* contribute her share of bringing and giving joy and happiness for both of you.' She closed her eyes in an effort to visualise the man in the photograph. The face of Grant was imposed too strongly, so Jane wiped the frame and glass carefully, replaced it in position.

The telephone summoned and it was Julius. 'Hi, Jane. Checking on the state of affairs—how's everybody?'

'Julius, I'm glad you phoned. We're all fine, Sandy hasn't caught it, thank goodness. Gran, how is she—and Mara?'

'Gran's tummy gave her hell yesterday and practically all night. She's as weak as a kitten today, But I think the worst is over, her temp is normal. Mara—well, I feel sorry for her. For the uninitiated it's not pleasant, especially nursing an old person, but she's been super and I'm fantastically surprised at the grit she's shown.'

Jane sympathised. 'I do hope it's over for the old dear

now, Julius, and I fully agree that Mara deserves a medal.' She sensed a presence and turned to see Grant leaning against the wall, his arms folded across his chest.

'Are you still with me, Jane?' Julius reminded in her ear.

'Yes—what was I saying? Oh yes—even trained nurses would find it distasteful, and her spirit is to be admired. I've got off lightly and—and Julius, Grant is here now if you want to speak to him.'

'Actually Mara wants a word with him. She still hates my guts, although recent events almost made us sort of buddies, if you get my meaning! Right, Jane, put him on. Just a minute—any signs of the little green devil and—here comes Mara—tell me loud and clear how much you care for me, my little brown dove?'

Jane laughed and coloured under the direct scrutiny of disturbing eyes. 'Really, Julius! This is a party line! No signs of what you asked, and—well, I have a great regard for you——'

Grant levered himself from the wall and started to walk away.

'Grant!' Jane clutched the phone to her breast. He turned. 'J-Julius wants to speak to you.' She held the instrument the length of her arm. Grant walked back and took it from her, eyeing her flushed face with a grey, glacial stare.

'A great pity party lines aren't visual. Local biddies would derive ultimate pleasure—yes, Julius, you've put a becoming blush on tender cheeks and only I can see the delightful confusion—how regrettable. Now the maiden has stampeded in graceful retreat. What do you want with me?'

The deriding voice followed Jane and turned her ears a vivid puce. 'I really do positively hate Grant Saxon at times,' her lips moved angrily. 'He's sarcastic, horrid and—and his bossiness is enough to shrivel any love a body might have— like a chameleon, nice one minute and then—a Jekyll and Hyde—he makes me boil!' She tidied the magazines with precise angry hands—and realised she could hear every word that was being voiced.

'Hullo, sweetie. Why not—but you are, darling——' saccharin and honey dripped from his tongue and the listener at the magazine rack muttered wordlessly, 'Humbugging, Mara, watch it!'

'Everyone's doing fine—keeping an eye on Sandy, so far merely a sniffle. Hmm?—she's still here and kept busy—we'll see about that. She's just spoken to Julius—eavesdropping? That's nasty and I don't imagine she can hear what you're saying, so carry right on——'

Jane made for the door leading to the verandah, her breast throbbing with a mixture of indignation and guilt. *She* was not interested in their honeyed talk and didn't care a fig what Mara was saying!

After the evening meal Grant once again made for the study. Jane cleared the table, helped Polly with the washing up and then walked out to study the closed door with curiosity. She longed to be with him, if only to help, but that door looked too forbidding, evidence that he wished to be undisturbed. She smoked one cigarette then went inside, bathed, brushed her hair and climbed into bed feeling weary, at odds with herself and the rest of the world. The sooner she decided on a definite course the better for her peace of mind; the bitter-sweet, close association in this house must end. Jane crossed her arms under her head and, under closed lids, a vision of a tanned, arrogant face and steel-grey eyes floated unchecked. Yes, far better to leave; distance would dim the picture, other work would numb, crush the yearning for reciprocated tenderness. Before she made a complete fool of herself.

Tomorrow she would ask—no—she would tell him to replace her in the office. She would plan her future. A future in which Grant Saxon did not figure ...

CHAPTER 12

MINNA Dut Toit was up and about, Sandy ran to meet Jane with her quota of healthy spirit and vigour and Polly's mother was back on duty, so Jane found herself back at the desk in the study. In Grant's absence—he was somewhere on the Estate—she tidied up the disorder of papers and found sufficient work to keep her busy till noon. He worked with her in the afternoon and just before closing time Jane set a firm chin and asked for five minutes of his time and attention.

Grant studied the set of her chin calculatingly. 'Any chap with half a brain can reckon on a troublesome five minutes, if that chin's anything to go by,' he sighed. 'Fire away.'

'I'd appreciate it very much if you would find replacement for my duties as soon as possible, please.'

'May I know the reason for this sudden wish to leave? Salary not good enough?'

'It's the best salary I've ever earned,' Jane admitted.

'Well then, do I have to drag it out of you ... what is or are your reasons?' Grant looked impatiently down at the paper on his desk.

'I have my reasons, private reasons.' Jane felt stubborn and more foolish in the face of his impatience.

'Private? Hmm ... like Julius, for instance?' Grant lifted wintry grey eyes briefly.

What could she say; that the sole reason was himself and her close regard for him? She should have planned her strategy beforehand. 'He might just be one of the reasons!' came recklessly from her lips.

'I see. Respect and trust for an employer is not evidently to be considered.' Grant held her defiant, mute stare for a coolly controlled space of time, and then shrugged a shoulder resignedly. 'As you wish, Miss Wheeler. You'll kindly continue as usual until I advise you of the termination of your services.'

'Grant!' Jane took a step towards him.

'Yes?' His eyes were blank, enigmatic.

'Please, I apologise if I've disappointed or angered you. I'm behaving very badly, but won't you just take my word that I would like to leave, without any special reason?' Her appeal came from the heart. He stared at her as if studying an alien specimen. 'Please stay friends with me and understand.'

Genuine puzzlement ousted the coldness from his eyes. 'Other times I've know what to understand, but this, friends are made for confidences?'

Heartened by the warmer look Jane stumbled eagerly, 'Grant, please accept that ... it's something within me, something that must be withheld even from a close—friend——' she stammered to a tongue-tied stillness and watched him take a cigarette and light it smoothly and silently. Her voice calmed. 'It has nothing to do with the Estate. I've been happy here and everybody's been very good to me, but I guess I'm what they call a career girl. There's no future here. I'd like to try my wings alone and further afield. As for Julius——'

'He might clip them before you even find the chance to flutter them.' A small smile played at the corners of his mouth. 'I wouldn't have typed you exactly a career girl.'

'How would you type me, then?'

'I haven't considered seriously, to be frank.' As he was ordinarily a man of quick judgement, that bland statement hit Jane like a blow in her solar-plexus: She was of such little account that he hadn't even bothered to 'type' her! Grant continued almost absentmindedly, 'But a random guess types you as a potential home-body, requiring a firm hand to guide and keep you out of mischief.'

'Thank you very much! Your random guesses aren't always spot on,' Jane felt haughtily compelled to point out.

Grant's attractive smile framed very white, healthy teeth. 'Time will tell. The agency at Nelspruit will give prompt and friendly service in the matter of supplying—replacement. Girls falling over each other for a job like this.' He started to rustle the papers on his desk.

Jane walked back to her chair feeling inexplicably dampened by his noncommittal acceptance of her resignation. It mattered not greatly who did the office work as long as the female was fairly efficient. Oh well, she had asked for it and hadn't expected him to fall at her feet, begging her to stay because she was absolutely indispensable, highly valued or irreplaceable! A sad hollow made a lonely vacuum under her ribs and gave a disconsolate droop to her mouth when she forgot to guard her expression. She forgot quite frequently and, after a miserable time had passed, happened to raise her eyes to find Grant watching her quizzically.

'Do cheer up, lass. You look as if you have one big tum-ache,' he said, densely unfeeling. 'Mara's coming back to-morrow and Julius sent word that he'd be obliged if I slacken up on you. He desires some of your time and has much to tell you. That should cheer you up somewhat.'

Which good cheer only made the hollow echo deeper against her backbone. 'It sure does, he's a nice guy,' Jane said sourly.

'Well, blow me down, the child sounds like doom. No joyous bells ringing, no butterflies fluttering madly?'

She managed a watery smile and Grant suddenly scraped back his chair, threw the heavy ledger on his desk and strode purposefully towards her. Jane's eyes widened like a startled fawn when he gripped her arm and drew her to her feet. 'Come on, Doc Saxon will apply the remedy. A dash of purifying air through hair and clouded brain.' She was steered firmly through the door, down the steps and round to the back of the house. He bundled her into the car, and by the time Jane had recovered breath they were out of the gates and away!

'My bag——' she gasped weakly.

'To blazes with your bag. Unpin your hair and get set!' Grant pressed a button and the hood retreated smoothly to an invasion of late summer breezes which made of Jane's hair a flying silky pennant.

Up and up the winged monster flew, rounding hairpin turns and twisted pine-edged ribbons of road, down into breathtaking fairy valleys, verdant and lush with nature's bounty.

And then they were in a wide cleared space with a high steel structure towering above them. 'Look-out tower.' Grant switched off and looked at his windblown passenger. 'Care for a bird's eye view, touslehead?'

The keen-eyed Bantu keeper walked smartly to greet them. He had his own shack here and did constant patrol work. Jane felt quite breathless when she reached the top of the steep stairway and peeved at the ease and normal breathing of her companion as they stood on the high platform. The view was superb.

'Headache gone?' queried Grant.

Yes, her 'headache' had gone. In the clear air, high above petty worries, who could not but feel exhilarated and cleansed. Of course, it could depend immensely on one's company; and whom would she wish for but the very one at her side?

Grant took the return journey at a leisurely pace and the evening star winked brightly at her paler satellites as they drew up behind a familiar stationary car in the driveway of Bart's home. 'Julius, I do declare.' Grant mused, with a sidelong glance at Jane. His hand fluttered an inch from the material covering her left breast. 'Heart fluttering like a caged birdie?' He laughed at her indignant denial and mostly at her involuntary gesture of protecting her body from his hovering hand. 'It's all right, honey, I only touch what's mine.' He moved his arm across to open her door and Jane only just caught his murmured, 'Very tempting, though ... oh, strength, where is thy weakness!'

Mara waited languidly on the top step. Her green eyes were not so languid as they strayed from Jane's confusion to the tall figure of the man who walked towards her. 'Hi, Grant,' she said softly, reproachfully, and waited for him to reach the step below her. Two slim arms fondled across his shoulders and the man's hands lifted to encircle her waist.

Jane walked past them with a dazzling smile for Julius while her mind churned on six little words ... 'I only touch what is mine.'

Julius had no such inhibitions. She was enveloped in a bear hug.

'Darling Jane! I was beginning to despair of ever seeing you again. We've been waiting ages, Minna told us Grant took you home and what do we find? No Jane, no boss. My thoughts were sadly following the elopement and dear Mara was just trying to console my great loss, by begging me to receive her affection to replace a lost love, when you materialised. Saved by the gong!'

Mara tore her green gaze from Grant's face long enough to stab Julius between the eyes. 'If present company can believe that pretty speech then they don't know the shyster, or are themselves solid bone from the neck up!

'And where were you two this afternoon?' she demanded of Grant and Jane.

'Above the planets, touching the silver lining of a puffball,' said Grant.

Mara's eyes flicked from his face to that of the quiet girl next to him. Her eyebrows arched with sarcasm. 'Your poetic strategy may lure a little mackerel, darling,' a sideways slant of her lashes at Jane. 'I know them so well—was the puffball gratifying?'

'Absolutely, wholly satisfying.' Grant lighted two cigarettes, passed one to Jane and drew deeply on the one between his brown fingers. 'The silver came off on our fingers, never to be erased in our lifetime.'

Bart came to join them. 'Grant, I have some information from Sergeant Mason—could you spare a moment?'

'Surely.' Grant excused himself and followed Bart inside.

'Flip Olivier is wanted for robbery, in Nelspruit. He managed to evade the police and all cars were stopped at a roadblock. A salesman admitted to giving a man of Olivier's description a lift. He got worried at the wild manner of the man and, on the spur of the moment, told him he, the salesman, would have to return to the hotel for an imaginary briefcase. The man muttered angrily and ordered him to put him off at that spot. The police believe he's headed this way. The sergeant is aware of his hatred for you and phoned your place. You weren't there, so he asked me to pass on the message, to be on your guard in case Olivier gets nasty. Derek Cross—you know him—his house was entered by an open bathroom window, quite a few valuables stolen.'

Grant rubbed his chin. 'Thanks, Bart. Wonder what made Olivier turn to robbery? A private house—hmm, I know the Cross family. Olivier is the type to seek vengeance when cornered, or when he imagines he's been ill-used. We'll have to do something about the womenfolk if the police haven't tracked him yet ... I'll contact them at home, keep a wary watch this end until you hear from me. Liza and Jane must stay at home tomorrow ... I'll send Tom over tonight when I reach home, as an extra precaution. That day when I brought Mara and Jane home in such a dishevelled condition ... they had a nasty encounter with Olivier ... I'll find the whole truth from Mara if I have to torture her!' They walked back and Grant decided to leave immediately because Minna and Sandy were alone in his house. He cut short Julius's protest. 'I'll take Mara home if you'd like to visit longer, Julius. A good idea because Bart can pass on the message from Sergeant Mason and you can contact your home as a precautionary measure. I must go now ... thanks for the supper. Come on, Mara.'

She was hustled into the car and swerved away in a flurry of gravel.

'What gives with the sudden haste?' Janet was intrigued.

'Nothing to worry about ... I hope.' Bart drew on his pipe, related the doings of Flip Olivier and Grant's instructions for safety measures. 'The police may have tracked him by now, but if not, he has a grudge against Grant and therefore it may involve us. The mind of a man like Olivier works in devious ways, and that encounter Jane and Mara had with him will rankle in a wild mind.' His eyes were on his niece. 'The story is that he got fresh with you two and you used a bit of judo on him before Grant arrived on the scene?'

'Yes ... Uncle,' Jane answered. A shudder of apprehension went through her as she recalled the man's nasty attitude and Grant's contemptuous order for him to leave the vicinity. A robbery put him outside the pale and his jealous, vicious mind would fasten on the estate owner as the cause of his downfall. Would Mara, in view of this latest development, confess the true details of that ugly encounter in the woods to Grant? Jane had an urge to tell her uncle all about it, but decided to await events. The police might have caught him already, so there would be no point in clarifying Mara's strange presence with him. The truth was, Jane was still puzzled herself at Mara's lack of propriety.

The burglar was forgotten as Jane lay in bed that night. Her thoughts dwelt on Grant and Mara. When would they announce their engagement—or wedding—and why was he procrastinating? Were there still snags concerning a man marrying his brother's widow? The way Mara had greeted Grant showed clearly that she was determined on a show-down and she had affected dislike for Julius in no mean terms. Julius could forget about his vow to alienate her affections. If only the Saxons would declare their alliance it would spur Jane on in her decision to leave ... she was only prolonging the agony of being near to him, allowing herself the exquisite torture of his sudden, lovable traits of concern ... like today when he hustled her out for a breath of mountain air. Why didn't she stop being a weakling for punishment, pack her bags and get out? Why wait for the pain of their announcement? Jane sat up and pounded her pillow to a softer bolster for an aching head.

Jane was outside, breathing fresh morning air, when the Land-Rover stopped in front of the house and Grant's long stride covered the distance between them with swift ease. He saluted her with a hand on the brim of his disreputable hat and Jane invited him in for a cup of coffee. Janet and Elizabeth were at the kitchen table, lingering over cups of aromatic coffee, the boys were with their father in the backlands, taking care to keep the house under careful surveillance.

The big man straddled a chair and Jane placed his coffee on the table.

'Thanks.' A generous helping of sugar followed. 'No sign of our vagabond. I doubt he's in this vicinity, too hot for him. In his boots I'd streak clear across the country.'

'Then I may as well get back to work ... there's stacks waiting. Have you come to fetch me?' Jane looked down at her faded jeans and loosely hanging shirt.

'If you would, Jane. That's why I've come. Mara is edgy about the job she promised to do in Johannesburg. I can't take her all the way and won't allow her to drive alone, so the only thing to do is drive her as far as Nelspruit and put her on the train. A couple of hours and I'll be back. You needn't change, that rig's serviceable and you still have clothes at my place. I'm taking further advantage in asking you to stay on again until the scare is over or until Mara gets back, whichever's the shortest length of time.'

'Sure, I'll do that,' Jane said quietly.

Jane managed to wade through the stacks of work on her desk that had stealthily piled up in her short absence. She then took a breather by walking outside in the immediate surrounds of the house, keeping in mind Grant's explicit warning to all of them not to wander out of sight. She didn't feel like Mara or Sandy's company, or anyone's presence. She eventually walked into the house and met no one en route to the bathroom, showered and changed into fresh undies, green linen frock with saddle-stitching and thonged sandals. Her hair was brushed with uninterested ministration into a ponytail and she was not conscious that this severe style defined the pure lines of cheek and brow as no elaborate coiffure could.

Grant followed her into the dining-room where Mara and Sandy were waiting. He too looked freshly showered and virile in brown slacks, silk shirt and cravat. Minna, who was now fully recovered, put finishing touches to the serving dishes on the sideboard, from where the family usually helped themselves and did so now.

'Who were you speaking to on the phone, Grant?' Mara asked. 'I was dressing so couldn't answer and then I heard you talking.'

'Did you follow the gist of my conversation?'

'Of course not. One can't hear from behind a closed bedroom door.'

'Well then, I'll tell you.' Grant lowered his soup plate and sat down. 'My talk was with someone who, most conveniently, will save you a trip by train.'

'Someone going through by car? That will be fine. Who,

Grant?'

'None other than Julius Davenport. He's taking Granny for a check-up and we'll meet him at the crossroads and you'll be whisked off to your destination after he offloads the kids at their hostel ... what's the matter, you look explosive?'

'I feel explosive. Why must it be that damned man, he's been in my hair far too much ... I'd rather travel by train!' Mara exclaimed angrily.

Grant was amused. 'Come now, girl, Julius is a fine chap and he sent a special promise to treat you gently and behave in a manner dear to the sensitive hearts of Victorian misses. After all, Granny will be with you.'

'Oh, did he! I don't know which is the lesser of two evils ... a trip by train or a few hours in obnoxious company.' Mara drummed her fingers while Jane and Minna passed the roast and vegetables. 'Excluding Granny, of course. I'll go with him only because she'll be with us and your mind will be easier. I know you always worry when I travel alone and he can save you considerable time and miles by taking the kids as well. And Jane need not stay here with Sandy and me away.'

'Actually I'd prefer for her to stay, until Olivier is apprehended. Can't risk him accosting Tom on the road unless I personally take over the transportation.'

'She can surely stay at home until the roads are safe?' Her bored question hid a slight crack of green anger.

'This is my busy time. I need Jane.'

The following morning Grant passed on the news that the boys and Sandy would not be going back after all. Until a full complement of healthy children returned and no further outbreaks of 'flu were reported. He and Mara left soon after breakfast, with his promise to be back as quick as time permitted. He had hesitated at the car door with his grey gaze on Sandy and Jane. 'Would you two care to come along for the ride?'

'Yes, please!' Sandy dashed down the steps, but Jane stood her ground.

'Thanks, no. There's plenty of work for me, remember?'

Jane waved to Sandy and walked purposefully to the office. Mara's affronted stare, at Grant's impulsive offer, floated between pages of calculations and notes . . .

Such was her concentration that the piles of work lessened rapidly and shortly after lunch was satisfactorily completed. Jane walked to the kitchen in search of the housekeeper. Minna was setting out the tea cups.

They sat at the table and Minna enjoyed her occasional cigarette with Jane. 'Minna,' she said, wondering why she suddenly wanted to know, from this woman, something about the Saxon affairs, and if Minna Du Toit would deem it unseemly to discuss her employer. 'Minna, was Mara really engaged to Grant—before she married John?'

Minna's questioning glance shifted from Jane's face to the tip of her cigarette, thoughtfully. She knew, instinctively, that this sudden probe would go further than one innocent question; she either had to answer that one and others or refuse to discuss the situation completely.

'Grant and Mara weren't exactly engaged, there was a sort of understanding. They've been friends from childhood and we—everyone took it for granted—you know how people are?'

'But weren't they in love with each other?' Jane wasn't sure now if she wanted to hear an affirmative answer or a denial and became confused and sorry that she had started the question. 'Please don't answer if you think I'm prying into things that don't concern me. I—I won't mind at all.'

Minna smiled at her companion's sudden shrinking. 'It's all right, dear, the Saxon affairs are common knowledge and it all happened ages ago—I mean that part of it. What's to come no one but themselves know—at least, Grant believes he has a promise to fulfil.' Minna's face became strangely sad, as if with some secret memory.

'Just talk about the family,' said Jane. 'What were his parents like? Did you know them well and were Grant and John nice little boys or utter devils?'

Minna sighed. 'Mr. and Mrs. Saxon were a charming pair, and John was lively but sort of dreamy too. Grant was the little rapscallion—not what they call delinquent these days—full of lively curiosity about everything living and growing and happening. Their father passed away first and Mrs. Saxon did a mighty fine job of rearing her two boys to manhood. They loved her, specially Grant—I mean he showed his love more than John, who was more reserved and sort of secretive. Mrs. Saxon died after Grant came back from University, he passed degrees in agriculture and forestry or whatever it's called. He worked like a trojan on the Estate, it wasn't so big as now, and was with his mother when she had a heart attack and died in his arms. He went sort of grim after that and didn't laugh and enjoy life as he did before. I expect John felt as deeply, but he was away at college and we didn't see much of him until he came back and married Mara.'

Jane sighed. A clear picture of the young Grant formed; unruly dark hair, grey questing eyes and a laughing mouth that became firm with grief and responsibilities. The image stamped on her mind, never to be erased.

Minna said, 'I was Nanny to Miss Mara, she and the household kept me busy, so I really can't tell you more about the Saxons. A real tomboy she was, and Grant and John were her constant playmates, Grant more so because John would come over, find a book and live a world of his own. Mara spent a lot of her time here too ... what a time I had with that one!' She forbore to follow up that last statement and Jane did no more prompting.

'Grant escorted Mara to the odd entertainments, but she was often mad at him for not bending a knee at her every beck and call and for preferring to "slave", as she called it, on the Estate. She eventually left to take up a course in modelling, and did extremely well. As she was the only girl that Grant really noticed, we naturally presumed they would marry, and it surprised most of us when she suddenly showed preference for young John when he came home for three months.' Minna looked through the window with a remembering, rather grim gaze. 'Perhaps I did know ... and didn't want to believe. We had a flaming row one day when I was presumptuous enough to accuse her of ... certain things. From then on she showed a sort of contemptuous indifference towards me. People don't like their secrets rammed down their throats, and I reared that child, so knew her very well.' The housekeeper suddenly looked uncomfortable, as if she had revealed more than intended.

Jane was far too intrigued now and simply had to know more. 'So Mara and John got married? Here?'

'No. John returned to Pretoria and Mara to Johannesburg. They motored back together and, some weeks later, the two households received telegrams announcing their marriage.'

'How very deceitful!' Jane exclaimed scornfully.

'Well, I was surprised at John, I can tell you, but knowing madam's impulsive ways ... anyway, John came home a short while later. What he said has never been revealed, but there was no change in the affection between the brothers. Grant actually acted as if—as if he were happy for John and unconcerned about Mara's preference. When Sandra was born Mara insisted that they make their home in Johannesburg and I suspect John was not pleased. Then came the accident ... and Grant's promise to a dead brother.' Extreme sadness clouded Minna's eyes.

'A promise to a dead brother ... was Grant with John when he died?' Jane asked softly after elapsed moments.

'No, Jane. John was killed instantly. But I heard ... I'm going to tell you this in complete confidence because I trust you and it's been a burden on my soul. I was the only one present when Grant uttered that promise.' Minna pressed her hands together and leaned her forehead against them.

Jane sat quite still.

At last the grey head lifted. 'I took him tea, one night, to his room shortly after the funeral, and he had John's photo in his hands—and oh, Janey, the grief was pitiable on his face. He said, taking my hand in his, "Toicky, stay and bear witness to this pledge I make to a beloved brother. I will endeavour, to the utmost of my ability, to care for his family ... his wife and child. I will comfort them in their grievous loss and may they never know want or lack of love as long as I live. Amen."'

'Oh, Minna!' Jane laid her hands on wrinkled ones and the two women sat in deep silence.

Minna said, 'John provided well for his wife and child, but my heart fears greatly that Grant will now marry Mara just to keep that pledge.'

'But why does your heart fear, Minna? If they love each other surely that will be right?'

'Do they?' Minna gathered the tea things. 'Grant never once showed a grievance or jealousy ... may he not be deluding himself that the old love is still there, merely because of that pledge and also for a secure future for Sandy, whom he adores? Miss Mara was dumbfounded when Grant inherited, instead of John ... she cares for Grant and has a thing about security.' She lifted her eyes to Jane in a direct way. 'Forgive me, Jane, but you too care a great deal for Grant?'

'I do, Minna,' Jane admitted quietly.

'So you see, Jane, I don't know what will happen, I just don't know.'

Mara telephoned two evenings later and Grant joined Jane on the verandah after a lengthy conversation on the instrument. He gave a quiet chuckle as he took up a favourite seat on the wall. 'Mara's having a spot of bother with Julius. He's evidently casing her place of work and making sure she's not being exploited by leering male buyers, and, she says, he even had the cheek to advise her not to model *revealing* garments.'

'Julius, for all his advanced ideas, is plain old-fashioned and nuts!' Jane exclaimed. 'Surely he knows that Mara can look after herself, she's experienced in her job and has learned how to handle that sort.'

'Well, according to her, he's making an old-fashioned nuisance of himself.' Grant studied Jane for a long disturbing moment. 'Does the thought of him being away and with Mara upset you?'

'Upset me?' She felt slightly bewildered by his abrupt question. Then remembrance came; Grant was still under the impression that Julius meant more to her than just a friend. 'No,' Jane met his eyes directly, 'it doesn't upset me one iota. Mara's silly words that other day are quite unfounded. Julius is my very good friend and I love him as such.'

His glance held hers and became almost like physical contact.

'*Love* him as such?' The emphasis on love was strangely questioning.

'Julius can be a staunch friend and there are different kinds of love. I love him in a what's commonly called platonic way——'

Grant cut across further explanation, 'Do I rate a kind of love from you, Jane, and would it be platonic? Or haven't you made up your mind yet to which category I belong?'

'I—I don't put people into a categorical filing system.' Jane declared, alarmed at the turn of questioning. His sudden probing might well unleash her wayward tongue into voicing irretractable avowals. She turned quickly back to the original conversation. 'Julius is my friend, Grant, but I think you should watch him. I respect you too and I think you should know that he's trying to woo Mara away from you.'

'Well, I'll be damned!' Grant came upright. 'Thanks for the respect bit, but Julius wooing Mara? If that's what he thinks he's doing by dogging her footsteps—I'll be triple damned—wow! Jane, you're quite priceless, what a dear little old-fashioned word!'

'Call it what you like, but aren't you being just a little too sure of Mara? There's many a slip 'twixt cup and lip.'

Sudden laughter came from Grant. He leaned down, took Jane's hands and pulled her to her feet. 'I haven't heard that cliché for some time. Now who told you that I hold that particular cup?'

She felt again the electric tremor pass from his hand to hers and stammered confusedly;

'E-everybody knows that you and Mara—she told me—I mean she was your girl——' and came to a tongue-tied stop.

'Do they now, did she tell you? And yes, she was my girl.' Laughter was gone, replaced by searching stony eyes. 'Quite a problem on my hands, wouldn't you say?'

'I don't see it as a problem, Grant. All you have to do is—is——'

Grant interposed, 'Honour a promise.'

Jane dropped her eyes from the pain in his. She knew,

from Minna, what he meant. But why should it be so difficult to honour that promise if he and Mara loved each other? 'Are there legal difficulties?' she asked diffidently.

A short humourless laugh followed. 'Doubtless there would be that ... Mara spoke to you about her and myself? That seems to settle, rather definitely, one of my problems.' Grant lit two cigarettes, passed one to Jane almost absent-mindedly. 'No wonder you were, some time ago, so indignant with Saxon, the sexy philanderer.'

'At that time I thought you were married to Mara,' Jane explained, and Grant listened in amazed silence.

'Again, I'll be damned! If you'd know then what you know now, would you have played along?'

'There's no point in pursuing the subject.' Jane suddenly felt tired and weary of talk. 'I'm going to bed.'

His hand was on her shoulder. 'Jane, if things were different, believe me, if they were—I'd stake my claim in no uncertain terms. Sleep well, child.' Her shoulder felt the firm, gentle pressure of his hand and then he was walking down the steps and night swallowed the sound of fading footsteps.

So there were obstacles in his path to happiness. 'If things were different...' A dull ache followed Jane to bed.

CHAPTER 13

DAYS followed nights like gold and black beads in the hands of benevolent weather. Grant found work for himself, aside from the office, within the radius of the house. He did not believe that Flip Olivier, still at large, had left the vicinity of home ground. Jane asked tentative permission to return home nightly, but a curt negative came from her boss, which she obeyed with outward nonchalance. Inwardly, it was sweet torture to be with him constantly. Although there were no more intimate talks or quiet company in the evenings. Grant retired to his study or spent the hours after dinner perusing books and business circulars. Jane filled in the hours by chatting to Minna and helping Sandy prepare for school, retiring early.

Saturday morning dawned, clear and bright. At ten o'clock Sandra disappeared.

Jane looked up from the list of hostel clothes and toilet items she was checking when Minna walked into Sandy's room.

'Tea's ready, Jane, I thought Sandy was with you?'

'No.' Jane fitted the list into the pocket inside the case lid and checked the metal fasteners. 'Have you called outside? She was with Lemmy behind the garage about half an hour ago.'

'I called and called but the little witch didn't answer. Up to mischief, I'll bet,' Minna said distractedly. 'I'm worried, Jane. Tom went to the compound on some errand and promised not to be away long. Do you think the children went with him?'

'Tom would have told us if he was taking them.' Jane bit her lip vexedly. She straightened suddenly and made for the kitchen door. 'I'm going to the storeroom.' She ran across the yard, past the garage to the shed where, among other tools and equipment, the fishing gear was stored.

Two short rods and reels were missing!

'They've gone to the river against Grant's explicit orders! Oh, Jane,' Minna wailed, 'what shall we do?'

Jane's mind raced. 'Not to worry ... I'll take Mara's car. The child's wickedly talked Lemmy into a last fishing spree before going back to school. I'll tan her small hide with her own fishing rod when I find her!'

It took her a controlled five minutes to study the roadster gears, back out of the garage and swivel on to the road with a prayer in her heart that the youngsters would be where she hoped to find them. It was quite a walk and they must have left within the last hour. She'd have to leave the car on the roadside and cut through the grass and trees on foot. The car flew under her trembling hands and, at a spot she reckoned would be nearest the river, Jane brought it to a stop on the grass verge.

The fishing rods were lying side by side in the favourite fishing place, somewhat haphazardly. Jane's heart gave a jump of relief but started palpitating unpleasantly with anger and then fear as she turned and searched and called without avail.

'Oh, God!' Sturdily shod feet faltered as a plume of smoke met her searching eyes. At right angles to her advance and the rising rock. 'Not that, Sandy, not a fire, you stupid child!' Jane started running, her breath hammering more from fear than physical effort as she foresaw the destruction that silly action would start.

Then she was close enough to hear Sandy cry out ... close enough to hear deep, uncontrolled laughter answer that piteous, frightened cry! Smoke veiled the figures and Jane tore past the outer rim of orange, leaping flames.

To come to an abrupt halt at the tableau that met her scorching eyes.

Flip Olivier towered over two very frightened children. Their hands were tied together with a grubby strip of stretched dry cowhide and he held the end of it in a tight grip. The man's pale blue eyes were alight with fascinated glee as he watched the crackling sparks fly.

Jane seemed to materialise like a genie out of the smoke and his glee was wiped out suddenly as he stepped back a startled pace before recognizing the furious demon that confronted him. Instinctively he dropped the lead from his hand.

Jane wasted no time. 'Run for that big rock, kids! You, Olivier, take off your jacket and help beat down the flames. Move!' Her own jacket came down forcefully on the spreading rim of fire.

Flip Olivier's jacket came off in obedience to her peremptory order. He started to lift it and then dropped his hand and began to laugh again, a mad pitch of laughter that held a spice of insanity. 'Gees!' he shouted, 'I've scooped the kitty —Saxon's kid, his girl and a sweet fire to help him to hell!'

Jane ignored him and looked despairingly at the small headway her futile efforts had made and noticed that the fire was spreading in a circular run, with the rock slap in the centre. She turned back to glare at him in contemptuous anger. 'Use your jacket, you damned fool!'

He suddenly lunged forward and whipped his jacket around her arms and body. 'Nobody calls me names and gets away with it! Try your clever tricks now, Miss Mighty!'

Jane fought furiously, the hot breath of flames on their backs as they struggled on the uneven ground. Her efforts to loosen his hold only goaded him to further angry laughter. 'I've waited just for this—Saxon has it coming—this will even up the score quite a bit. Better give up if you don't want to be burnt alive——' he grunted as she kicked him hard on the shins. 'Damn you! I'm joining the kids on the rock and you're coming with me if I have to drag you by the hair. Saxon's empire's going to burn like Rome did!'

Jane winced as his fingers viced cruelly into her upper arms. Quite suddenly she stopped fighting his straitjacket hold on her.

'You're right,' she panted, 'we may as well watch. The fire is right behind you—be careful.'

Olivier slackened his hold suspiciously at her sudden capitulation and pushed her and himself away from the blasting heat of the approaching flames. The grass was higher and dryer on the rise to the edge of the rock. The children were huddled specks on its smooth grassless surface.

Jane stood docilely while Olivier still gripped the jacket, pinioning her arms. He turned his head to stare at the destruction he had started. Soon it would reach the trees and then the real fun would start. Dry wild brush crackled fiercely as hungry flames seized on them.

'Just dig that, sister,' he said, mesmerised.

Jane acted. Her body and legs collapsed like a deflated rubber doll, completely and limply, bringing her tormentor down on top of her, completely off balance. Two feet hit his stomach, Jane's legs straightened and Flip Olivier flew through the air with a flail of legs and arms to land beyond her head. Then she was up and running for her life.

Olivier made no attempt to follow her.

Jane only realised this when she turned her head to see if he was gaining ground. He was still lying as she had thrown him and the fire was creeping very close to his head. She stopped for a stunned moment, and then began to run back. That trick couldn't—unless—his head lay at an unnatural angle.

'No ... no!' She knelt beside him, the heat searing her skin. And then Jane saw the stone and the wound it had made when his head had contacted. No time for a closer look; he was either concussed or—her blood ran cold with terror—dead. She had to move him before the fire overwhelmed them both.

Slipping her arms under the limp shoulders, Jane began to drag him by straining and walking backwards. He was a dead weight (her lips moved in silent prayer), but she managed to drag him a few yards before stopping to inhale fresh breath into her pumping lungs.

Two figures appeared beside her. 'Please tell us what to do,' Sandy sobbed. 'We can help—Jane, you're both going to be burned!' Lemmy tugged at the man's legs.

'Wait, Lemmy.' Jane looked back and glimpsed Flip's jacket, where he had dropped it. She ran back and snatched it from a lapping, fiery tongue, ran back and placed it on the ground above his head, then took up her former position, arms under the shoulders, and talked steadily to the children. 'I'll lift him and drag him on to the jacket and then you two stand either side, grip the jacket tightly and drag with me. Now!' she managed with desperate strength to lift the inert body on to the jacket.

Heaving, dragging, straining, they started to make headway. At last they reached the rock, haven of safety, with hungry tongues of fire spitting dangerous sparks on clothing and hair in a last demon effort to capture its prey.

In various positions of utter exhaustion the three mortals gasped, choked in a pall of smoke and clapped feebly at clothing and hair. Flip Olivier lay as he had been dragged, inert and a bedraggled mess of torn, dirty clothing; his shoes had come off somewhere on the way and the backs of his heels were skinned and bloody. Jane became terrified of even looking at him ... if he was unconscious at the start, not dead, then that struggle to rescue him had certainly worsened his condition. Her mind blanked at the thought and her body became too paralysed to inch nearer to test his breathing.

'Thank you, kids, that was a stout effort ... we're safe now.' The dear smudged mites managed weak grins and then Sandy sat straighter and charged excitement took over.

'I can hear something, Jane, I can hear cars!'

The Land-Rover, vengeance on wheels, braked to a halt on the ashes of a smoky but dead grassfire. Jane thought hazily, not a demon of vengeance but a mere haloed, heavenly astral vehicle, and the angel alighting could take over, body and soul and all.

Jane sighed softly, 'They're getting mighty careless in heaven these days, darling, no wings ... I killed him,' and fainted in a very old-fashioned way.

She came to life with her head pillowed against a hard chest, exactly where that aching head yearned to be, vibrating against her ear with Grant speaking to someone. 'Our firewatchers are on the ball, poppet. The alarm went forth at the first wisp of smoke. Now everything's under control.'

'Is he dead?' Jane whispered to the chest against her cheek.

Grant tilted his dark head. 'Feeling better? That was a silly thing to do, passing out at this stage—sort of anticlimax, don't you think? Lucky you postponed the first one until out of the burn, wise child.'

Jane stammered, 'when I saw you it—it just happened.'

'That's because I'm more devastating than fire!' Grant quipped lightly, but the convulsive pressure of his arm belied the flippancy of words. 'If you can sit up I'll help you to the Rover. The ambulance men are coming with stretchers.'

Jane's eyes strayed to the quiet form and her stomach turned as she noted the jacket covering head and chest. Grant must have examined him while she was in her faint and the covering could only mean ... Grant hadn't answered her question.

'How did they know to send an ambulance?' Sandy queried as she and Lemmy followed Grant and Jane to the vehicle.

'That's part of the fire-fighting unit, in case of casualties.'

181

Grant settled them in the seats and prepared to walk away, obviously to meet the oncoming men.

Jane guessed his purpose; he wanted to speak with them and leave before they examined Flip Olivier. She simply had to know. Now.

'Grant, please wait for them. I want to know.'

He turned away without further argument and joined the white-coated men. Vision was obscured by their broad backs and to Jane time became interminable, agonisingly endless before Grant lifted from his heels and walked back.

'He's alive, badly concussed.'

Relief almost made Jane faint again. A small voice came from the back of her, 'I think I'm going to be sick ...'

Grant lifted Sandy out. 'Do so, poppet, you'll feel better.' He held small shoulders while the child heaved, Lemmy nonchalantly climbed out the other side and did likewise. Jane ached with tender pity for both of them.

At home at last, Minna and Polly were waiting, each taking a child in loving arms. Grant turned to Jane. His arms helped her from the Rover, wandered round her body and she was held close.

'Jane, Janey, how can I ever thank you for what you did for two helpless children? What was in that madman's head, how did they fall into his trap, what were his vicious plans once he had them?' The arms around her tightened as the big man seemed to lose control; as if his hold on her prevented, helped him from breaking apart and brought back sanity. His body shook as if in fever spasms.

'And you, Jane Wheeler, had to be mauled ... thank God for your quick brain, clever tricks ... and brave heart.'

A measure of slackening came finally, one arm freed completely so that the attached hand could stroke back wildly disarrayed hair from off her face. Her nose unwound from his breastbone and air seeped back into her lungs. He tugged her hair gently back to tilt her face and look long and hard at her features, his grey eyes circling with a deep look of wonder in their depths. 'Do you feel better now?'

'Except for a burst spleen, yes. Do *you* feel better too?' Jane countered.

'Burst spleen——' Grant saw the glint in brown eyes and his arm came away from her waist. 'What do you mean, do I feel better?'

Jane felt like biting her tongue clean off for depriving her of that exciting arm. Well, it was good while it lasted.

'An erupting volcano had nothing on you, Grant Saxon, a few seconds back! You've got it out of your system now, nobody was hurt except the villain and that was by accident. He hit his descending head on a rock and I'll pray for his recovery and repentance. Not too much damage was caused by his little arson game. Kids recover from shock rapidly, no lasting harm done and that's that!'

'That's all you know. Things are going to move my way at last.' Grant took her shoulders, shook them slightly while some deep, secretive look made his eyes almost black. 'I have a telegram in my pocket right now——' he stopped and his eyes moved over her shoulder, 'but that can wait for a more suitable moment. Take yourself to bath, girl, wash away your aches and dirt and I'll consider the bed-going bit.' He winked deliberately and turned away.

An hour later, bathed, changed, her hair swept into a neat chignon, Jane moved about the sitting-room, Uncle Bart proudly at her side, and smiled composedly at the excited questions flung from all sides. Old friends greeted her with familiar pride and new friends were welcomed courteously. Through the open french doors a group of men clustered, Grant in their midst. His quizzical eyes strayed often, above their shoulders and heads to follow Jane's progress. Sandy and Lemmy, clean and exuberant, came in for their share of telling and praise.

Sergeant Mason cleared his throat selfconsciously. 'I truly regret that I can't stay. This gathering that started off so fearfully is obviously going to turn into a jolly "do" and it's always my lot to have to push off when the going's good. However, duty calls——' he bowed gravely towards Sandy and Lemmy. 'The police personnel gratefully extend thanks to Miss Sandra and Master Lemmy for flushing out the enemy, which our entire squad couldn't accomplish!' He walked to Jane's side and put a large hand on her shoulder.

'Dear ma'am, on behalf of my colleagues, present company and myself, accept our deepest esteem for your brave act. I am personally sending a recommendation for citation to courage, quick acting in moments of danger *and* unbelievable compassion for a scoundrel who deliberately victimised two small children, committed arson and is a robber wanted by the police—and assaulted your person——'

'—vice versa,' Grant cut in softly.

'Don't put an official off stride, it's illegal.' Mason waited for laughter to subside. 'Again, thank you, Jane. I'm also deeply thankful that neither you or the children came to no harm. We'll call on you tomorrow, at your convenience for a little statement of events—will you be here or at Bart's home?'

Jane felt shaken to the point of tears at the sincerity of his intense and orderly speech and her own mind shook at the sergeant's unspoken conjecture of what might have happened to two innocent children. Grant answered for her.

'Miss Wheeler will be at her uncle's home tomorrow and you may call on her when she's rested suitably. Bart will contact you when she's ready.'

'Thank you, Grant. That suit you, Jane?'

'Y-yes, Sergeant Mason. I'll be at your service any time in the morning.' Jane stammered slightly. All of a sudden she was being sent home; of course there was no danger of being waylaid and—something clicked in her memory ... Grant had mentioned a telegram received this morning ...

Her hand was shaken warmly and the sergeant took his leave. From then on she had little time for thoughts. She didn't realise that not only the stiff drink but reaction was settling on her stiff shoulders. She stretched her eyes wide, closed them and repeated the exercise; opened them again to meet Grant's scrutiny across the length of the verandah. He put a hand, motioning for silence, and all eyes turned to him.

'This seems to be the time for more startling disclosures and, believe me, I have much to disclose. Firstly, Pat and

Peter have finally settled their wedding date, three weeks from now.'

Grant lit a cigarette, then slowly lifted a hand to slide an orange envelope out of his pocket. And Jane's insides curled witheringly as she remembered his remark about a telegram. It could only be from Mara; she was coming back. Grant wouldn't make a thing of it if it only meant her return; this was something of great importance and he could not wait for Mara's presence to announce the shattering news contained in that envelope.

Jane shuttered her mind while his maddening coolness iced through her veins. She had a fierce urge to scream at him, to get it over, let the hammer fall; let the knife cut sharp and viciously—damn you, get on with it so that I can go home and die alone!

After a million years Grant spoke and the words came strangely stilted: 'Secondly, I have here a telegram,' he looked up from the paper in his hands and, though his lips smiled, the challenging stare that pierced across space to transfix one girl held a grimness that belied his nonchalant appearance. 'Another startling bit of news—Cupid seems to be working overtime.'

He should have waited, Jane thought dumbly, for Mara to be at his side. She loved the limelight and would have been delighted in being the star of the day...

'Julius Davenport and Mara Saxon were married in Johannesburg at ten-thirty, yesterday morning.' Grant raised his voice above the sudden murmurings. 'I'll read further. "I married her to control mischievous intent. Stop. Love her madly and found surprising reciprocation. Stop. Don't be mad."' Grant hesitated, his eyes strayed across the form in his hand, and then he folded the missive. 'That's all.'

Murmurs became prattle and Peter and Pat were warmly congratulated. Curious looks were cast at the Estate owner and conjecture written plainly on puzzled faces. Grant, quite composed and affable, began to walk towards Jane. Her eyes followed his progress hynotically. Three metres from her, reaction and shock collided. Jane whispered sympathetically, 'Oh, you poor dear man!' and Grant was there to catch her in his arms as she folded limply for the second time in one day.

Elizabeth walked with him to Jane's bedroom. At the side of her bed Grant turned, the girl still in his arms, and gave an anxious mother a beatific smile. 'Tell the chaps to push off now, Elizabeth. I'll take good care of our Jane and bring her home in due course. You can all go home.' His bright grey eyes took the sting out of the summary command.

Jane opened her eyes and hazily investigated the arm that circled her, the close warm body . . . and lifted her lashes fully; the bed was familiar, the setting sun comforting against drawn curtains and, most of all, the pure delight she experienced at the quiet voice in her ear.

'Sleep, child. Sleep, dearest one.'

Jane blissfully obeyed and slept.

'Is she sick—is Jane sick—is she——' the frightened little voice penetrated. 'Minna didn't want me to come, b-but I had to come. Is she very sick?'

Jane opened her eyes to a shaded lamp, felt the movement of Grant's head and closed them again quickly and just listened.

His free arm moved carefully to stroke Sandy's shining hair. 'Jane is perfectly all right, poppet. Only very tired. Absolutely nothing to worry about.'

Sandra breathed deeply. 'Thank goodness—'cos it would be my fault if Jane is sick 'n then I'd die too. Do you want some tea?'

'No, sweetheart. You and Minna pop off to bed now and I'll stay with Jane till she wakes up and take good care of her.'

'Okay. G'night, Grant.' At the door, in a piercing whisper, 'I'm glad Mommy married Uncle Julius 'n I'll teach him to be a fine new dad. And I think Jane belongs to you, 'cos you're sleeping with her!' The door closed.

'I'll say!' Grant shifted slightly to look at the face in the crook of his arm.

Wide open eyes stared back at him.

'Hello, darling,' he said.

186

'Hello.' Her voice held enchantment. 'You're not to be mad at Julius and you don't have to console me. He didn't mean a thing to me—I just passed out because I feel so sorry for you.'

'Yes, love, I know that. You have such a wonderfully compassionate heart.'

Jane lifted her head from his arm and rested on her elbow to gaze at him earnestly. 'You didn't finish that message from Julius today. Please don't let it hurt you too much, Grant.'

'If I were hurt deeply, would you be willing to help me, Jane, to try and forget?'

Jane said miserably, 'If that's what you would want.'

'Would you give me anything I wanted?' His finger-tips traced the contour of her face and lips.

'Y-yes, Grant.'

'Unconditionally?'

Nut-brown eyes glistened mute confirmation.

'Say it! Say you love me unconditionally, heart and soul, with every breath in your beautiful body!'

Jane sat up straight, away from his thrilling touch. 'I've loved you from the time I met you, so you might as well know. Even when I thought you were married. My mind was disgusted, but my heart was irrevocably yours.'

'How lovely you are, my Janey. Julius did me one hell of a favour; I was beside myself with torment, because of a self-made promise—to John.

'Now I'm released. Julius, bless his scheming heart, released me from a course I almost took before you came, and when I saw you it became torture to contemplate sticking to that promise and I became a cowardly procrastinator. Thank God I waited! The telegram from Julius ended thus: "I know where your heart belongs. Stop. Ask and ye shall receive. Stop." '

Grant's eyes met hers levelly, a deep shimmering flame in grey depths.

'Dare I ask and will I receive, and do you know where my heart belongs, now and for ever, hazelnut?'

Jane's own breast became an erratic, joyous drumbeat.

187

'Do you know? Answer me, Janey. Well, come here and I'll show you!'

Grant pulled her down beside him and began to kiss her eyelids, worked his way to her smoothly fragrant neck, keeping her mouth for last, the sweetest of all.

Finally his lips lifted an infinite speaking space from hers.

'My darling dumb one, do you know that we belong?' he breathed, with rough passion, and Jane's answer was to seek his lips again with sweet ardour. To whisper:

'Yes, boss.'

'This is why I must take you home ... some time. And bring my wife back ... soon.'

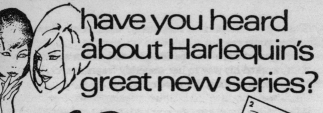

Three of the world's greatest romance authors.
Don't miss any of this new series!

ANNE HAMPSON

- [ ] #1 GATES OF STEEL
- [ ] #2 MASTER OF MOONROCK
- [ ] #7 DEAR STRANGER
- [ ] #10 WAVES OF FIRE
- [ ] #13 A KISS FROM SATAN
- [ ] #16 WINGS OF NIGHT

ANNE MATHER

- [ ] #3 SWEET REVENGE
- [ ] #4 THE PLEASURE & THE PAIN
- [ ] #8 THE SANCHEZ TRADITION
- [ ] #11 WHO RIDES THE TIGER
- [ ] #14 STORM IN A RAIN BARREL
- [ ] #17 LIVING WITH ADAM

VIOLET WINSPEAR

- [ ] #5 DEVIL IN A SILVER ROOM
- [ ] #6 THE HONEY IS BITTER
- [ ] #9 WIFE WITHOUT KISSES
- [ ] #12 DRAGON BAY
- [ ] #15 THE LITTLE NOBODY
- [ ] #18 THE KISSES AND THE WINE

To: **HARLEQUIN READER SERVICE, Dept. N 308**

M.P.O. Box 707, Niagara Falls, N.Y. 14302

Canadian address: Stratford, Ont., Canada

- [ ] Please send me the free Harlequin Romance Presents Catalogue.

- [ ] Please send me the titles checked.

I enclose $_____ (No C.O.D.'s). All books are 75c each. To help defray postage and handling cost, please add 25c.

Name _____

Address _____

City/Town _____

State/Prov. _____ Zip _____

N 308

Golden Harlequin Library

A Treasury of Harlequin Romances!

Many of the all time favorite Harlequin Romance Novels have not been available, until now, since the original printing. But on this special introductory offer, they are yours in an exquisitely bound, rich gold hardcover with royal blue imprint. Three complete unabridged novels in each volume. And the cost is so very low you'll be amazed!

This very special collection of classic Harlequin Romances would be a distinctive addition to your library. And imagine what a delightful gift they'd make for any Harlequin reader!

Start your collection now. See reverse of this page for **SPECIAL INTRODUCTORY OFFER!**

v